CW00747211

What people have said about *Jeanne de Winter at the Wars*

Very lively and enterprising... Producers seeking film and television rights should form an orderly queue...

Godfrey Smith, *Sunday Times* book critic

David's novel is as authentic, enthralling and engaging as the great original, *Rebecca*...

Robert Robinson, TV personality, critic and author (most recently his autobiography *Skip All That!*)

I was delighted with your novel...

Archduke Otto von Habsburg, Pocking, Germany

I could not put your book down until I had read it from cover to cover...

Captain J F T Bayliss JAG RN

We much enjoyed your masterpiece, of special interest to those of us ex-SOE [Special Operations Executive] combatants who in my opinion were, collectively, Enemy Target Number One...!

Brigadier Billy Beyto, Nerja, Spain

To Fay Wilkins,
"The First Lady of New Zealand", xx
sent on behalf of the first
Lady of Linton, the saintly
Rebel Elizabeth,

JEANNE DE WINTER AT THE WARS

The Wartime Sequel to Rebecca

David Roach Pierson

"Stalwart support to her
friends & superb homemaker"
quoth Elizabeth, with
the author's best regards &
respects
David Roach Pierson
4/10/99

MINERVA PRESS
LONDON
MIAMI DELHI SYDNEY

xx And a St Cuthbert's Lady, to boot!

JEANNE DE WINTER AT THE WARS:
The Wartime Sequel to Rebecca

ISBN 1 85863 043 2

First published 1996 by
MINERVA PRESS
315–317 Regent Street
London W1R 7YB

2nd Impression 1999

Printed in Great Britain for Minerva Press

JEANNE DE WINTER AT THE WARS

The Wartime Sequel to Rebecca

To Nigel Douglas, Prince of Operetta Performers and Translators, this novel is dedicated. As well as being one of the finest interpreters of Benjamin Britten – his Captain Vere (Billy Budd) and von Aschenbach in Death in Venice are still vivid in my memory – he also introduced me to the music of Emmerich Kalman. His translations have put back the verve and the fun, and the jokes, into operetta, and made one hear them as the original Viennese would have done!

'Nimm, Zigeuner' from Kalman's Die Csardasfürstin

Translated by Nigel Douglas

with grateful acknowledgement to Josef Weinberger

FERI: Come Zigeuner, take your bow
And let that fiddle sing,
Child of night call up the devil,
Make the rafters ring!
Where's the tune that laughs and cries?
Where's the tune that sobs and sighs?
Where's the tune to set the aching heart on fire?
Where's the tune to touch the chords of deep desire?

Strike up, Zigeuner,
Drive our sorrows away,
Play gipsy, play Till night has turned into day.
Fortune's a lady who does not like to wait,
And tomorrow may be too late!

SYLVA,
BONI & FERI: Strike up, Zigeuner,
Drive our sorrows away.
Play gipsy, play
Till night has turned into day,
Who knows how long this sad old world will survive?
And at least we are still alive!

SYLVA: Play, oh play a soothing song
To mend a broken dream,
Any song you like as long

Jaj, Ma-mám, Bru-der-herz, ich kauf mir die Welt! Jaj Ma-mám was liegt mir am
lum-pi-gen Geld! Weißt du wie lan-ge noch der Glo-bus sich dreht, ob es
mor-gen nicht schon zu spät!
Tanz
Furioso Presto (schneller Csárdás)
16
17
18
1.
2.

As love is not the theme.
Where's the tune to stop the heart
Tear the pain and grief apart,
Where's the tune to show me heaven after hell?
Play and let the Csárdás weave its magic spell.
Strike up, Zigeuner,
Drive our sorrows away,
Play gipsy, play
Till night has turned into day,
Fortune's a lady who does not like to wait,
And tomorrow may be too late!

SYLVA,
BONI & FERI: Strike up, Zigeuner,
Drive our sorrows away,
Play gipsy, play
Till night has turned into day.
Who knows how long this sad old world will survive?
And at least we are still alive!

BONI: What's the point of people mourning
In this vale of tears?
We'll have all moved on elsewhere
In roughly fifty years!
Why should life be sad and grey?
Let it be a cabaret!
So bring on the dancing girls and pink champagne!
Maybe we shall never have a chance again!

SYLVA,
BONI & FERI: Strike up, Zigeuner,
Drive our sorrows away,
Play gipsy, play
Till night has turned into day,
Fortune's a lady who does not like to wait,
And tomorrow may be too late!

Remember you, that buy this book
What agonies the creation took:
From Hell and Hades to Gehenna –
We hope you'll feel it's worth a tenner!

David Roach Pierson

Contents

Preface

Homage to Daphne du Maurier

Why another sequel to *Rebecca*? My purpose is to give *Rebecca* the kind of romantic sequel, a novel of action and atmosphere, that I think Daphne du Maurier might have enjoyed, to give Maxim a good war, and to pay my personal tribute to one of the finest storytellers of the twentieth century.

Why this personal tribute? Because I met Daphne du Maurier in my years in Oxford, and thereafter she was an icon for me, setting a standard of excellence in lively story-writing that for the next half century I have tried vainly to emulate.

Daphne du Maurier impacted briefly on my life when I was studying at Oxford, at the end of the forties, after doing my military service in Libya. Her play, *September Tide*, with Gertrude Lawrence playing the lead, Stella, was given its pre-West End premiere at the New Theatre, Oxford, in the winter of 1948.

It was an appropriate venue, for not only was Daphne's husband, General Sir Frederick 'Boy' Browning brought up near Oxford at the Rectory, Rousham, at , but Oxford was then at its most brilliant post-war best, a period referred to as 'the Golden Generation', some eight years of coruscating characters, which saw Tony Benn, Margaret (Thatcher) Roberts and Ken Tynan at its start, and Michael Heseltine and athlete/politician, later writer, Jeffrey Archer, at its conclusion; and a host of names: Jeremy Thorpe, (Lord) William Rees-Mogg, (Sir) Alastair Burnet, Shirley Catlin (Williams), Antonia Pakenham (Fraser), Brigid Brophy, (Sir) Martin Jacomb, (Sir) Peter Parker, Rupert Murdoch, Dick Taverne, Alan Brien, Lord Justice (Tony) McCowan, Michael Codron, Nigel Davenport, Jeremy Isaacs and so on, and countless other great names in between, giving modest men an inferiority complex for life!

Daphne du Maurier at this time was at the height of her powers, with many more novels in her quiver, and married to the war hero,

Brigadier 'Boy' Browning, of Arnhem fame. *September Tide* was one of her first plays, and there was a kind of strange chemistry between her and her leading lady, Gertrude Lawrence, which resulted in the play being suffused with a kind of brilliance.

Gertrude Lawrence was then a living legend, from her association with Noel Coward and the Cochran revues of the 1930s. Coward tailor-made plays to match her brilliance, and Gershwin wrote his musical, *Oh Kay*, as a star vehicle for her, as did other popular composers and writers of the day. She was the perfect matinée idol, and as she made her entrance down the stairs, in *September Tide*, the audience always broke into spontaneous applause.

All Oxford flocked to the play, in order to see the fabulous Miss Lawrence, and all who could contrive it went on to the reception after the triumphant first night, to meet Miss Lawrence and the author, Daphne du Maurier. I attended as one of the theatre correspondents for the *Isis*,amid the hubbub of a Ken Tynan party.

I have to say that the diva of musical comedy, Gertrude Lawrence, rather overshadowed Miss du Maurier, who seemed quite content that Gertrude, as ever, should steal the limelight. Gertrude sat there like a queen on a state visit, receiving the homage and adoration of the undergraduates. One nervous young man (would it had been me) confessed to Miss Lawrence that he had agonised all evening before plucking up the courage to approach her. "Young man," said Gertrude grandly, "you lack confidence. You need a woman." My own encounter with Miss Lawrence was brief and unmemorable, no good quotation for the *Isis*, but I did speak a little longer with Daphne du Maurier, after telling her my family had served with General Browning in two wars, and asking how she went about writing a novel. She was gracious and vivacious, a charming lady of talent and intelligence, and though I do not recall a word of our conversation, I recall her warmth.

You left her feeling you had made a friend; Gertrude Lawrence left you with the awed feeling that you had met a star.

I later met Tessa Browning, then at St Godric's, having been introduced to her at a *fête champêtre* at New College, by Bill Shelton (later MP, knight of the realm, head of an advertising agency, and one of the Tory cabal who was to get Margaret Thatcher made leader and later Prime Minister, a few years later). Bill knew everybody at Oxford, and nearly every pretty girl at university; I envied his easy assurance.

I recall that Tessa was a very pretty girl, if a little serious, and seemingly a little overawed at having brilliant parents. It was a phenomenon I observed then among children of famous people, and particularly girls; like Elizabeth Cairns, daughter of the famous brain surgeon, her mother being one of the tribe of Smiths that dominated Balliol and Oxford - Lady Cairns, Lady Barrington Ward, Lady Clay, Lady Bullard, all descended from the famous Master of Balliol; or Antonia Fraser (then Pakenham) with her father, the lovely eccentric Lord Longford (then in the Labour Cabinet) and her historian mother Elizabeth; and even Shirley Catlin (Williams) by Professor Catlin out of novelist Vera Brittain, were all a little overawed by having famous parents. This was also the case with Daphne du Maurier, whose subconscious was dominated by the larger than life personality of her adored father, the actor-manager, Gerald du Maurier, which as we shall see, provided the germ of the plot of *Rebecca*. This did not prevent her, or Antonia Fraser, or Shirley Williams, from having very successful careers, outside the family influence, but it did create something of a complex, especially for Daphne du Maurier.

Tessa Browning was not a star at Oxford, unlike Ann Younghusband, descendant of the famous explorer, whom I met at the same *fête champêtre,* her full-blooded red rose in full flower personality rather making Tessa seem a virginal white rose in bud. Great things were expected on Ann in later life, but they remained largely unrealised.

Oxford stars, or young lions, rarely made it in later life. Who now remembers Uwe Kitzinger, Oleg Kerensky, David Williams the actor, Sally Seed, Anthony Besch, David Raeburn? Edward Boyle died young, Jeremy Thorpe sparkled and fell like a great comet, Ken Tynan and Robert Pitman had their brief moments of glory. Only William Rees-Mogg made it to the deathless establishment.

Even the young Lions that succeeded, did so in different ways than one expected. Robert Robinson, expected to be a great author, became a TV figure. His wife, Josée Richard, the uncrowned queen of Oxford Theatre, was expected to be a second Bernhardt on the West End Stage; she has become a very influential president of the League of Catholic Women.

Peter Parker, whose celebrated *King Lear* (Josée was his Regan and Shirley Williams his Cordelia) led people to say here was a new Olivier, ended up as a Captain of British Industry, and a famed Chairman of British Rail. Tony Richardson, the *enfant terrible* producer at Oxford, is remembered now for Hammer Films and siring a dynasty of young actresses, from his marriage to Vanessa Redgrave. Robin Day, expected to be a great lawyer, became a major TV inquisitor and interviewer.

But the great names of our day came from those unnoticed at Oxford in their day, Margaret (Thatcher) Roberts, Rupert Murdoch, Martin Jacomb, now a vast power in the City of London (he was expected to be a backbench Tory MP), Sir Alastair Burnet etc. And of all the would-be novelists, many of whom became establishment literati, the only one to be a mega-writer was Jeffrey Archer, whose ambition was to be a leading Tory politician and tycoon, until a bankruptcy turned him into a popular novelist.

So Daphne du Maurier is associated in my mind with the glories of the golden days of Oxford's 'Golden Generation', with walks on Port Meadow with Jeremy Thorpe as he improvised a whole brilliant speech, to be delivered at the Oxford Union next night, from a single phrase: "inordinate girth": "The Tory Party is like an elderly dowager of inordinate girth, unable to proceed with any speed in any direction except ponderously, in mortal fear of tripping over her own feet, which are invisible to her beneath her splendid bow-window of bosom and belly…"

I associate her in my mind with the splendid productions of the OUDS in my day, *The Tempest* of Neville Coghill in Worcester College, with Charles Hodgson running out over the surface of Worcester lake as the liberated sprite Ariel, and of John (*Midnight Cowboy*) Schlesinger in the same production as the drunken butler Stephano. Or performing with Josée (Desdemona) and Bob Robinson (Cassio) in Alan Cooke's *Othello*, mercilessly parodied by Michael Codron in the subsequent OUDS smoker. All the nostalgia of those days, Tyrone Guthrie lecturing on Shakespeare, Dame Ninette de Valois, with Margaret Fonteyn in attendance, talking about ballet; making periodic speeches at the Oxford Union with the flute-voiced William Rees-Mogg, President of the Union, in the Chair (I cannot conceive… Shame!); writing for *Isis*; visiting Blackwells, of course, manifold activities which caused my tutor, Vere Somerset, to complain to my Provost, Sir John Masterman, "I think Mr Pierson is a little too much of a social butterfly…" All these things are bound up with my recollection of Daphne du Maurier.

Not surprisingly, Daphne du Maurier became something of an icon to me, and over the following years I bought all her books as they appeared and vainly tried to emulate her technique and her vivacious style; *Frenchman's Creek*, *My Cousin Rachel*, her semi-historical novel on Mary Anne Clarke, mistress of the Duke of York, Commander in Chief in the Napoleonic Wars, who through Mary Anne was involved in the big army scandal about the procurement of promotions via *douceurs* paid to Mary Anne, I devoured them all, and even that strange last novel, recalling wartime rationing and privations, of Cornwall declaring UDI from Britain, in protest at EEC regulations. It was called *Rule Britannia*, and proved that Daphne, even in her last years, could be both topical and prophetic.

So Daphne du Maurier was my icon, my standard of value, against which my prentice works had to be measured, right up to the time of her death. Because of her easy friendliness, I mourned her as a lost friend, as did many of her readers; and also as the last standard bearer of the popular narrative novel, the cult of the story teller, in a tradition that ran unbroken from Dickens to Arnold Bennett and H G Wells.

So I was delighted to learn that the distinguished writer, Susan Hill, had gained the ukase from the du Maurier estate to produce a sequel to her best selling novel, *Rebecca*, carrying on the narrative tradition.

Rebecca had never been my favourite of the du Maurier novels, on first reading it, it had had too many jagged nerve ends for my taste; I preferred the passion and sweep of her first novel, *Jamaica Inn*.

It was only when I saw the film of *Rebecca*, with Laurence Olivier, rather younger than the forty-five year old Maxim of the novel, that I began to perceive what might have been the impetus and force of the book and its raw quality.

It was, I perceived, a subconscious message of love by Daphne to her dead father, the celebrated actor-manager, Gerald du Maurier.

There must be few people alive who will remember Gerald du Maurier in his heyday, at the end of the First World War and during the 1920s, and the influence he imparted to the West End. Such was his fame that a cigarette, the du Maurier, was actually created in his honour, which continued to be sold successfully for several decades, to people who had long forgotten the actor after whom it was named.

Gerald du Maurier was the gentleman actor par excellence, a master of light comedy and light drama - I think he created on the stage the gentleman cracksman, Raffles, typically. His image was a debonair man-about-town in a dinner jacket, a cigarette negligently held in his fingers. His one near flop was as an unshaved escaped convict, despite the much praised excellence of his acting, his public could not stomach this deviation from his smooth and urbane image. Plays were written as vehicles for him, and comedies like Freddy Lonsdale's *Last of Mrs Cheyney* were inspired by him. All the younger actors of the day, Noel Coward, Laurence Olivier, Sir John Gielgud, were influenced by him, consciously or subconsciously.

Gerald was as popular offstage as on, a social lion much sought after by society hostesses, a principal guest at country house parties. The great ladies of fashion, and the most elegant actresses of an elegant age, doted on him.

In *Rebecca* I seemed to hear the voice of the teenage Daphne saying, "Daddy, leave these glitterati! They don't love you as I do!" *Rebecca*, the dazzling society beauty of the novel, epitomised this brittle society that, so often, claimed Gerald, and took him from daughter Daphne. There was also an element of anger.

So, in the book, Daphne has her revenge. Rebecca turns out to be a bad lot and it transpires that Maxim, the fictional representation of Gerald, murders her. Daphne gets him in the end, though Manderley, his world, has to burn down.

That combative old Cornishman, A L Rowse, snorted angrily in my presence of having a Cornish grandee "with the fine old Cornish name of Maxim de Winter!" But de Winter is not all that different a name from du Maurier, and one knows where Daphne got the name. The villainess in Dumas' *The Three Musketeers*, beautiful and deadly, was "Milady de Winter", a clear indicator that Rebecca in the novel will turn out to be a bad lot. (The curious friendship between Daphne and Gertrude Lawrence was itself significant. Gertrude Lawrence was the last of the great glitterati of the 1920s.)

Bearing in mind that Maxim was a representation of Gerald du Maurier, he could be nothing less than heroic; he is the book's star. I imagined a sequel with Maxim and his wife enduring the Blitz and the wartime privations (to which Daphne alludes indirectly in *Rule Britannia*) and I also expected that Maxim would emulate General Browning's war exploits, as a leader of men. I also envisioned a heroic role for the "I" of the story, perhaps as another Odette of the French Resistance.

Alas for my hopes! Maxim and his wife seemed to have missed the war altogether, in Susan Hill's sequel, skulking in Switzerland as the great events passed them by. In the post-war climate they would have been despised. As Olivier left Hollywood at his peak, to join the Fleet Air Arm, so Maxim must, or should, have come back.

As I read *Mrs de Winter*, I had the conviction that this novel, about as cheerful as *Jude the Obscure*, with death waiting round the corner for the various characters, was not the sequel Daphne du Maurier would have wished, despite Miss Susan Hill's narrative powers. Maxim in particular, round whom the first novel rightly revolved, seemed to be relegated to a subordinate role.

So, on a whim and for my own pleasure, I determined to write my own sequel, which would be a novel of action, in which Maxim and in particular "I", would have heroic roles, in a Second World War setting. If Daphne du Maurier might have not approved, I felt she would have been amused, especially at my efforts to create a family pedigree for the de Winters.

Thus inspired, I dashed off the novel in a few weeks. I had all the materials to hand. The setting of the lakeside Swiss villa I picked out of the film *Claire's Knee* of the great French film-maker, Max Rohmer. I had visited the Auvergne, staying at the Château of the *Comtesse* de Matherel near Issoire, and had met the local gentry, the de Montmorins, the Dillons and the D'Arcys, the two latter descended from the ennobled Wild Geese, Scottish and Irish soldiers of fortune serving King Louis. This, and my knowledge of Voltaire and his mistress Madame du Châtelet, gave me the family history.

I wanted my heroine, christened Jane/Jeanne, to have an intelligence role, in World War Two, but I did not want her to cash in on the heroism of the girls of SOE and the French Resistance. Then I read of General Carton de Wiart, said to have been the prototype of John Buchan's Richard Hannay, and how he had posed for some months as a Boer storekeeper in the First War in South Africa, listening and watching and being part of the furniture. That was the role I wanted for Jeanne, in the German Army headquarters in Paris, a silent observer who merged into the background. And who is the girl who becomes part of the furniture at any social gathering? Why, the girl who plays the piano.

So the idea built up. What sort of music would the Germans like to hear?

Obviously *limonades*, popular songs from the operettas and musical shows, Lehar, Kalman (was not the *Merry Widow* Hitler's favourite entertainment?) as well as more serious fare, like Chopin, Weber and Beethoven.

Then I remembered a conversation with the operetta expert and opera singer, Nigel Douglas, after he had created a new book and lyrics for Kalman's *Gypsy Princess* at Sadler's Wells. This operetta, *Die Csardasfürstin* in German, had run and run in Vienna throughout the First War, with hit tune after hit tune, which must have been whistled in the trenches, or sung; German soldiers were great singers.

One number '*Nimm, Zigeuner*' ('*Spiel, Zigeuner*', in verse two) had a very ominous ending: "Tomorrow is far too late!" Nigel said he imagined German officers would clasp the hands of their girlfriends at these words, and look soulfully into their eyes, implying that soon they were going back to the front. Many girls were willing to surrender their virtue, after hearing this repeated three times, at the end of each of the three verses.

I realised that this could be the way that Jeanne could get into the confidence of the German military. I envisaged Maxim and Jeanne going on an intelligence mission into Switzerland in 1938, at Carton de Wiart's request, to find out the strength of anti-Nazi feeling in the German Army, from the senior officers holidaying in Switzerland for the last time before the war, and salting away their valuables in Swiss banks at the same time. Playing the *limonades* and '*Nimm, Zigeuner*' would work on their nostalgia and sentimentalism and gain Jeanne the *entrée* and the friendships which she could profit from, when she set up her one-woman intelligence operation in Paris.

I knew there was, in fact, great debate in pre-war military circles as to whether the German Resistance and the German Army were thoroughly reliable or penetrated by the Gestapo; the Foreign Office and MI6 were very insistent that with UK help, the anti-Nazi elements in the German Army would launch a coup against Hitler. The Resistance, as it proved, was penetrated by the Gestapo, and a credulous MI6 operative who arranged a meeting with his Resistance counterpart on the French-German border, was hijacked by the Gestapo, who carried him over the border, so that he spent the war in a German prison.

The idea of Carton de Wiart having a private army is a pure invention, but he was the kind of larger than life character who might have done. Several novelists used him as a model, notably Evelyn Waugh, who based his Brigadier Ritchie Hook in *Officers and Gentlemen* on Carton de Wiart. Carton was also a considerable linguist, who had an eventful war. The idea of Maxcol was taken from Kingcol, Brigadier Kingston's force that went across the desert from Amman to overthrow the pro-German regime of Rashid Ali in Iraq in 1941.

I have to end with an apology. You remember the plot of Kalman's opera, *Countess Maritza*, in which the heroine, an heiress beset by suitors, tries to put off the pursuit by inventing a fiancé, Count Czupan, only to find a gentleman of that name arriving on her doorstep the following day, saying, "I understand from the papers that I am engaged to you. This has come as something of a surprise!"

When I wrote my book, I invented, or so I thought, the title of the *Vicomte* de Langlade. Re-reading the book, I realised that one of the ladies I met in the Auvergne in the late 1940s was a Madame de Langlade, who had spent the war in Australia. I apologise to her and her. family, for having involuntarily stolen her name. After all, Daphne du Maurier borrowed the name of de Winter from Alexandre Dumas!

I have enjoyed writing this romance, and hope Daphne du Maurier, whose books are still in print, would be tolerant of my presumption. It had not been my intention to publish this *jeu d'espirit*, written for my own amusement, had not a beautiful French girl, Suzanne Morel, to whom I passed it to check my indifferent French, insisted that I find a publisher. Thanks to a legacy from my late and very dear cousin Eveline Beal, and the efficiency and courtesy of the Minerva Press, this is now happening. I commend this labour of love to my readers, in memory of the wonderful Daphne du Maurier.

David Roach Pierson
Brashiers Cottage, 1996.

Chapter One

I Get a Name

It was Maxim who 'christened' me, Maxim looking up to find me before him, as he sat at his desk in the library at Manderley, reading the morning papers. I had gone into the library on some trivial errand, to find out what vegetables he would prefer with his luncheon. Finding him absorbed in his paper, I had stood there, marvelling that this masterful handsome being, with the head of a Greek god, had chosen me as his wife; had plucked me out of the servitude of being companion to an odious old woman, like King Cophetua elevating a beggar-maid to be his queen. It was a constant source of wonderment to me, surrounded as I was in Manderley with all the living memories of Maxim's first wife, the brilliant and lively Rebecca, whose death, I had believed, Maxim still mourned...

I was awakened from my reverie by the awareness that Maxim, over the top of his paper, was observing me with a mixture of amusement and exasperation.

"Oh, girl," he said, smiling that smile that always made me a little weak at the knees. "Why do you creep in here like a timorous little mouse, and stand there looking at me with your great big eyes? You remind me of Jane Eyre in the presence of Mr Rochester. I think I shall call you Jane until you mend your ways. You are the mistress of Manderley. Assert yourself until everyone, and especially your husband, trembles before you."

"I don't think I could do that. I'm not built to be a tartar," I replied as spiritedly as I could. "But if you want me to assert myself, I shall say that we are going to have broccoli for luncheon, whether you like it or not. And if you want to call me Jane, that is fine with me. It is better than the names my parents inflicted on me."

"Very well, Mélisande Yolanda, or Emma, as you have become, you shall be Jane forthwith. And as it happens, broccoli is my favourite vegetable," he said. We laughed and I left him to his paper.

The sheer cruelty and thoughtlessness of my romantic, opera-loving parents in naming their wretched offspring Mélisande Yolanda, because the last opera my mother had attended, before going into labour, was *Pelleas et Mélisande*, is something I have found hard to forgive my parents for. People should realise that children have to bear the names they have been inflicted with at christening in a hard and unsympathetic world. I have never managed to work up any enthusiasm for the composers of the late Romantic period, Debussy, Ravel, Richard Strauss. Even if I had inherited a sort of talent for music, my tastes were for keyboard and orchestral music and not opera, though I made an exception for operetta, whose vivacity I found infectious. But the piano was my instrument from early on, and my only love.

My parents did not survive long enough to know of my lasting displeasure. I was born in 1914, shortly after the start of the Great War, as we called it then. My father was a lecturer and tutor of mathematics at Oxford, so my earliest memories are of big untidy gardens and Victorian houses at Boar's Hill.

My professor father always seemed busy and preoccupied, though kind enough. He carried an air of sadness with him. So many of his best pupils had gone to the trenches, and so few had survived...

My mother, working on her own book, was also very affectionate when she saw me, which was about twice a day. For the rest I was left to the care of Nanny, who fed me and dressed me and took me for walks, and said how hard the poor professor worked.

When I was five, the professor went out of my life for good. With the coming of peace my father took advantage of an offer he had nursed during all the war years: of going to deliver a series of lectures in the United States. Unhappily, though the killing had finished in Europe, a particularly vicious influenza epidemic raged through America in the winter of 1918-19. My father arrived at the tail end of this epidemic early in 1919. He was hit by the virus and instantly succumbed even before my mother, coming over hotfoot on one of the latest liners, was able to reach his bedside.

She was desolated by his death, because they had been very close. She returned in a daze of mourning and literally pined away. She had lost the will to live, and six months later, a heavy cold turned to pneumonia and she gratefully joined my father in death. I was left an orphan.

There were, of course, any number of relatives who were happy to rear poor orphaned Melly, particularly since my father had left adequate provision for my keep and education. I was raised by various aunts with their boisterous families, and settled easily into the role of poor relation,

"Be nice to poor Melly, Children," was an injunction I frequently heard. On the whole, my cousins were nice to me, but I had become accustomed to being an only child and preferred to be solitary with my books and later my piano. I was just poor Melly, part of the family like the furniture was, to be remembered at birthday and party times.

I was sent off to boarding school as soon as that could be conveniently arranged. I was popularly supposed to have been desolated by the loss of both my parents. Though in truth, I hardly knew them; except as smiling and absent-minded adults whom I visited from the schoolroom, to be hugged and scrutinised twice a day, and returned to Nanny.

Nanny was kindly and taught me my letters, and I could read by the time I was three, which pleased my bookish father, when he remembered me.

At my schools I continued to be bookish and solitary, getting good marks while continuing not to make much of a mark. I continued to hate my name, which led my insensitive schoolmates to torment me with choruses of "Smelly Melly" in the school playground, from time to time. I accepted this as the natural order of things.

I had my piano – fortunately all the schools I attended had good musical traditions – and sympathetic staff. My ambition was to be a concert pianist. It was not until my teens that it was borne on me that I should never be more than a competent performer, and that it would be a waste of money for me to seek to go on to music college. My father's legacy, diminished by the crash of 1929, just would not run to it. My future seemed to lie in becoming a schoolteacher, governess or companion to some rich female.

I was a natural conformist, and accepted my fate. My one spurt of revolt had been when I went to my public school, and I finally announced, to everyone's surprise, that I was fed up with being "Poor Melly". Henceforward, I declared to my relatives, I would be known as plain "M" or Emma. My relatives responded by calling me nothing at all to my face.

At the age of sixteen I was thrown upon the world with a minuscule private income. I was qualified for nothing, though in my last years at school I had been taught domestic science, to qualify me for the brilliant marriage girls at my school were expected to make.

As my chances of matrimony seemed by my teachers to be slight, "Such a quiet, colourless girl, Emma," I was also taught the rudiments of shorthand and typing, to qualify me for the great world of commerce; a revolutionary step proposed by a new and worldly headmistress, though the Old Guard at school still regarded it as unladylike. But then the new headmistress had spent some time in America, and was rather progressive.

It was through this headmistress, Miss Clement, that I made the acquaintance with my future employer, Mrs van Hopper. Miss Clement had a correspondence with a friend in Boston, and learned from her that a distant cousin, a rich widowed Boston lady, had decided to reside in Europe, and needed a biddable companion.

I met Mrs van Hopper in Claridges and she was all graciousness, delighted to oblige any friend of Cousin Mary, and sympathetic that the American flu virus had carried off my father, as it had carried off the late Mr van Hopper. She professed herself deeply fond of music and hoped that I would oblige her on the piano every day. She might, she hinted, arrange some concerts for me with her influential friends, and, "Then, my dear, who knows?" I soon became so indispensable to her, that this promise was conveniently forgotten, though I did play for her when her hypochondria called for restful music.

Uncomplaining, I entered into her slavery, as her companion. In the ensuing years, I endured her temperaments and attacks of temper, smoothing down hotel officials whom she had offended, and making her wandering life comfortable in the various hotels in Europe through which we made our ill-tempered and complaining way. I was content to be a smiling doormat, to be periodically trodden on, but always to come up smiling.

It was from this slavery that Maxim rescued me, as I have related elsewhere, and brought me wondering to be mistress of Manderley, faced with the indifference of his family, the malice of Mrs Danvers, the housekeeper, and former lady's maid, and the awful brooding presence in the house of the brilliant and adorable Rebecca, Maxim's dead former wife, who seemed to be everything in charm and assurance that I was not. Only later did I learn that Rebecca was, in reality, a veritable monster, and that Maxim had murdered her.

Chapter Two

Manderley and After: We Go Abroad

Not even the abdication seem to have provoked more headline stories than we did in the popular press in the early part of 1936, with the double revelation of the suicide of Maxim's first wife, Rebecca, and closely following on, the burning down of Manderley.

"Society Beauty Suicide," screamed one newspaper headline, with a huge picture of the smiling Rebecca accompanying it. Another blazoned the words, "Cornish Death Mystery Solved." "'It was suicide,' says coroner." "Cornish Tragedy," was another familiar billboard caption. What the papers would have made of the true story, that the suicide chosen by the capricious Rebecca was to goad the hapless Maxim by taunts into killing her, is too awful to contemplate…

Hardly was the ink dry on those sensational news paragraphs, than the papers had another sensation to record: the burning down of our country house in Cornwall, Manderley. "Manderley, the ill-fated," "Double Tragedy for Cornish Family," "Accursed Cornish Mansion Ablaze," were just a few of the more lurid headlines, with pictures of poor gutted Manderley and of ourselves constantly shown.

Journalists were despatched from London to Cornwall, to see if the two tragedies could be interlinked…

"Servant Dies As Cornish Mansion Blazes," was as near as they could come to the true story, that the obsessively devoted Mrs Danvers, Rebecca's lady's maid, made crazy at her mistress's death, had burned down Manderley in an act of revenge against Maxim, whom she believed, instinctively, had murdered Rebecca. But happily there was no evidence of Mrs Danvers' mad act, which was useful when our agent, Frank, filed the insurance claim on our behalf. Poor mad Mrs Danvers. She did her best to make me feel an interloper and to make trouble between Maxim and myself. But it was a terrible way to die, as bizarre a suicide as that of Rebecca herself.

Understandably, the hotel to which we resorted after the blaze was soon besieged by journalists and the phone was never still. Maxim coped with unwearied courtesy. But the persecution continued even after we moved to London, to another hotel, and we were reduced to taking shelter in an unknown address, from which Maxim continued to issue statements, and arrange interviews, by letter. Even his patience finally frayed.

"I never want to see England or Cornwall again," he said grimly, adding, "Nor do I ever want to read another English newspaper."

Accordingly, as soon as we could get away, we escaped abroad. Maxim wanted to go to some country, and some part of that country that spoke no English and had no English visitors or residents, where we could start a new life. He already spoke several continental languages, and I was willing to learn.

We finally settled on Switzerland, buying a villa on a lake in a French speaking canton, where few foreign visitors came. As we live there still, and value our privacy, I shall not reveal its name.

Frank, our agent, visited us as soon as we settled in, bringing with him one of the few things that had survived the fire at Manderley: Maxim's father's hunting horn. Maxim was delighted since his father, Colonel Jack (Maximilian) de Winter, who had died leading his battalion at Ypres, carried this hunting horn with him on the battlefield from 1914 onwards.

"That is a good omen," he said smiling. "This hunting horn has survived the shot and shell of the trenches, and was found on my father's body in no man's land, and brought back to me. Now it has survived the burning down of Manderley. I think it proves that the spirit of the de Winters is indestructible."

Frank was pleased that we had chosen Switzerland. Though Manderley had gone, the Manderley estate was still considerable, and the income large. It would be easy to remit that income to us, by a Swiss bank, and there was still the money from the considerable insurance claim to come. Even if there was another war, it should still be possible to get the funds through, as Switzerland would almost certainly remain neutral. We should not have to worry about money: we should be very well-off.

Maxim signed a full power of attorney to Frank, and told him to regard the Manderley estate as his to command, and make what improvements he might wish. Unless we were to have an heir, the properties would be bequeathed to him.

"You are now the Squire of Manderley, Frank, so throw your weight around! Above all, don't let my sister Beatrice bully you. You are the boss," Maxim said. Frank coloured and shook Maxim's hand warmly, saying he would be a good steward of the property.

When he was gone, it was as though we had cut our last links with England, though it was to claim us back. We settled down to begin a new life in Switzerland, as Monsieur et Madame de Winter.

Chapter Three

Paradise Found

To my surprise and infinite satisfaction, the next three years were the most tranquil and happiest of my life, in our oasis in Switzerland by Lac du Brenets, close to L'Abbaye, and Le Lieu. The world seemed to have forgotten us, and we were very content to be forgotten. We had left no forwarding address, and Frank, our one contact with England, was resolute in not revealing it. All letters, from Beatrice and others, were being directed to our bank in Zurich. We ourselves sent only vaguely addressed cards to relatives and friends at Christmas. We were quite cut off.

Moving into the villa by the lake ended our period of mourning for Manderley. When first we came to Switzerland, we had been like wounded animals seeking a cave in which we could crawl, and lie remote from the world, while we licked our wounds and healed.

Our 'cave' was a second-class, small hotel, of very moderate quality. Its strength was that none of our friends, nor any besetting journalists whom we had come to consider as our enemies, could find us. We both smoked too much, and Maxim discovered a fascination for the progress of the Test Matches, though they were over before the English papers came to us. The rest of the English papers he threw away unread. Then one wonderful morning he came down to breakfast, a letter from Frank in is hand, not with the mask of pain that I had come to fear, but with the restless irritation that I remembered from Manderley, when things were not to his liking. He looked up at me, sitting expectant, and about to pour what the hoteliers liked to imagine was English tea, and growled, just like the old days.

"I am always disagreeable at breakfast, but the food here is vile, and the service not much better. Why on earth do we go on staying here?"

My heart leapt. This was the aggressive old Maxim.

"Why, indeed? Let's move out, today. Shall we find a better hotel, a bigger one?"

"Not another hotel. I should hate to meet any of our acquaintances yet, or your Mrs van Hopper and her sort. But I've had a letter from Frank, and a copy of the farm accounts. We aren't paupers, and we don't need to live in this way. Why don't we find ourselves a villa, buy it and furnish it ourselves? At least we should have our own things around us."

"A villa by a lake...?" I asked tentatively.

"Certainly. I can take up sailing again."

Now I knew he was cured. I went over and kissed him.

"Welcome back, Maxim. And can I have a piano?"

"Don't be too sympathetic," he growled. "We should have done this months ago. And of course you must have your piano, the best that we can find."

And so over the indifferent breakfast table we made our plans, and our new life in Switzerland began.

We furnished the villa modestly, from local sources, to suit our own tastes. I discovered Maxim had a fine eye for colour, and a talent for picking up attractive pieces at local auction sales. The villa, at the end, bore our own hallmark but was essentially Swiss. We were very pleased with it. Our few luxuries were a boat for Maxim to sail on the lake, and in due course, to instruct me in the niceties of sailing; a good piano for me, to indulge my taste for unflamboyant music; and also, a necessity rather than a luxury, a large, comfortable and not too ostentatious tourer car.

I had feared Maxim would get bored and fretful, and inclined to brood on the past. But I was wrong. He welcomed the leisure, the freedom from having to supervise the day by day management of the estate, and its battery of dependants, all with their feuds and complaints. He had leisure, he said, to do what he had always wanted to do, to research the history of the de Winters.

"I want to find out how a family with a name like de Winter, which is neither French nor English, came to be great landowners in Cornwall. And I want to nail the rascal who caused every eldest son in our family to be inflicted with the name of Maximilian."

By good fortune or wise forethought, the family archives of the de Winters, such as they were, were kept in deed boxes with the family solicitor in London, so had not perished in the fire.

This provided Maxim with a starting point, and soon he was carrying on a lengthy correspondence not only with London but with Paris and Edinburgh, and experts and historians in several different countries. Fortunately the villa had several spare bedrooms, one of which became our private archive room, full of filing cabinets, and document-storing receptacles.

I had my piano and Maxim liked to hear me play as he worked. I had no aspiration now to be a concert pianist, but was a competent performer of unexacting works, and popular tunes. I had my favourite classical pieces, mostly Chopin, which I was able to augment in shopping forays to Bern and Zurich. I also had a good repertoire of musical comedy numbers and popular tunes, some of which I picked up on the wireless and was able to play by ear. I have a good ear.

It was my playing that first gave me my debut into the local Swiss society. A neighbour heard the music as she was passing by, which gave her the notion of coming in and introducing herself, begging that I would attend her next tea party. Being English, I was permitted the eccentricity of answering the door myself, and not having a maid in white gloves to attend to that function.

My playing at the tea party was extravagantly admired, and other guests hoped that I would come and attend their soirées. I had my debut in polite local society.

Maxim was amused when I told him of my social success.

"That is admirable, my girl," he said. "Now you have the opportunity to learn French properly, as a child learns it, by listening. Your French is adequate now, but by listening, you will pick up the nuances of real spoken French. When I first went to Europe, as a boy, my father told me to think of myself as a young boy from a grammar school, posted to a smart Guards regiment. I must smile a great deal, but say only the absolute essentials, like "Pass the mustard." But I had to watch and listen, and hear what people said, and the way they said it, the gestures and body language. When I had mastered those, I would be speaking the way they did, and be accepted as one of them, without question."

With my mouse-like past, I was very good at smiling, and being sympathetic and listening to the conversation around me. Being on the piano stool makes you particularly anonymous, part of the furniture. So I smiled and listened, "*L'Anglaise au piano.*"

I soon discovered, to my joy, that I had an ear for languages similar to my ear for music. I made myself a phonograph disc for audial sensations. I found that, like an actress, I could retain and repeat back whole phrases and conversations, which I would bring back in the evening to Maxim, and relay back, word for word and gesture for gesture.

"I can absolutely see these matrons, clacking away like hens. You have missed your vocation, girl. You should have been an actress," he said, wiping the tears of laughter from his eyes. "You would have been as famous as Sarah Bernhardt by now."

"Oh, no, " I said. "I cannot play a part. I am just a phonograph, recording and playing back what I have heard."

"You always underrate yourself, my dear," he said. "You have unusual talents."

That set me thinking. My growing knowledge of French had given me a mask, behind which the shy, gauche Jane could hide, and like a Greek actor in a mask, in classical Greek drama, could create a part to perform. I remembered how Alec Guinness and other actors and actresses I had seen, were dull and colourless people in themselves, or when they played themselves. Give them a flamboyant part, they were totally convincing, submerging themselves in it. Perhaps I could do the same, looking out dispassionately from behind my mask and playing a role I had set up for myself?

From that time, I had my first mask, that of Jeanne de Winter, the sympathetic hostess in this provincial Swiss society. As my fluency grew, I was still never the gabber, but the chosen confidante of my friends, always willing to lend a sympathetic ear to any tale of marital infidelity or social dispute. Dear Jeanne would never gossip; she was a real friend. I continued to be a loyal performer on the piano at my friends' tea parties, and an accompanist of singers, which was something of a strain when the talent was small, but I still managed to be smiling and sympathetic. I also played the piano at dances for Maxim's yacht club.

Maxim was a popular member of the local yacht club, a good fellow who was never ostentatious. or throwing his weight or his money around. His nickname was '*L'Historien*'. We were popular members of the community. Within a year, we had become wholly absorbed, and few people thought of us as '*Les Anglaises*'. My moment of pure bliss came when a newcomer thought that I was wholly Swiss, and spoke disparagingly of those foreigners across the lake, who do not know how to behave as we Swiss do.

Maxim had taught me how to sail, and I enjoyed it, but only when I was with him. He called me the perfect crew member.

"You remember everything I tell you, and have no clever ideas of your own."

That caused a tiny cloud to come between us, momentarily, because we both remembered Rebecca, who always had her own ideas, and got her own way.

Maxim liked to go for walks in the mountains, and sometimes I went with him, happy to pit my lesser strengths against his, knowing instinctively when he wanted to talk or to be silent.

"Oh, my love," he said to me once, "your silence is the most beautiful thing I have ever heard." And my cup was full. Then there were times when I felt he wanted to be alone, and then I made excuses, and spent the day happy in the villa, thinking of what dishes I would leave waiting on the table for him, when he returned, relaxed and ravenous.

"I am so late that I expected the dishes to be thrown at my head, rather than on the table arranged in my honour, " he said on one occasion. "What have I done to deserve so perfect and compliant a wife?"

"If you had suffered an accident, I should have known," I said. "But if you had met with some delay and had to stay overnight, I would not have worried. We have thought transference, you and I."

"I think we have," he agreed, smiling. "But happily you are not the worrying kind. If I came in covered with blood, having fallen down the mountain, you would patch me up and send for the ambulance, and never turn a hair. You can't know how reassuring that is for me."

"I did all my worrying in Manderley," I said. "Nothing can worry me now."

Maxim's work on his book and my development as a society hostess continued. We began to entertain more – Maxim's friends from the yacht club, and my friends, who in many cases, were the same people. We had become natives of Switzerland.

As we saw our guests away from the villa, profuse with gratitude for a really enjoyable evening, Maxim said to me, smiling,

"I little knew when I married you, that sweet gauche girl as you were then, that I would be marrying a perfect society hostess."

It came out.

"You mean, another perfect society hostess," I said. He smiled, not offended.

"No, you are better than she was. She thought only of herself and dazzled everyone. You care about everyone else, and think of yourself hardly at all. After being with her, one thought what a brilliant evening it was. After being with you, people say, 'How brilliant *I* was that night!' People really enjoy coming here, just because of you." His kindness made me blush, and he embraced me, saying, "You will never believe how wonderful you are, however much I tell you."

Only one cloud shadowed our happiness. Maxim, I knew, wanted a child, and I could not give him one. We never spoke of it, but I sensed his disappointment, which was as great as my own.

Some day, perhaps...but that some day never came.

Still, I had my music, my increasing fluency in French, and I had Maxim. I needed no more for happiness.

It was gratifying to be mistaken for French, and to overhear myself being discussed one day in the yacht club.

"Dear Jeanne...do you mean to say that she is not French at all...? You would never think it...she must come of very good family...better, I think, than her husband's..."

When very diffidently I repeated this conversation to Maxim, he roared with laughter.

"How very percipient of your friend!" he laughed. She's probably right. From what I've been able to learn of my ancestors, they were the most shameless sort of adventurers, with a penchant for marrying rich heiresses."

"Maxim! You've traced them?"

"Back to the Highlands of Scotland, and the rebellion of 1715, when they first went on their travels. And I've managed to trace the villain, and he was a right villain, a revolutionary and a Jacobin, who inflicted on us the name of Maximilian, and endowed his ill-gotten fortune to his son, on the stipulation that every eldest son would bear the name of Maximilian, or strictly Maximilien, after one of the great villains of history."

"Tell me about it," I said, eagerly.

So sitting by the fire, Maximilian, named after Robespierre, did just that.

Chapter Four

Where We Came From

"As far as I've been able to discover," said Maxim, "the Winter family, not de Winter yet, straddled the Scottish borders. Whether we were originally an English family that migrated to Scotland or a Scottish family some of whose members came south, I've been unable to discover.

"There was certainly a branch of the Winter family established in the Midlands when James I came to the throne. There were certainly two brothers, Sir Robert Winter, and Thomas Winter, who served as a mercenary soldier in the Low Countries, and recruited Guy Fawkes, an expert on siege tactics and controlled explosions, to be a member of the Gunpowder Plot. But I haven't established any direct contact with them.

"About the same time there was a Scottish branch of the family, known as Winter or McWinter – the names seem to have been interchangeable at that time – who were a junior clan of the McGregors, Catholic and Jacobite. Our direct ancestor seems to have been the Laird of McWinter. He and his son were involved in the 1715 rebellion. They turned out for the Old Pretender, James Stuart, son of James II. You remember that there was a very inconclusive battle of Sherriffmuir, when both armies ran away? Well, the old man, the Laird, Roderick McWinter, managed to get himself killed at that battle. He probably fell off his horse.

"After the battle, his son, Alastair McWinter, now the Laird, decided Scotland was too hot to hold him, and decamped to France, where he became a mercenary soldier in the armies of King Louis XV. The king was just a child and the real ruler of France was the Regent Orleans, who gave him a cadetship in the musketeers.

"One of his fellow cadets was the military engineer Vauban. Another who was to have greater influence on his life was FlorentClaude du Châtelet-Lomont, later Marquis du Châtelet, and a Marshal of France, who has gone down in history as the cuckolded husband of Voltaire's mistress, Emilie du Châtelet.

"He was about twenty in 1715, a great bull of a man over six foot, but a very good soldier. Florent-Claude and the Chevalier de Winter, as he was now known (a translation of the Laird of McWinter), became close friends and companions of war. They were joined by Charles, *Vicomte* de Langlade, and the three got the reputation of being the bravest of the brave. '*Les Insepérables*', the Army called them. Interesting, isn't it? You can probably see the germ of *The Three Musketeers* of Alexandre Dumas, in their story.

"The three served in the campaigns of Landau and Freiburg, with Florent-Claude the brightest star. He was a Major General before he was thirty, and second-in-command at the siege of Phillipsburg. Of course he looked after his two friends, and got them good commands, but Charles de Langlade was too dashing once too often at Phillipsburg, and a cannon ball took off his head. When the Army went into winter quarters at the end of 1724-1725, the two young men went on leave.

"Florent-Claude went on leave to Paris, where he met the beautiful Emilie de Breteuil, daughter of the chief of protocol at the court, the rather dim Louis-Nicholas, Baron de Breteuil. He discovered, to his surprise and horror, after his wedding night, that he had married the most brilliant woman in France, and could hardly understand a word she spoke, though he soon became well aware of her extravagance.

"He fled back to the front at the earliest opportunity, leaving word with the tradesmen that he would not be responsible for any debts incurred by his wife, not personally countersigned by him. Emilie obliged him with an heir and then a daughter, Gabrielle-Pauline, and was unfaithful – first with the Duke de Richelieu, and then with Voltaire – to the Marquis's relief, since Voltaire understood what Emilie was talking about, regarding Descartes, physics and Newton's theories, and could support her in the style to which she imagined she was entitled.

"The Chevalier de Winter also got himself a wife. He went down to Charles's home in the Auvergne to give his old father, the *Comte* de Langlade, details of how his son had died. He found that as

Charles was the only son, the heiress to the château in the Auvergne and the family fortune was Charles's sister, Gabrielle-Pauline de Langlade (she was godmother to Florent-Claude's daughter, who took her name, a very popular one in the de Langlade family). Whether from love or self-interest, or because Gabrielle-Pauline resembled so closely his dead friend, the Chevalier married her, being able to call himself thereafter the Chevalier de Winter de Langlade.

"The Chevalier went to join his friend Florent-Claude at the wars, which continued intermittently throughout the 1730s and 1740s. The crowning glory of the War of the Austrian Succession was the victory of Fontenoy over the British, which must have given the Chevalier a certain satisfaction.

"Honours were conferred like confetti on all the senior officers, of which the Chevalier was now one, Florent-Claude, second-in-command to the Marshal de Saxe, being especially singled out.

"The Chevalier was given his heart's desire: a title. As the *Comte* de Langlade, his father-in-law, had just died, he was allowed to take his title in his own right, becoming the *Comte* de Winter et de Langlade. His young son was accorded the courtesy title of the *Vicomte* de Langlade, the title the long-dead Charles had borne.

"The *Comte* de Winter, as he was now known, retired to the château in the Auvergne, where he became known as a mighty hunter, but little was left of the dashing Highlander that he had once been.

"But blood, they say, will out. Though his son, the second *Comte* de Winter, followed the dim, rich, pompous and right-wing views of his de Langlade ancestors, his son Louis Xavier, *Vicomte* de Langlade, was soon to display in the 1770s and 1780s, all the quixotic wildness of the Highlander.

"He refused to use his title and called himself *Citoyen* de Winter. As the French Revolution approached he allied himself with Robespierre and the extremists. His father, the right-of-right Count de Winter, disinherited and disowned him. When he died, shortly before the French Revolution, he petitioned and gained consent from King Louis XVI to leave the title and the entailed estates to his younger son, Philippe.

"The Jacobin, as Citizen de Winter was now known in the family, was quite content with this arrangement and remained on the best of terms with the new *Comte* de Winter, his younger brother. He had married the sweet, adoring daughter of an apothecary and was having a high old time playing politics. When his wife gave him a son, in 1787 or so, he named him Maximilien, after Robespierre.

"But again, heredity will out. The Jacobin soon sickened of the Terror, but remained on good terms with Robespierre. Robespierre, despairing of all the corruption around him and having to fight a war, called on his old friend, who was at least honest, to take charge of supplying the armies of the Revolution.

"The Jacobin had found his true *métier*. When Robespierre fell from power, Carnot, 'organiser of victory', begged the *Citoyen* de Winter to continue in the post. So did the First Consul, Napoleon Bonaparte, when he seized power.

"As a result the Jacobin remained at his post until almost until 1814; he took retirement just before Napoleon's Russian campaign, after telling the outraged Emperor that if he went ahead with what he considered was a very foolhardy campaign, he despaired of ever seeing his supplies again.

"He retired to Switzerland for his health, and did not return to Paris until his younger brother, the *Comte* de Winter (whom the Jacobin had protected throughout the Revolution), secured an amnesty for him.

"The Jacobin ended his life in the château in the Auvergne, which he had redecorated from top to bottom with his great wealth. He left all his papers and documents and a considerable sum of money to his brother when he died, having seen the Bourbons replaced by King Louis Philippe d'Orléans, son of his old friend, Philippe (Orléans) Egalité.

"But what happened to the Jacobin's son, Maximilien de Winter? To his father's despair, he became an ardent Bonapartist, joined the navy as a cadet, became a dashing lieutenant, and was taken prisoner by the British, after Trafalgar.

"He was taken to Falmouth, where he stayed as a paroled prisoner, much admired by the ladies for his romantic French appearance. At the end of hostilities, he scandalised Cornish society by eloping with a Cornish heiress, Miss Pengelly, and carrying her off to France.

"He appealed to his father, the Jacobin, for support. The Jacobin, remembering his own marriage to an apothecary's daughter and being repudiated by his father, and because Miss Pengelly was very pretty with winning ways, gave his blessing to the marriage. He endowed his son hugely, but only on the proviso that the first son had thereafter to be called Maximilien.

"The young couple returned, laden with French gold, reconciled with Miss Pengelly's family, and proceeded to buy the biggest house available in Cornwall, called Manderley.

"And there," concluded Maxim, "we have remained ever since, until the great fire. And that is why, I and all the eldest sons of my family have been blessed with the name of Maximilian."

"What about the younger son, the *Comte* de Winter, and his family? Do they still live in the château in the Auvergne?" I asked.

"Indeed they do," said Maxim. "There is a *Comte* de Winter, in his seventies, who lives in the château. In fact, he was one of the starting points for my research. In my father's war diaries, which is a book I carry everywhere with me, like a bible – that was how it wasn't lost in the fire at Manderley – I'd remembered that my father had mentioned meeting a colonel at French headquarters, a Count de Winter, who was some sort of French cousin.

"Later he wrote that my cousin, the Count, writes that his second son has been killed in the trenches, poor devil, and how he feels for him. He has written down the Count's address, the Château de Langlade, Issoire, Dept Puy-de-Dôme, in order to remind himself to send a note of commiseration. But he himself was killed on the battlefield a few weeks later, so the letter was never sent.

"Well, I took a chance and wrote a letter to the Count, saying I had found his name in the war diaries, and was interested to know a little of the family history. We have had quite a correspondence, and he has invited me to go down to the Auvergne to see him and to look through the family papers.

"Apparently, the first Maximilian, for all that he pretended to be the complete English gentleman, used to spend at least three months in France most years, to do the French season, and regularly visited the château for a few days, to pay his respects to the old Count Philippe, and after his death, to his son, his cousin.

"He left all his papers to be kept in the château after his death, including, the Count thinks, his correspondence with Alexandre Dumas, whom he knew, and who used the de Winter name in the *Three Musketeers*.

"The Count says he also has correspondence which the Jacobin had with Voltaire, when he was a very young man and Voltaire was a very old man. The Count says it is amusing because it is virtually the only occasion that the Jacobin used his title in correspondence. He had written to Voltaire as plain M. de Winter, and had had no reply. Someone suggested that Voltaire, for all that he pretended to be such a liberal, was really an old snob. So he wrote again as the *Vicomte* de Langlade and Voltaire replied by return."

"It's snobbery that makes the world go round!" I said flippantly, little thinking that before very long I should be the beneficiary of that snobbery.

"So we have an open invitation to visit the Count in his château in the Auvergne, any time we choose. I'd like to do it. The old man is quite alone now with only his granddaughter, who must be about your age, to look after him. He may not live long."

"If he dies you can claim the title back," I said lightly. "You are descended from the elder son, after all. And I should be a Countess."

"I prefer you as plain Mrs de Winter. Or Madame Jeanne, as you have become. Should we take out Swiss papers and live here forever?"

"Live here forever, certainly. But I rather like being British."

"So do I, actually," said Maxim. "Perhaps we could work it that we have two sets of papers. You can do anything here, if you have money."

In the end, we did manage to get two sets of papers. And very useful they were to prove.

Chapter Five

In Which We Get Our Marching Orders

"There will be war within the year," said Maxim matter-of-factly, looking up from the newspaper.

Since the beginning of the German propaganda war against Czechoslovakia, midway through 1938, with the call the reunification of Sudetenland with Greater Germany, Maxim had broken the rule of life established in 1936, and had begun to receive the English papers as well as our usual Swiss ones. It was the first step of two recluses to come back into the world.

The English papers, after an absence of two years, seemed exceedingly trivial. Maxim, who detested Dawson the Appeaser, as he called the editor of *The Times*, said it was worse than trivial. There was a concerted conspiracy, implicitly agreed, among the English pressmen, to turn their backs on events that were happening outside England.

The Munich Agreement had been signed, and so attention could be directed, to the great relief of the English public, away from those far-off countries of which we knew little, like Czechoslovakia ("It's not a country, it's a disease," giggled some clever diplomat), and the Civil War in Spain.

I looked over Maxim's shoulder at the October 10th edition of *The Times*, with a slightly nauseating fulsome account of Prime Minister Neville Chamberlain appearing on the balcony of Buckingham Palace with the King and Queen, and being motioned forward by King George VI to the edge of the balcony, to receive the cheers of the assembled crowds.

"Do we have to read this?" I asked.

"We need to know what the British people are thinking and what bromides and propaganda they are being fed by the press," he replied.

I returned to Maxim's remark.

"Do you really think it will be war, this time round?"

"Not a doubt of it," he said. "After the Munich sell-out, Hitler will believe that he has only to push and the British and French governments, and everybody else, will fall on our backs like puppies, with paws in the air. He will break his word over Czechoslovakia, and occupy the rest of the country, probably early next year. The British and French governments will be aghast, and will guarantee the integrity of Hitler's next target, Poland. He will ignore these guarantees also and invade Poland, probably at the end of next year. And so it will be war. I only hope Chamberlain will have used the breathing space to re-arm."

I felt my paradise was already lost.

"What will you do, Maxim, if war comes?" He frowned.

"Go back to England and join up, I suppose. My family has been involved in every war going since the 1715 rebellion, so I don't think in all conscience that I can sit this one out."

"But will they take you? After all, you're over thirty, Maxim."

He laughed.

"How percipient of you to raise that point! Yes, I am over thirty, but I'm fully fit, I can climb mountains, I can sail a boat, I can shoot and ride, and until I came here I was a countryman, able to move silently through rough ground at night, and navigate my way by the stars. I think they will need these skills in the next war. And, yes, I can drive a car, strip it down and put it together again, all useful attributes in a soldier, not to mention all my languages, including German.

"The next war won't be static and a war of attrition, a war of the trenches, like the last one, despite all the investment in the Magnet Line and the Siegfried Line.

"I think the next war will call for small and very mobile forces, very fast moving, living off the land: an armoured war of small mobile units. Just the sort of war envisaged by Marlborough when he set up my father's old regiment, the Duke of Cornwall's Mounted Infantry."

"Mounted infantry? Isn't that a contradiction in terms, like the Horse Marines?"

Maxim laughed.

"It sounds like that, I know. But the infantry of the Duke of Marlborough's day were very slow moving. Not only did they have to lug around their muskets, heavy cumbersome things, but they carried a great deal of other equipment as well.

"The Duke wanted infantry to be able to move fast on a battlefield, so that if there was a weakness in his line, he could shore it up, or if the enemy fell into disarray, he could exploit that weakness, and throw fresh men into the battle fast.

"So he formed this elite corps of soldiers who could ride and were good sharpshooters under a protégé of his, Colonel John Carmichael. He'd keep this corps in his reserve, and when the decisive moment came he'd say, "Send for Carmichael."

"Then Carmichael and his troop of mounted infantry would ride hell for leather to the point of weakness, dismount and charge, usually at the point of the bayonet. Very effective they were. The Army nicknamed them Carmichael's Devils. They were very effective in messy wars, like the American War of Independence, when the Army was up against sharpshooting irregulars, and they were very useful to General Cornwallis when he carried out a mounted blitzkrieg through the Southern States, later in the same war.

"During the South African War, when my father was a subaltern, the regiment was very useful in fighting off the Boer mounted commandos. Of course they lost their horses in the Great War of 1914-1918, and became just another infantry regiment. But in the next war, they could be very useful, with armoured cars taking the place of horses."

He was becoming quite enthusiastic.

"When do you make your next move then, and join up?"

"As soon as possible. If I am going to get a place in my father's regiment, and there may be a few left who remember Colonel Jack, the sooner I apply the better. If I wait till the war starts, there will be conscription, and I may be sent anywhere. This way I can be fully trained when the shooting actually starts."

"Well," I said. "If you are going to join up, then so am I."

He looked surprised, but pleased.

"I never thought about it, but that is exactly what I would have expected you to say. You're very courageous, my dear, and I'm not the only one who underestimates you. Let's go to London as a fighting couple, the tiger and his mate, and see what London can offer us."

I went straight to my piano and began to play one of my favourite airs from Massenet. Maxim looked on, amused.

"What are you playing?"

"It's Manon's aria: 'Adieu, petite table'. She sings it as she bids farewell to the little room she has shared with her young lover, the Chevalier des Grieux, and goes to be the mistress of the tax financier, to live in glorious luxury and to have her every whim gratified, down to the last diamond tiara!"

Maxim laughed outright.

"Very appropriate, my dear. But don't start mothballing the villa entirely. I daresay the Army won't be able to employ us for months. We probably won't be gone more than a fortnight, at the outside. But if you like, we can arrange to spend Christmas in London, and look up all our old friends. If we have any friends left," he concluded cynically. So that was what we decided on.

We had a neighbour, a widowed lady called Madame Gossard with time on her hands, who delighted to look after the villa whenever we went away for a few days, usually when Maxim was visiting Zurich to consult the bank and to discuss our financial affairs. Now that the insurance company had paid out on Manderley we were very comfortably off, and Frank was sending regular cheques from the rents of the Manderley Estate.

I went to Madame Gossard, and told her we were spending Christmas in London. She was delighted to have the run of our larger villa, as well as her more modest one, and said she would come in every day, to dust and forward our mail.

She seemed touchingly concerned that once we were back in England, we might like it so much that we should not come back. I assured her that we were devoted to Switzerland and would assuredly return. She asked where she should forward our mail. I asked Maxim, engaged on a letter to Colonel Julyan, whom he thought might still have contacts at the War Office.

"Tell her to forward any mail to us care of the Savoy Hotel, London. It's close to the War Office and we want to splash out a little, before the balloon goes up," he said.

So about a fortnight later, grace of Imperial Airways in Croydon, we were back in London again after nearly three years.

The capital had not changed much, though I sensed a feverishness of gaiety which I had not remembered before. The fashionable restaurants, like Gunters, were full with well-dressed people drinking champagne. The shops also were busy, with Selfridges and Harrods doing record business. Other people than us, it seemed, were determined to enjoy themselves before the balloon went up.

As French Ambassador M. Paul Claudel is said to have remarked during the Wall Street Crash, "Between the Crisis and the Catastrophe let us take a glass of champagne." The comfortable people in all the cities of Europe: London, Paris, Rome, probably Berlin too, seem to be doing just that. From the Folies Bergère in Paris to the Café de Paris in London, tables were full and trade was good.

Most nights we would dine in the Savoy Grill Room, listening to the music of Carol Gibbons and surrounded by women in exquisite evening gowns and men in full evening dress, resolutely having a good time.

The last days of Pompeii," Maxim murmured to me as he caught my wandering glance.

All this contrasted with our daytime activities. Colonel Julyan had been one of our first visitors. He congratulated me on my new-found beauty and brought with him a list of old comrades from the last war now in responsible positions in the War Office. Daily, Maxim set out to the sandbagged War Office following up mew contacts. He spent much time in the War Office in meetings followed by the inevitable business luncheons. I sometimes wonder if any decision of war, business or politics could be resolved without those formal sessions of serious eating and drinking.

We also entertained the current Colonel of Colonel Jack's old regiment, white-moustached and brisk, who remembered Colonel Jack very well in the trenches and said he was a legend in the regiment. He had many anecdotes. But after almost a fortnight we were no nearer employment.

The Duke of Cornwall's Mounted Infantry had divided. The first battalion, as Maxim predicted, was equipped with armoured cars and the second battalion remained a purely infantry unit. But there were no vacancies. The regiment was not yet on a war footing; officers who had waited for a shooting war, and the possibilities of casualties and promotions, would not be standing down when war seemed imminent.

The Colonel promised Maxim a commission as soon as a vacancy occurred, and everything was on the move. But in the meantime...

We were almost ready to pack our bags and go back to Switzerland, once the now rather hollow Christmas celebrations were over, when Maxim visited one of the last contacts on his list in the War Office.

He came back with a curious smile.

"I have an appointment with a very senior General in the War Office who wants to speak to me, and you, Jeanne, are to accompany me!"

Chapter Six

The Interview and the Mission

An interview with a General? Maxim and I together? My mind reverted immediately to the banal.

"Good heavens, Maxim, are they interviewing wives now with their officer husbands, to see they know what forks to use at table, and that they have the right form of small talk so they don't let their husbands down at ladies nights in the mess?"

He smiled.

"Probably it would be no bad idea. Often it is the wives who run the husbands, or provide the motivation to make them run. My father told me, or I overheard him telling mother, that one General in the Army, and a very good one, had only got to his exalted rank because his wife was so extravagant that he had to climb the military ladder in double-quick time – just to keep pace with his wife's spending. Actually, it may be because I told someone of your remarkable gift for languages and your facility of total recall."

"Oh, my old phonograph talent. Have you been bandying my praises all round the War Office?" I asked.

"When you have attended as many interviews as I have, and the lunches that follow them, you begin to run out of topics of conversation. A pretty wife with a talent like yours seems a good safe subject, and makes me out as a model devoted husband."

"So you trot me out in conversation, when it is beginning to flag, as Fido, the performing French poodle? I wonder what will be expected of me when I get to the War Office? Some risqué French cabaret numbers?"

He laughed and said,

"I really don't know. I imagine it will be some high level liaison work with the French Army. General Adrian Carton de Wiart is very senior, and being half-Belgian, is quite a linguist. But I don't think he would be seeing us unless it was important. Carton de Wiart served in the South African War and the Great War. He has the reputation of being very bright indeed. More than that I don't know. Cheer up, girl. When we came from Switzerland we said we'd hunt in pairs, tiger and tigress. Now it seems we're getting our chance."

It was a strange situation. I found myself unconcerned about the interview, *che será, será*, but extremely concerned about what I should wear.

To be over-dressed would create the wrong impression if I wanted to help Maxim get the appointment. So furs and a saucy hat were out! So was too great a profusion of jewellery, and too conspicuous a scent. On the other hand, to be totally mouse-like would not help him either. I had to give the impression of self-command, and competence, to indicate that I was the ideal helpmate of an officer on the way up.

In the end I chose a deceptively simple dress I had bought in Switzerland; neither too fashionable nor too tweedy, but conveying a slight and discreet air of affluence. My jewellery was good but discreet. Only my gloves and my handbag looked expensive. I was pleased with my appearance in the mirror. I looked like a Frenchwoman of taste which I instinctively felt that this half-Belgian General, with the impossible name, would appreciate.

I remembered a phrase from a Saki novel, "She wore her pearls with the indefinable air of having better ones at home, a gift which few are able to achieve." This was precisely the impression I was trying to achieve, the mask that for this occasion, I was going to put on.

As it happened, I had instinctively chosen the right mask. We were shown deferentially into a small room in the War Office, the secretary seeming to convey by her bearing that we were being accorded a very great honour given to few. Then a door opened in the back of the room and the General entered.

General Carton de Wiart has become so much of my life since, though we have met only on a few occasions, that I find difficulty in remembering what he looked like on that occasion. He seemed a very large man, though that might have been the impression of the small room, with this figure in his khaki and red tape, whose personality seemed to dominate it. He had a mobile, intelligent face but the thing that dominated his features was the black eyepatch that covered one eye, making him look like a pirate.

He was civil, cordial and business-like.

"Mr de Winter, how kind of you to come and see me, and to bring your charming wife along. I had wanted to meet you because I was a little acquainted with your father, Colonel Jack de Winter, in the Great War."

Maxim smiled.

"Everyone in the War Office seems to have met my father in the last war."

"Well, he was a very commanding personality. Once seen, never forgotten. And in any war, the people at the front line are quite a small select mob. You always seem to run into the same people, the fighters, everywhere you went and if they survived, you were part of a very elite body, rather like the men of the Forlorn Hope in the wars of Wellington. But I am neglecting your wife. Forgive me. Do you prefer to be addressed as Mrs Jane de Winter, or Madame Jeanne de Winter? "

I shrugged my shoulders.

"Personnellement, cela m'est égal."

Why had I chosen at this moment to lapse into French? I shall never know. Perhaps it was the French accenting by the General of my name, Jeanne de Vinterr.

At all events, the General switched effortlessly into French and began to interrogate me in that language, about my life in Switzerland, my interests, my piano, my friends, and what they were like. I warmed to this man, and had no difficulty in answering him, giving little character sketches of my various friends and their mannerisms, as I did for Maxim. The General listened, entranced, interpolating a question now and again. I ended up with bravura, saying that I was now "*une vraie Suisse*", and that I never wanted to see England again, except for the pleasure of meeting a "*vrai soldat Anglais*" like himself.

The General laughed and switched his attention to Maxim, questioning him about his life in Switzerland, his friends at the yacht club, his book about the de Winters, and the French connections of his family.

Then the General, still speaking in French, gave an admirably concise account of the political and military situation, touching on the likelihood of war, and the intentions of Germany. Then he turned to me.

"Répétez, s'il vous plait, Madame de Winter."

I had subconsciously known that this would be my test, and had relaxed, taking it in point by point. I found that I was able to repeat it back to him, almost word for word, in the exact nuances of phrase and action he had used.

Carton de Wiart listened, intrigued.

"Fascinating, Mrs de Winter," he said. "You have a most unusual gift. Oscar Wilde used to be able to thumb through a book and repeat back whole passages. But I have not met someone before who could repeat back word for word something he or she has just heard, as you have just done. Could you do the same in German?"

"Not the nuances of speech and pronunciation, I think. Of course I speak German, as it is the second language of Switzerland, but I have never been exposed to a lot of German speech. Perhaps I could, I don't know. I don't even know that I could do it in English."

"How good is your German?" the General asked.

"I speak it with a strong Swiss-French accent."

"That need not be a disadvantage," he said. I became aware that the conversation had slipped imperceptibly back into English. Carton de Wiart settled back in his chair, pleased with events as they had turned out, and now prepared to show where our colloquy was leading.

"You will probably be wondering what this is all about. All you want, Mr de Winter, is to join your father's regiment, and here this old buffer has been chattering on in French.

"I knew your father, Colonel Jack, as I've said, and I know the present Colonel of your regiment. I say your regiment, because I think I can arrange for you to be gazetted to the regiment, in absentia, so that you don't lose your seniority when war comes. But I hope that if I arrange this, you will consent to undertake a mission for me which may take some months, you and your wife?"

"I'm sure Jeanne and I will be happy to undertake a mission for you, General, when we know what it is, free gratis and for nothing."

"You're uniquely qualified to carry out the mission which I am about to explain, you and your wife operating as a team..."

"Intelligence work?"

"A very special type of intelligence mission for which you are ideally qualified, by the fact that you are not professional agents, and have no connection at all with intelligence work…

"This may not go beyond these four walls. We in military intelligence have become extremely worried at MI6. They seem to be utterly obsessed with the idea that there is a strong anti-Nazi movement in Germany, in the German Army and among influential German civilians, and MI6 feels that we should give them all our covert support to help them overthrow Hitler. They are constantly bombarding the Foreign Secretary, Lord Halifax, with memos.

"Now, I know Germans and I am highly sceptical that there is the extent of broad-based support that MI6 claims there is.

"Remember Thucidides? He said, somewhere, that one had to beware of the estimates of exiles. I know there are good men among the anti-Nazis, like Adam von Trott and Helmuth von Moltke. I've met them and they are sincere. But they aren't the kind of people who carry out *putsches* to overthrow the established governments. They'll be fine as the good Germans who will take over after all the dirty work has been done, if they don't get killed in the process. I know there is, what Hitler calls, his Green Freemasonry in the Army; officers of aristocratic backgrounds, all related to each other, in a network across the Army and all anti-Nazi. But there is no general disaffection in the ranks. It is the captains and corporals of an army who go out and take power, not the Generals, and they will go anti-Nazi only in a situation of defeat.

"If there was to have been an Army *putsch*, it would have happened before Munich. When Hitler got all he wanted at Munich, it was a diplomatic triumph, then all the anti-Nazis in the Army disappeared into the woodwork.

"This is the gut feeling among my friends in Army intelligence, and I've been given some discretionary funds and told to find out what the real situation is. It is all very unofficial; we can't openly be seen to be questioning MI6's judgement.

"Now an occasion has arisen where you two could be very useful to us. You're clean, no one in the intelligence game knows you. You speak excellent French and you know Switzerland.

"As part of my intelligence private army, I have a few people in useful positions. I have a contact in one of the biggest travel agents in Germany, the ones that arrange trips for the leading Nazis and senior officers of the Army. I've another good friend in one of

Zurich's leading banks. He'll be your contact in Switzerland, by the way.

"What our man in the travel agency has reported is that there are a surprising number of senior Nazis and officers who have opted to take holidays in Switzerland in 1939, either on the ski slopes or in the lakeside resorts of the German cantons of Switzerland.

"This makes a lot of sense. If the Germans know that a war is coming at the end of 1939, this will be the last occasion that they will be able to take a holiday out of Germany, but be near enough to get back to their posts if any crisis blew up.

"There is a second motive. The Germans don't know that they will win any war they undertake. They think they will, but there is a deep-seated insecurity among all Germans, ever since they saw the mark lose its value in the 1920s, that makes them want to hedge their bets, Nazi and anti-Nazi alike.

"So, as Switzerland is a place that you can deposit money, with no questions asked, all these high-up Germans are going to Switzerland, ostensively on holiday, but actually to deposit all their spare capital in Switzerland, to have a nest egg there, which will be safe however the war goes. The Nazis know it is going on but, because they are all doing it themselves, they wink at it. My banking man in Zurich says it is an open secret that this is going on.

"This means that a lot of very influential Germans and their wives are going to be in the Swiss resorts in the first part of this year. They can be tapped for their loyalty to the Führer, and for any battle plans that they may inadvertently reveal, either the men themselves, or their wives.

"So, what I propose is that you and Jeanne, Maxim, will spend the early part of 1939 in these resorts, posing as aristocratic French people. The Germans all adore aristocrats. You listen to their conversation, befriending them as French aristocrats who want to unite the gentlemen of France and the gentlemen of Germany in a crusade to prevent another Armageddon from happening. That must be your particular bugbear, Maxim, and you must give dinner parties to influential Germans to try and put over this crackpot philosophy."

"Aristocratic French people...?" said Maxim reflectively.

"You told me, when you were speaking about your book, that you had discovered French cousins who were the Counts de Winter?"

"You don't miss much, General," said Maxim, smiling. "Yes, there is a Count de Winter, an elderly cousin, who might let me borrow his title, for the sake of France. As a matter of fact, as the descendant of the senior branch, who was disinherited in the eighteenth century, I may have a better claim to the title than the present holder. But there is one snag..."

"What is it? Is it insuperable?"

"I don't know," said Maxim frankly. "But to bear the name of de Winter, whether I am a Count or not, might be inadvisable. You say I am clean and I am, as far as intelligence work is concerned. But at the time of the burning of Manderley, and the enquiry into my late wife's suicide, I was front page news in the popular papers. A lot of pictures were taken of us.

"I seem to remember that the only people in Switzerland who had read about the Manderley business were German. They seem to have a passion for our sort of scandal sheets and I imagine *The Times* is read in Berchtesgaden. I might just be recognised."

"But Maxim," I said. "Doesn't the Count have two names, de Winter, yes, but also de Langlade? Could we not appear as just Monsieur and Madame de Langlade, authentically French, and without any de Winter hang-ups?"

"That seems a good compromise," said Carton de Wiart. "I suggest you visit your French cousins at the earliest opportunity, and see if patriotism will induce them to lend you their name for a six month period. I should like you to begin on your mission to the Swiss Alps as early as possible, say March at the latest, and go on to the summer resorts about April."

"Let me fully understand what you want us to do," said Maxim smiling. "You want us to pose as aristocratic French people, rich and idle and having a crackpot gospel to disseminate. But that will mean staying in the very best hotels, Jeanne wearing the most fashionable of clothes. I should have to hire a showy yacht. Are you sure you have considered the cost? We shall be the most gold plated flies on the wall in history! I am counted as a rich man, but I don't think I could afford it."

The General smiled broadly.

"I think the discretionary funds I have will cover it. I also have a secondary source of funds, from business interests in South Africa, who are very interested to know about the likely commencement of hostilities so as to make contingency plans. I think that even if your wife were to spend a fortune in the Paris couture houses and you should live in the best rooms in the best hotels for six months, we can still cover your costs.

"My banking friend in Zurich will make the necessary transfers of funds. You are to live like lords, literally, at government expense, for the next six months. That is an order."

"It is an order that we shall be very happy to obey," said Maxim.

"I am sure His Majesty's Government will get their money's worth. The Germans can be most surprisingly indiscreet, and I don't doubt Madame Jeanne of the phonograph memory will provide us with some most important titbits. And we shall know for certain how strong the opposition to Hitler is. I am concerned about MI6. I am sure their sources are penetrated and tainted but, of course, one mustn't say it."

"We are staying at the Savoy and can be reached there," said Maxim. "We are just spending Christmas there, and then as soon as we get a reply from France, we shall visit our cousins in the Auvergne and get their blessing for our masquerade. After that, it is just spend, spend, spend."

"The Savoy is a very discreet place. I shall arrange for your sealed orders to be sent there. It would be a place to which to send your reports. For Mr Sidney."

For once Maxim was taken aback.

"Mr Sidney?"

I provided his edification.

"Sidney Carton, the hero of *A Tale of Two Cities*. 'It is a far better thing I do now than I have ever done...'"

"Exactly," said the General, and rose to show us courteously to the door. He shook my hand and bade farewell to me.

On passing, he said, "I am so glad to have met you *Vicomtesse* de Langlade. I am sure your sympathetic face and your title will enable all the German wives to seek your acquaintance and confide in you."

"It is my new mask," I said. "I have still to come to terms with it."

"Do you think in terms of masks, as well? I knew we were kindred spirits, Jeanne. May I call you that? My friends call me Carton and I feel we three are destined to be very good friends and comrades in arms. We both have the ability to merge into our backgrounds, a very great gift. For six months, in the South African War, I posed as a Boer mule driver, and I was never rumbled. John Buchan said he based his Richard Hannay on me, though I could never see the likeness. I think we will see great things from you." Then he went back into his office and was gone.

Chapter Seven

In Which We Visit the Auvergne and are Ennobled

We returned to the Savoy a little bemused by the interview, but elated and excited by the prospect of our new mission.

"Maxim," I said, the prospect of our masquerade running like champagne through my veins, the parallel indicating my frame of mind. "Do you really think we can carry it off?"

We were back at our suite in the Savoy. Maxim sank luxuriantly into a comfortable chair.

"Of course we can. We shall write our own script and perform it to perfection. I shouldn't wonder if we can't bring your piano-playing talents into play. A pretty girl playing at the piano...that provides a cover under which indiscretions can be made, which she can overhear. But I must get my letter off to the Count."

As planned, we celebrated Christmas at the Savoy, and held court for such of our friends and relatives as could spare the time to come up and visit us. Frank Crawley, of course, came early and stayed for a couple of days, protesting that we should not have to bear the cost of his hotel room.

Frank brought the accounts of the Manderley Estates with him in two big suitcases, much larger than the modest case that contained his clothes. He and Maxim pored over the accounts, Maxim full of praise for the excellent improvements Frank had set in train. The estate was in very good shape indeed, but Frank absolutely refused to take a percentage of the improved income, which we begged him to accept.

"Certainly not, Maxim," he said resolutely. "I am only doing what I am paid to do. Besides which I live rent free in a very lovely farm house. I want nothing more, I assure you."

The increased income did enable Maxim to increase Beatrice's share from the estate, which he was enabled to backdate two years.

Beatrice was delighted, and came, with her dull stick of a husband, Major Giles Lacey, and her two boys, to thank him personally. She was quite unchanged, still as bossy as ever, but I was now able to cope with her, a dear familiar ogre, and when she tried to patronise me, I slyly paid her back in her own coin.

"I like you a lot better than I did, Jane," she confessed. "You were such a frightened little mouse. Now you can answer back, and I feel much more at ease. You're so much prettier and so much more *soignée* than you were. I hope you're able to cope with Max. He always was a selfish devil."

I assured her that I could cope.

There was only one moment of awkwardness, when she asked, rather tactlessly and bluntly, and in company,

"No sign of any kids on the way, then?"

It was a delicate point and it caught me on the raw. An uncharitable comment like, "It's none of your damned business!" hung on my lips, but happily Maxim intervened.

"You should felicitate us on not producing an heir, Bee. If I fall under a bus, you and your children stand to inherit the whole Manderley Estate. But don't count on it yet. With the world about to blow up, I'd think twice about bringing a kid into the world. But we have earmarked a couple of sons with the stork for when peace comes again."

Beatrice's husband Giles tactfully made some comment about the risk of war receding, and everyone joined in a discussion about the political situation.

Under cover of the conversation, Beatrice said to me in a low voice.

"Sorry, Jane. Shouldn't have asked that. Tactless. You should have told me it was none of my damned business."

I found I was able to laugh.

"As a matter of fact, Beatrice, that was exactly what I was about to say, when Maxim and your husband intervened."

She grinned.

"Pity you didn't. I don't want the estate. Maxim provides for me very generously out of it. But you would make such a good mother that it seems an awful shame you don't have kids."

"We shall some day, I hope," I said.

"Well, don't leave it too long," she said, and we dropped the topic. We managed to get seats for Beatrice her husband and the two boys to see *Me and My Girl*, then the fashionable show in town, and they all enjoyed it hugely, as did I. There was a marvellous quality of innocence about Lupino Lane's performance as Bill Snibson, the dustman who inherits an earldom, that it made a most joyful show. I bought a copy of the musical score to add to my repertoire. It was ironic too, that within a few weeks, I should be masquerading under a title. Beatrice and family returned to the country, still voicing their gratitude.

Our sealed instructions came from Carton de Wiart, being brought up to our suite by a fairly gnarled old retainer who said confidentially, "The General and me were comrades in the war, Ma'am. If you need to get in touch with him, private like, drop a message to the Savoy, care of Albert Robinson – that's me – and I'll see it's got round to him, double quick time."

It seemed that, like us, Albert was a member of Carton's private army. We also received a letter from the *Comte* de Winter, from the Château de Langlade, Issoire, Puy-de-Dôme. Maxim had written in French but the *Comte* replied in English.

"Dear Cousins, Come when you like and stay as long as you can. I shall expect you any time from the last week in January. Just cable your time of arrival. Gabrielle-Pauline sends regards. Henri Xavier de Winter."

"He has a very good command of English," I said when Maxim passed the letter over to me. "But who is Gabrielle-Pauline? His wife? "

"No, his granddaughter, I think. She must be the daughter of the elder son. He married an American nurse, I think, who went back to America when he was killed. She remarried an American, and the child insisted on staying with the grandparents... She must have been born about 1917, so she must be just over twenty now, I suppose.

"We must take her a present. And one for the Count, too."

We debated much about what present we should take. Finally Maxim called a taxi, and we went to Old Bond Street. He took me to an old-fashioned shop called Hunt & Winterbottom, the sales outlet of a very ancient cloth merchants from Stroud – they provided the uniforms for Prince Rupert's armies in the Civil War – and bought a bolt of thornproof tweed for the Count, and had me choose a bolt of more fashionably patterned tweed for Gabrielle-Pauline.

"English cloth is always admired in France, and if war comes, they may not be able to get it for quite a few years," he said.

I expected we should go directly to the Auvergne, but Maxim said we should go back to the Swiss villa first.

"That is where they will expect us to go, and we must not act out of character."

The sealed orders had also given the name of a bank in Zurich, where Carton de Wiart had a contact, and we were to have a safe deposit box. There we would leave any messages to be transmitted to London.

The contact name in the Zurich bank was a Herr Coppelius.

"We are into romantic ballet," I exclaimed. "It must be an alias."

Maxim proposed we fly to Geneva, and find out if our Zurich gnome really was an actual person.

But Herr Coppelius proved to be very much a man and not a myth. When we asked for him in the bank, giving our names, there was a pause, and then an assistant cashier came out and motioned us into a private room. He was far from gnome-like, but was very fair, rather like a Swede, tall and bespectacled. He motioned us to sit down and began in English.

"Hello, I am Coppelius, and you I understand are Mr and Mrs de Winter. But now, if you will excuse me, we play games. I must interrogate you, if that is agreeable."

We nodded.

Coppelius began brightly.

"You are part of Carton's private army. So am I. But a lot of money is riding on this, so we must be sure that you are you, and I am who I say I am. You agree?"

Again we signified our assent.

"You say you are from Mr Carton, and wish to open an account. Is he your only reference?"

We had remembered our sealed orders. Maxim said,

"We also have a reference from Madame Sidonie de la Savoie."

"Sidney from the Savoy. Sidney Carton. Very well. You have the number of the safe deposit in this bank?"

Maxim gave it. It too was in the sealed orders we had memorised.

"Good. Carton will communicate with you via that deposit box, and you with him. Do you have the number of your bank account here?"

"No, you are to give it to us."

"And in what name will be the account, for you and your wife?"

Maxim paused. This was not in our sealed orders.

"De Winter," he said.

Coppelius paused, as if expecting more.

"De Winter..."

I realised the implications before Maxim did.

"De Winter de Langlade," I said.

Coppelius relaxed.

"Good. Now we can do business. You could not have known all this unless you were briefed, and nor could I. Even if a third party was to have somehow got details of the transaction, forced it out of you, or me for that matter, there were some things they could not know. Now I have deposited quite a large sum in the De Winter de Langlade account. Do you wish to draw anything out now?"

"I don't think so. Most of our expenses will be in Paris, outfits for Jeanne, a complete new wardrobe, and fashionable ski clothes for both of us. I assume you can make the necessary arrangements with your Paris branch."

"It has already been done."

"I shall need to hire a rather flashy yacht when I come to Interlaken in April. Can you arrange that? And reservations for a very opulent suite in the best hotel?"

"I shall see the reservations are made. And for the ski resort we shall choose for you. You shall be informed which one through the safe deposit box."

Maxim considered.

"We have Swiss papers in the name of de Winter. When we return from France, we shall probably be calling ourselves de Langlade. Can we have papers made out in that name? It may be a case of our inheriting a title, which causes a change of name."

"A routine matter. I shall see to it. A letter from a notary, to the authorities. I shall see it expedited. No problem."

Finally Maxim said,

"I think we shall need to buy a new car. A smart car, a tourer, to create the image of hereditary wealth. Nothing flashy, but giving an air of substance, and a slightly sporty ambience. Could you assist us in this?"

"I can recommend a good garage in Zurich, very discreet, and accustomed to dealing with the aristocracy. He will suggest the right sort of car for your purposes. Good second-hand, of course. And he will purchase it back from you discreetly, when the mission is over."

Our business was concluded. But before we left, I could not resist asking,

"Herr Coppelius, is that your real name?" he laughed.

"So you would know my secret, Madame? It is my business name. I have a perfectly good name, under which I pay my taxes, but it is Polish. My father had some disagreement with the Czar of Russia, about the turn of the century, and thought it prudent to move to Switzerland. His name, and mine too, is Czytarowski.

"Now you cannot succeed in business with a name that few can pronounce and no one can spell. So when I joined this bank, my employers and I agreed that it would be better to have another name, which people could spell and would remember. So we decided on Coppelius, from the opera. It has served me very well... There has been a very great migration from Eastern Europe this century, and people have taken German, American, and even Scottish names in order to assimilate to their new countries. You yourself, Madame, are about to change your name to Langlade, to make yourself sound more French."

I felt properly rebuked for my curiosity and presumption. But Adam Coppelius and I have remained good friends since.

We chose a handsome Hispano Suiza tourer, for our trip to France, suitable to our new *sportif* image. We left it in Zurich, as we paid a last visit to the villa, as Monsieur et Madame de Winter. We told our neighbour that we would be touring in France and Europe for the next few months, asking that all mail be forwarded to us, care of Mr Robinson, at the Savoy, London.

I looking nostalgically at the villa, until so lately my haven of peace, while Maxim packed a bag with papers on his research and other necessaries. We slept a final night, and made love. Then it was back to Zurich to find our new car, to get papers in the name of de Langlade, from Coppelius. Then we set out to drive to the Auvergne.

*

The Château de Langlade had been a fortified citadel in the French Wars of the Religion and probably even earlier and it stood like twin towers joined together on its own low hill, round which the cobbled roadway wound upwards. The grey stone walls looked as if they could withstand a modern siege.

Because we were expected, the heavy gate into the yard was open, and we nosed our way in. The courtyard was large and wide, almost the size of a parade ground, with the entrance to the house, a wide seasoned timber door, up some stone steps, and under a sort of arch.

Facing the house, on the other side of the square were the stables and farm buildings, and at the far end of the courtyard was a high hedge and gate, beyond which was the parkland of the château.

A girl, saddled and mounted, was walking her horse in front of the stables. At our arrival she put spurs to her horse, which careered away. She gathered in expertly, and the horse jumped clear over the high hedge, scorning the gate, We watched horse and rider disappear through the trees and over a little hill.

"That girl can ride like a Cossack," said Maxim admiringly.

"I wonder if it was the granddaughter, Gabrielle-Pauline. I hope she doesn't resent us calling on her grandfather. Young girls can be very possessive."

Maxim manoeuvred the car so we pulled up outside the door of the château. From this door there emerged a grey moustached man in his seventies, very straight and military, albeit leaning on a stick. From his bearing there was little doubt that this was the *Comte* de Langlade.

"Mr and Mrs de Winter, I have waited so long to meet you," he said in very excellent, unaccented English. "It was most kind of you to telephone from your hotel in Vichy the time you expected to be here. You should not have wasted your money on a hotel. You should have come on directly here, never mind the hour.

Maxim said,

"We had to make ourselves presentable, before meeting our most distinguished noble relative.

The Count laughed.

"Oh, we do not keep ceremony here. Two old servants, my granddaughter and myself. We dress for dinner, of course, but apart from that, no ceremony. I am sorry my granddaughter is not here to greet you. But she is very shy of strangers. She will come in after her ride. But come in, both of you. It is a fine day for January, but you should not be standing about in the wind. Louis, my old batman, will bring in your things. And Marthe, my housekeeper, will show you presently to your rooms."

He led us through to a large, shabby, but very comfortable sitting room with deep chairs, and poured us each a sherry.

"It was a habit I got into, when serving with your army in the war. That was where I learned my English, though my sister and I did have a good grounding from our English governess, sixty years or so ago. But you do speak French, I hope? Gabrielle-Pauline for all that she has an American mother, is a little shy in speaking English. She would not go back to America with her mother, and her new husband. 'Non, non, non,' she said. 'I will stay in France with *Grandpère* et *Grandmère*.'

"I am afraid my daughter-in-law, Caroline, did not press her too hard. So Gabrielle-Pauline stayed with us, and was a great comfort to us, and to me, when my wife died, ten years ago."

"I think we can make ourselves understood," said Maxim with a smile.

The *Comte* was not deceived.

"You English! I know you of old. You have this terrible modesty. You ask a Frenchman or a Frenchwoman if they play the piano well, and they tell you, 'Yes, I play very well.' But ask an English person and they are immediately self-deprecating, 'I don't play very well, no'. Then you find he or she is a concert pianist."

Maxim laughed.

"Modesty forbids me to talk about myself, but Jeanne has been complimented in Switzerland on her effortless French, and yes, she plays the piano remarkably well, though she will never admit it."

"And Maxim speaks very good French very well. We lived for two years in Switzerland, and spoke nothing else."

"Maxim?" said the General. "Of course you are descended from the Jacobin, Louis Xavier, who insisted that every heir of his line should bear the name of Maximilien Robespierre, *mon Dieu*! You must see his picture in a little while. I am so glad you speak French, Madame, because Gabrielle-Pauline needs a girlfriend of her own age. We must get you to show us your musical talent tonight, after dinner. Now Maxim, if I may call you that, you said you were on a confidential mission, and needed my help. How may I be of assistance to you?" But before Maxim was able to reply, Marthe, the housekeeper, came in to say that we should like, would we not, to be shown our rooms, which were now ready. The *Comte* said we should discuss the mission at dinner time.

*

Our room was palatial, a great bedroom, with a four poster bed, and two dressing rooms, one for Maxim, one for me. Marthe remarked that King Louis VIII had slept in that bed.

We unpacked, and Maxim said he would take the *Comte's* bolt of cloth down to him. I was left, admiring the beautiful Louis Quinze chairs and the delicate oblong of a gilded mirror, when I heard a voice behind me, low and faltering,

"*Cousine…pardonnez-moi…*"

Through the mirror I could see a dark girl with imploring eyes, behind me.

I turned. Gabrielle-Pauline, the girl I had last seen riding boldly into me distance on her bay horse, was standing before me. She was tall and gauche, and wore an old-fashioned dress, though clearly a very pretty country girl.

She stammered in French

"Forgive me, I should not have ridden off like that when you came… I should have been at my place beside *Grandpère*, to welcome you. But we see people so seldom at the château, and I am very nervous in front of strangers…"

My heart went out to her. She reminded me of the mouse I had been at Manderley, and how I too was gauche and awkward in front of strangers. I went over and kissed her.

"But *cousine*, we are not strangers, we are family. No need to put on a great show of ceremonial. Your horse was fresh, he needed exercise… You could not have dismounted. Do not think another moment about it! I am just happy to meet you at last. Why, has your *grandpère* been scolding you?"

Her chin came up.

"Non, point! I have not spoken to *Grandpère*. But I know my duties, and I neglected them. Do not make excuses for me. I was wrong and I know it."

"Indeed, not. But I remember, only a few years back, how I hated meeting strangers, when I ran a big house, and dreaded meeting new people. But let us put this behind us. It is not of importance. I have brought you some tweed from London, which you can make up into a fashionable coat and skirt. Do you ever wear trousers? You looked so smart in your jodphurs, so enviably slim, that I thought you would look wonderful in slacks. Everyone wears them in London, and in Switzerland, where I live."

I had struck just the right note. The floodgates were unleashed. In voluble French she assured me that she adored wearing trousers, but *Grandpère*, though a marvel, she assured me, and so kind and tolerant, was old-fashioned, and did not like to see young girls in trousers.

"I shall tell him, straightaway, what you have said about trousers being à la mode, and we must buy some fashionable trousers, tomorrow, *bien sûr*, in Clermont Ferrand where I get my riding gear. As to the cloth, it is a marvel, so smart to wear English tweeds, and such a delightful pattern too, and you must advise me of the exact style that is being worn in London this season."

In an instant we had become bosom friends.

I was bidden to come down to see her horse, and told he had such a gentle mouth. I assured her that Maxim was the expert on horseflesh. Did I not ride then? I must learn. There was a gentle old horse in the stable, she would instruct me. Everyone should ride. It was such pleasure.

And I played the piano? She sang a little, the old songs of the Auvergne that *Grandpère* liked. We must practise at once, if I was not too tired after my voyage, so that we could perform that night after dinner. Oh, how glad she was that she had so *sympathetique* a cousin. And how well I spoke French, for an *Anglaise*. It was a marvel. Since I had hardly spoken two words since the torrent began, I thought she was too generous. But I allowed myself to be taken downstairs, to where a grand piano stood, and we practised together for an hour, to mutual admiration. Her voice was young and true.

We might have practised longer, but the *Comte*, hearing us, came out of the library with Maxim.

Gabrielle-Pauline went up to the *Comte* and kissed him.

"*Grandpère*, I do like our new cousins, so much..."

He smiled indulgently.

"But, chérié, you have only met one of them yet. This is M. Maxim de Winter, who is a descendant of the Jacobin."

She gave him a level glance.

"You do not look like a Jacobin, Cousin. More like the Chevalier. Jeanne tells me you are a great horseman. Will you ride with me tomorrow?"

Maxim grinned, as the *Comte* protested,

"Gabrielle-Pauline, such forwardness..."

"I shall be delighted, Cousin."

Her mercurial mood changed.

"No, not tomorrow. Tomorrow we go into Clermont Ferrand so I can buy some trousers. Jeanne tells me that they are quite à la mode, *Grandpère*. Not fast at all. , And I must get an outfit made from my marvellous new cloth..."

"Petite, you must not run on," said the *Comte*. "Perhaps your cousins do not want to go to Clermont Ferrand tomorrow."

"Oh," she said, "Do you?"

"Nothing would give us greater pleasure," said Maxim. "And I hope there will also be time to ride with you tomorrow as well if we get up early."

"Oh yes," she said with a disarming smile, no longer gauche. "There is nothing better than a gallop before breakfast. I will come and hammer on your door at seven."

"So you see, Maxim," said the *Comte*. "Give these young girls an inch of rope, and you will live to regret it."

Before dinner, he took us round the portrait gallery.

"There is a tradition in our family. A staid one, followed by a wild one. Gabrielle-Pauline, she is a wild one. The Chevalier de Winter, he was a wild one, though he was tamed by the first Gabrielle-Pauline, his wife. Look at her, with her brother, Charles. Are they not alike?

"Now," he said. "Look at your ancestor, the Jacobin, painted by David, open-necked shirt, looking very romantic and Byronic. Would you credit that he ran the Army's finances for twenty years and more? There is his younger brother, Philippe, from whom I am descended, painted in middle age by Madame Vigée-Lebrun. What a sweet face he has. He was no troublemaker. His main interest was agriculture. And there," he said, pointing to an old photograph, "are my two sons. What a waste."

We were a little silent after that, all of us. I looked at the photograph of the elder boy, so assertive and protective of his younger brother, and could see a speaking likeness to his daughter, Gabrielle-Pauline, who stood beside us.

"I never remember him," she said sadly. "He was killed in 1918, when I was just one. But *Grandpère* says he was a great horseman."

After dinner, while Gabrielle-Pauline went to the stables to see her horses were bedded down for the night, we sat in the library, and Maxim explained our mission.

The *Comte* was very amused.

"Your Carton de Wiart, he is a good psychologist. The Boches, they love a lord. And they are very indiscreet. I am sure you will learn a great deal just from being around them. You, Jeanne, have such a sympathetic face. See how you brought out my gauche granddaughter. All the wives will confide in you. Listen, and you will learn.

"I am delighted you are going to go against the Boches. I am too old to fight them now, unless it is like 1870, with the Boches swarming all over the country. Then the château will be a centre of resistance, as it has always been. Oh, the arms that have been hidden in these cellars, the fugitives we have sheltered there!

"Why, even the Jacobin was concealed in the cellars, when King Louis XVIII came here to stay, and the *Comte* Philippe his brother secured a pardon for him.

"In every civil war in France, the Religious Wars, the Fronde, the Revolution, one member of our family has been on one side and another member on the other. And remained on the friendliest of terms. That way we had an insurance, that whichever side came out on top, our family would not lose. The secret passages we have in the cellars of this house; even I do not know them all!

"I see no objection at all to your using the title of the *Vicomte* de Langlade, the courtesy title of the eldest son. If the Jacobin had not been disinherited, you would be the *Comte* de Winter de Langlade. If you went to law, you could probably turn me out of the château."

"We should never do that," I said.

And Maxim added,

"The *Comte* de Winter and his two sons have served France well, in a way I can never do."

"Your father did," said the *Comte*. "He lies alongside my two sons in Flanders. He was such a character, your father, Colonel Jack. I cannot think of him without laughing."

"Most people remember him that way," said Maxim.

"But he was a good soldier. No one better at fieldcraft; a born survivor. Except when you have to lead a regiment through no man's land on the Somme, through fire from machine guns your Generals told you had been wiped out by the artillery barrage.

"No chance to use your fieldcraft then. But for patrols, and ambushes across the lines, to bring back prisoners from the Boche, there was no one like him. Reprimanded ever so many times, 'Colonel de Winter, you are a battalion commander, not an infantry subaltern!' And he would reply, 'I've got to see that my people are doing it right!"'

"You knew him well, then?" said Maxim.

"I had no choice. We bore the same name and the same rank. The first thing they said, when I reported to the French general headquarters was, 'Aren't you the mad English devil with the hunting horn?"

"The hunting horn?" I said. 'The only thing rescued from the Manderley fire,' I thought.

"Yes, a hunting horn. Colonel Jack took it everywhere with him, and made sure all his troops understood what the calls meant. The hunting call, he said, would penetrate the noise of battle better than a bugle, and would fool the Boche, because he knew the call for Recall or Advance on the bugle. And the soldiery knew when they heard the call that the Colonel was around, and that was a tonic for them. Soldiers said they heard the sound of the hunting horn at night on the battlefield, after Colonel Jack died.

Maxim got up,

"Will you excuse me for a moment? I have something to get you, which may interest you."

We continued talking and Maxim soon returned.

"These are Colonel Jack's war diaries," he said. "I should like them to go in the family archives, with the letters of the Jacobin and his son. This also I would like you to keep in the Château. It is Colonel Jack's hunting horn."

The *Comte* looked at it as though it were a holy relic.

"The hunting horn of Colonel Jack? Oh, Maxim, you have given our house an heirloom. Would you play it for me, one last time?"

So Maxim blew a view halloo on the hunting horn, and Gabrielle-Pauline, coming in from the stables, asked him to desist, as it was making the horses restive.

"So, *Comte*," said Maxim. "I have no more cause to love the Germans than you have, and when I make my speeches about the French and German aristocrats getting together to prevent a second war, I shall not hesitate to remind them of the two brave sons and the father who died in Flanders fighting the Germans."

"I am glad of that," said the *Comte*. "I would not like to think of a *Vicomte* de Langlade being remembered as a friend of the Germans, when his cousin and immediate predecessor in the title was buried in the mud of Flanders."

But it was I who became known as the *Vicomtesse Collaboratrice*.

*

The days at me château continued pleasantly. Being part of a plot against the Boches had given the *Comte* a new lease of life. He was no longer the sad survivor of his line, but had a purpose in life. Gabrielle-Pauline told me that our visit had transformed him.

When we visited Clermont Ferrand to go to the tailors, the *Comte* left us, saying he had to transact some business with his lawyers, being gone for more than an hour. He insisted that each of us should be photographed in order that we should feature in the portrait gallery.

Then, most wonderful to Gabrielle-Pauline's eyes, he suddenly elected to drive all the way to Paris, to visit old friends, and spend several days with an old comrade in arms, whence he returned wonderfully refreshed and in the best of spirits.

"*Grandpère* is hatching a plot," said Gabrielle-Pauline. "But it keeps him happy, so that is well."

Gabrielle-Pauline rode out daily with Maxim, and flirted with him outrageously.

"He is such a handsome man," she sighed to me. "What a pity you found him first."

"Come back with us to Paris," I suggested. "We may be able to find you a boyfriend."

"*Jamais*! I detest Paris, so many people, so much noise. I shall wait here in my enchanted castle, until my prince comes." (Which, at the beginning of the war, and from a very unlikely quarter, he did.)

The *Comte*, it was, who provided me with my secret weapon. We were in the library, where he was seeking to find a suitable place of honour for the hunting horn and the war diaries. The book was open and I read, at random.

"The troops were singing 'Good-Byey' as they came up the line. They seem in good heart."

I carried this phrase around in my head for a day and a half until I found myself at the piano, and began to play that haunting tune from the trenches,

"Good-Byey, take the tear, baby dear, from your eyey... Though it's hard to part, I know, I'll be tickled to death to go..."

The *Comte*, who was passing through the hall, stopped, transfixed.

"*Mon Dieu*, that tune... It was as though I had been transported back to Armentieres, with the smell of mud and blood and the cries of 'Stretcher Bearer!' The English Tommies always sang that song and others like it, as they came up the line. The Germans, too, they were great singers, you could hear them from their own trenches, when they were not far from our own. But I never remember the French soldiers singing. Curious, is it not?"

But from that convulsive reaction of the *Comte*, the germ of an idea was born.

The *Comte* called us into his library a few days later. Gabrielle-Pauline was there, looking serious.

"Maxim," the *Comte* said. "I have been thinking a great deal about your proposal. And the more I think about it, the less I like it. You taking our name, posing as a false Viscount among the Germans, with forged papers, and the likelihood of discovery. I cannot like it, and I will not permit it."

He paused, taking in our dismayed faces.

"I have a better alternative. You will go among the Germans as a real Viscount, the *Vicomte* de Langlade. I am proposing to adopt you as my son and heir."

If our faces expressed dismay before, they now showed stupefaction. Maxim finally began,

"But Gabrielle-Pauline...

"She is totally agreeable. You will let her stay in the château, I hope, till she marries, and everything I have that is not entailed will go to her. But I am quite serious. When I die the title and the château will come to you. The senior branch of the family, who lost their inheritance because of the Jacobin *Vicomte*, will get it back again."

We were too stunned even to demur.

"I have had the papers drawn up by my lawyers, and in two days' time, the *Maire* and the officers of the town will come here, and I will make a public announcement of your adoption. You will need papers in the name of the *Vicomte* and *Vicomtesse* de Langlade. I stole the photographs taken of you in Clermont Ferrand. These papers, and your French nationality, usually take time. So I went to Paris and saw my old comrade-in-arms, General Gamelin, explained your mission and asked for his help."

"The Commander in Chief!"

"One should always go to the top in these matters. Gamelin is very discreet, unlike some others of his colleagues. Your secret will be safe with him. He has promised to arrange everything in two days. So we old soldiers are not entirely without our uses."

As tongue-tied as ever Gabrielle-Pauline had been, we tried to express our gratitude.

He only said,

"Now I am your adopted father, perhaps you will listen to what I have to say. I do not approve of your encouraging my granddaughter to wear trousers, which I consider unwomanly, and I would ask you to refrain from doing it in future!"

So it all ended in laughter, and some tears, from Gabrielle-Pauline and myself.

She kissed me and said,

"I am so glad you are now really my sister."

Maxim said wryly,

"You make a mistake, chérié. You have lost a sister and gained...an aunt!"

Two days later, there was a procession of official cars to the château, and a proliferation of officials, lawyers and the *Maire* in his official sash. The *Comte* delivered a short address, to which the *Maire* replied, at rather greater length. The ceremony was a little marred by the noise of a motor cycle, as a despatch rider came in, saluted the *Comte* as "*Mon Colonel*" and handed over a package with the compliments of the Commander-in-Chief.

"He asked to be kept informed of any developments."

The *Comte* promised that this would be done.

So a few days later, we drove back to Paris, the *Vicomte* et *Vicomtesse* de Langlade, with all the passports, papers and nationality certificates to match. In the few days that we had been in France, we had been enrolled into the nobility.

Chapter Eight

In Which We Go Among the Enemy, and Make Friends

In Paris, we stayed at the George V Hotel, where else? (I have constantly in my mind a jingle from a forgotten musical, "It's not a crime to rob a bank, or break into the George V (*Cinq*), it's not a crime, it's manly sport, it can't be wrong if you're not caught...")

We were beginning our masquerade in style, and no, we were not caught out in our deception.

I decided to enter with gusto into my role of the *Vicomtesse* who expects the best of everything, a sort of French Mrs van Hopper, but with charm.

The first thing was to get the hotel on the hop. We were shown into our palatial suite, which was decorated with beautiful flowers, the compliments of the management.

This was my chance. I phoned the management immediately, charming but peremptory. This was the *Vicomtesse* de Langlade. I was most grateful for the delicate gesture of the flowers. But the *Vicomte*, you understand, was a martyr to hay fever, so could the flowers be taken away, at once please.

I was gratified by the arrival of a whole army of maids, and a perspiring, apologetic *mâitre d'hôtel*. The flowers would be removed at once. A thousand apologies, *Vicomtesse*. He was unaware of the *Vicomte*'s unfortunate condition. He virtually backed out the room bowing as he went, and still mouthing his apologies. I stood in command of the field, after my Pyrrhic victory, rather sad that the beautiful flowers were gone. But I had made my point.

Other phone calls followed. The *Vicomte* and the *Vicomtesse* wished to take dinner precisely at eight. Would the table be made ready for them at that time? We descended at precisely 8 p.m., and it was. Later that night, I phoned again. The *Vicomtesse* would like a tisane brought to her suite in fifteen minutes, if you please. By this means I established a reputation of being exacting, if fair.

I really need not have bothered. I had no idea what the impact of a title was, on the underlings. All our wishes were gratified almost servilely. We began to understand what living like a lord meant.

An early visit was to the beauticians in the hotel, having previously telephoned my wishes. The *Vicomtesse* would like an appointment. To the abject girls, I said languidly, that my husband had come into a title and an estate, and I felt that from living in the Auvergne, I had become a little, dare I say it, provincial.

I was sure *les mademoiselles* would understand. Perhaps my thick eyebrows could benefit from plucking... *Les mademoiselles* set to with a will, at the sound of my new wealth, saying they perfectly understood. Between them, manicurists, beauticians, they transformed me from top to toe, conveying me into the hairdressers who gave me a fashionable and modish crop.

There was method in my madness. Switzerland was not a large place, and I had the nightmare of being hailed in some German Swiss resort with a cry of "Jeanne!" I had to be sufficiently different, that I could turn, when I realised they were addressing me, and say in polite surprise "Madame...?"

This done, I did not extend my fashionableness unreservedly to my new clothes. They had to be pretty and elegant, but very understated. I did not want to dazzle the German Fraus with my magnificence and frighten them off. The *Vicomtesse* had to be the '*sympathetique* noble woman', so people were amazed at her approachability.

As I was transformed I looked in wonderment through my mask. Was this really me, saying languidly, that it was all a great bore, but one owed it to one's position in society?

Maxim was very kind about my transformation.

I looked disparagingly in the mirror in our hotel suite.

"I look like a *poule-de-luxe*," I said looking at my plucked eyebrows and my unfamiliar new clothes.

"Not a bit," he said with reassuring candour. "You look different, but that is what we want. But you are still the same wonderful Jeanne underneath. I have greater problems. I cannot even shave off my moustache, or I shall have to get new papers. And I have to be so careful not to appear *nouveau riche...*"

Maxim was in fact scouring the old quarter of the city, seeking out the vendors of good second-hand clothes which fitted him.

"Cloth improves with age, like wine..." he explained. "So all my clothes need to look at least ten years old, but still smart, as though they've been treated with love, by a devoted valet."

After some trouble, he found what he wanted. His only concession to his new role was a rather French haircut.

I too visited the old quarter, looking for music shops. To give an appearance of being a student, I put a scarf round my head, wore flat shoes, and a trenchcoat mackintosh, like Michèle Morgan in a French film. I partly succeeded and found with surprise that I was not accorded the deference I exacted as the *Vicomtesse*. It was quite a pleasant relief.

I was seeking music shops that sold German songs, of an earthy kind, not the *lieder* of Wolf and Brahms that I was constantly offered.

Finally I struck gold. It was an old and unpretentious shop in a side street, which bore the name of Gottfried Vogel.

Inside the shop, which was empty of people, I came across a middle-aged, balding Jew, with a kindly, intelligent face.

"Madame wishes for German songs?" he asked in careful French.

"Forgive me, monsieur, but were you in the Great War? On the German side?"

He looked around the shop to see if anyone else was there.

"It is a strange question, Madame. But yes, I was. Me, Isaak Rosenburg, I was a corporal in the Pomeranian Grenadiers, the same rank as Adolf Hitler. But I do not mention it much here. Too many French people have lost relatives, killed by the Germans. We are '*les Boches sales*' to them still. But why do you ask?"

And so I poured out my ideas to Isaak Rosenburg, German refugee in Paris. I wanted the kind of songs that the German soldiers sang in the trenches, I said. The kind of songs that would bring a lump to the throat of any German who heard them. And on an impulse I told this complete stranger all about our mission, the bogus *Vicomte* and *Vicomtesse*, going to seek out the Germans in their summer retreats, to win their confidence and spy on them.

He laughed long and loud.

"Madame, I have not laughed like that since I left Germany as a refugee. We refugees in Paris, we are at the mercy of the authorities became we do no have me right papers that the visiting Nazis have.

But an angel must have directed you to me. I am the one man in Paris who can give you what you want.

"Listen, I was an orchestra player, a violinist in the theatre before the war, and I was not called up until 1916. I played all these *limonades* for the German soldiers in the theatre. Later, in the trenches, I had my violin, and the soldiers would ask me to play so they could sing. I know exactly what you want.

"*Mein Gott*, what a comic idea this is, to spy on the Germans and woo them with *limonades*. That it what we called popular songs in the war. It is worthy of having an operetta written round it. I shall find you such a portfolio, you will not credit it.

"I cannot leave France," he went on. "I cannot even perform as a violinist, except occasionally in nightclubs, when the regular violinist is sick. But I would give a fortune to be in Interlaken, or wherever you go, when you first strike up the music I shall give you. They will be all round you, those old German officers, and probably in tears..."

"But will you be able to find all these tunes in France?" I asked.

"Madame," he said, his eyes bright with laughter. "For you and your escapade, I shall write down the words and music, and invent the accompaniment."

"You must be paid well for this," I said.

"No, I will do it for sheer love and for the fun of it."

"But you must. We have secret service funds.

He smiled.

"In that case, I will help you spend them. But my charges will not be large. I want to be a contributor to your masquerade. Come again in a week."

We shook hands like conspirators, and I went back to the George V and to my *Vicomtesse* masquerade. I had now put my summer wardrobe together, but we had still to buy our skiing outfits. delighted in the bright colours of the sweaters and anoraks, and because I was still slim I felt myself at my best in the tight, black, tailored ski trousers. Maxim also looked more like Maxim in ski clothes.

"We must be careful," he said with a smile, "in ski clothes you look more like the Jeanne I know and love, and less like my languid *Vicomtesse*."

"I shall wear them with a strong French accent," I retorted. Mention of trousers made me wonder if Gabrielle-Pauline had been able to wear the smart slacks she so coveted, and I debated whether we should send her a pair of ski trousers, in which she would look magnificent. Maxim pointed out we did not know her size, and that for family harmony at the château we should perhaps restrain our generosity.

The regular arrival in the hotel lobby of packages from the best French *couturier* houses, did not fail to make its mark.

"*Ce Vicomte, il est un Croesus,*" I heard one Frenchman in the lobby remark admiringly.

The week passed and I donned my student disguise and went to see Isaak Rosenburg in his shop in the Old Quarter.

There were all my songs, impeccably written out in his clear hand, and meticulously scored and annotated.

"*Mein lieber Herr,*" I said in German. "I cannot thank you enough." And on an impulse I kissed the old lined face.

"*Gnädige Frau*, you have anticipated me. I was about to embrace you, to wish you success on your mission."

"One good kiss deserves another," I said, and we embraced for the second time. We exchanged addresses, his in Paris, mine in Switzerland.

"Can you not leave Paris and come to us in Switzerland? We have plenty of room in the villa, and you should be our very welcome guest. I am sure I have friends who could fix you up with Swiss papers, and you would be able to work and play again.

His eyes were moist with tears.

"What a kind offer, Jeanne, if I may call you that. If I can avail myself of it, to be sure (*sicherlich*) I will come, if I have to walk across France and climb the Alps to get there. But I fear that I shall have to spend the war in France, and may not survive. But if I do, after the war, with pleasure."

"After the war I shall come to Paris to fetch you, Isaak. You have made a great contribution to the success of our mission. Or if you want to settle in England, I shall arrange it. Word of an Englishwoman," I concluded, laughing.

"Word of a German Jew, if I survive, you shall hear from me. But come to the piano, Jeanne, and let us run through some of these songs. There is one that is important, the blockbuster, as the Americans say.

"There was an operetta that ran and ran in Germany in the war. It was called *Die Csardasfürstin*, or as you say, in English, the *Gypsy*

Princess. All the soldiers on leave would bring their sweethearts along to it. And all became of one song, '*Spiel, Zigeuner*' ('Play, Gypsy').

"This song is mock Hungarian, very *csárdás*-like, but it was the last couplet that was the punchline. 'Children, make love while you can, for tomorrow will be too late.' '*Morgen ist viel zu spät*."' He sang it to me.

"At this point all the young officers would squeeze the hand of their girlfriend and look soulful. Tomorrow I go back to the front, I may be killed, that look would say. Let us have one night of happiness together. And it never failed," said Isaak triumphantly.

"More nice German girls lost their virginity because of that than you can imagine. Play that in Switzerland, and it will hit every German officer who was in the war right below his solar plexus, as Sigmund Freud would say, right below the level of their awareness. The sentimental songs of the trenches may leave them cold, but for the German officers and their wives, that will hit them, WUMP."

Isaak insisted I play it in a particular way "very *sentimentalisch*" and he concluded,

"You must sing, or if you cannot sing you must say, very loud, the last phrase, "*Aber Morgen is viel zu spät*."

We practised, singing and speaking.

"*Mein Gott*, but you play well, Jeanne."

"Just a hack musician, Isaak. Good for light music."

"Remember, Jeanne, light music requires as much care as serious music. Gigli, Caruso, they sang light music. There are only two kinds of music, Jeanne, good music and bad music. Never forget that."

I was sorry to have to say goodbye to Isaak. I was to see him again, when the masquerade moved from Switzerland to Paris, in the war.

Our preparations were almost complete, and Maxim had phoned Coppelius in Zurich to confirm that our reservations had been made. We were to go to Zurs (if I remember aright) to a big hotel there. Maxim told Coppelius how much we had spent in Paris and his only comment was, "So little?"

But there was one sentimental visit Maxim wanted to pay.

In Colonel Jack's war diaries, one name featured again and again, during his accounts of his leave in Paris:

"Went to Florians. Good meal with Tim and Blanche." "Went to Florians and got beastly drunk. Went round next day to pay for breakages. The patron would not accept money. Said he was always pleased to see *les Anglais braves*. Very decent of him." "Went to Florians and had singsong after dinner. What a din we must have made!" "Had dinner in Florians with French cousin. A bit low because his younger boy had recently been killed up the line. Tried to cheer him up." The last entry was, "Got a couple of bottles of champagne from Florians to take to the chaps up the line. This may be the Big Push we've been waiting for..."

Maxim had researched through the telephone directory and found a restaurant called Florians in Montmartre.

"Exactly the place that your father would have gone to unwind," I said hopefully.

"What can we lose? Let's dine there," said Maxim, and telephoned the restaurant to make a reservation in the name of de Winter. "Perhaps the name will revive memories, if it still in the same hands," he said. "But the clerk who took the reservation didn't seem to react at all."

"It is more than twenty years ago, Maxim," I said. "If it is the right restaurant, it has probably changed hands by now.

"Probably," he said. "But we can only hope."

The restaurant was away from the fashionable part of Montmartre, down a side street. It looked like a family establishment.

"It is the kind of friendly place Colonel Jack would have chosen," I said optimistically.

The restaurant was full of locals. Clearly not a tourist spot, yet. We were shown to our table and were served with a simple but excellent meal. In deference to our neighbours, and as had become our custom in public, we spoke only French.

Halfway through the meal, the patron came round and asked if everything was to our satisfaction. We assured him that it was. He hesitated before leaving us.

"Forgive an old man's curiosity, but your name is familiar. During the war, I used to entertain a Colonel of that name..."

We looked up expectantly.

"*Colonel le Comte de Winter*. He had two boys who were killed in war, fine young men. The elder was married to an American nurse, I think, whom he brought here. A red-haired girl, very pretty. The *Comte* came here for consolation when the second one died.

Poor gentleman. He was very *blessé au coeur*, but he would not admit it."

Maxim resigned himself to the inevitable.

"The *Comte* is my adopted father," he said.

"*Vraiment*? Then you must send my compliments to him."

He began to move away. I could not bear it.

"Monsieur," I said. "Do you not remember *another* Colonel de Winter? An Englishman? He was usually referred to as Colonel Jack."

The patron's face lit up.

"Ah, yes, of course I remember Colonel Jack! I had forgotten that they bore the same name. We called him always Colonel Jack."

"I am his son," said Maxim simply.

The patron seemed galvanised. He ran to the kitchen and called out,

"Mathilde! Mathilde! The son of Colonel Jack is here. You remember him in the war. The Colonel with the hunting horn... *Viens, viens*."

La patronne, very fat and cheerful, waddled out of the kitchen.

"*Figurez-vous, mon vieux, le fils de Colonel Jack*! What a rascal he was. What laughs we had."

The patron was animated.

"If you had spoken English, I would have remembered earlier. *Mon Dieu*, Colonel Jack. Yes, monsieur, you are very like him. You speak French so well I did not realise that you were not French.

"His diary is full of references to Florians."

"*Bien sûr*, we were his club almost when he was on leave, he and friends. Dead and gone now all of them, but never forgotten.

"First you would hear the hunting horn." He did a very passable imitation. "That warned us they were near. Then they would burst in, Colonel Jack still tootling on his horn. Then there would be babel round the bar... 'Alphonse, get me a Pernod,' 'Alphonse, we're starving, what's for dinner...?' 'Mathilde, you wonderful woman, give me a big kiss.'

"Then after dinner, they would sing, I can see them now, grouped round the fire, with my best brandy in great glasses in every hand... 'Tipperary', 'Roses of Picardy', 'There's long, long trail a' winding', 'When Irish eyes are Smiling', 'Good-Byey', all the old songs.

"People would come in from other *estaminets* to hear them, and cheer them on. Ah, those were the days when we were young, and could laugh. They are dead all of them, in those terrible trenches, and I think we all died a little with them. You know," he said confidentially, "when the night is dark and the wind whips down the street, sometimes I think I hear that hunting horn and hear those young voices, very faintly singing, 'There's a long, long trail a winding…"

He insisted that we drink an old bottle of wine from his cellar, for the good old times. He and Mathilde drank with us. But I was thinking, how the old tunes keep coming back! It was just possible that my secret weapon would work on the Germans.

*

We left the George V a few days later, our tourer loaded with expensive new suitcases, and made our leisurely way back to Switzerland.

"We are going up the line to the front at last," said Maxim. I was now to address him as Jean-Maxime. We had agreed also to resurrect my baptismal-name. Though Mrs Mélisande de Winter sounded impossibly pretentious in Cornwall, *Vicomtesse* Mélisande de Langlade had just the right ring about it.

"As long as the Germans don't start calling me Melly, Okay?" I had conceded.

My one concern was that I could not ski. It was deplorable that after two years and more in Switzerland, I had never learned to ski. But Maxim and I had shunned the ski slopes, fearing to find hearty English there, who might be distantly acquainted with us. Then, as now, we sought to shun the English.

This meant that we would have to divide our forces. Maxim, an excellent skier, who excelled at this as at all other sports, would be undertaking the difficult runs, while I should be among the babes, parents and novices on the nursery slopes. Little chance of getting information from such small fry, and young mothers.

In fact, it turned out differently. Often it would be father and daughter who would be skiing on the heights, while grandmother had the care and instruction of the small ones, and was very glad of a sympathetic stranger, able to take one of the tots by the hand.

I endured the patronising attitude of these pint-sized mannikins, "I can ski better than you, Fraulein." Everyone took me for an unmarried girl, until they met Jean-Maxime.

Jean-Maxime was on easy terms with the grey-headed skiers on the slopes, with his easy German, and his skiing prowess. He had managed to put his rank across unobtrusively, and it was "*Vicomte, schnell, schnell*!", "*Vicomte, kommen Sie bitter, hier*!" on the slopes with great camaraderie.

But it was I with my piano that made the first breakthrough. I was uncertain whether, with such a young company of junior officers and civilians, I should have any impact at all. But there was a piano at the *Gasthube* and, when the room was half full, I went to the piano and experimentally played a couple of my *limonades*.[1]

I finished playing and found a middle-aged, military-looking man by my side.

"Ach, meine liebe Frau. How that tune took me back! The terrible days of the war". but there were good times too. And great comradeship!" He clicked his heels and introduced himself. "Major Ernst von Ahremburg."

"I am Mélisande de Langlade," I said.

"Oh, you are French. How do you come to know this tune? I have not heard it these twenty years."

"I have German cousins. Or rather I had. Most of them died in the war, like my husband's stepfather, and his cousins. My husband, the *Vicomte*, is determined that there never shall be such a terrible war again, to cause such slaughter among our families."

"I could not agree more. It is the politicians who make the wars, and we who have to bear the brunt of them. But I must introduce you to my wife. Hedwig, this is the *Vicomtesse* de Langlade."

I was in.

Word of my prowess on the piano seemed to have spread like wildfire through the German community, and on the nursery slopes the following day several ladies with whom I was only on nodding acquaintance came up to me to say that they had heard I was an excellent pianist and hoped to hear me play.

On the upper slopes Maxim was also approached by several senior officers to arrange a concert which they could attend, and this duly took place in the *Gasthube*.

It was interesting to see these very reserved and formal middle-aged men in different parts of the room break into song as the familiar numbers were played.

---

[1] 'Lisa, Lisa, komm mit mir auf der Wiese' and 'Meine Darling, Meine Darling'

I only played half a dozen songs then said that perhaps the younger people would like to hear something more modern, and broke into some cheerful French dance music. This enabled the younger generation, a little relieved, I thought, to get up and dance, while their elders gathered at the bar to reminisce about the war, and where they had heard those tunes last. Maxim was of course at the bar, and began to put forward his gospel of how the gentlemen of Europe should combine to stop another Armageddon happening, sowing the seed for later conversations.

At the end of the evening, the patron approached me deferentially.

This had been such a jolly evening, he said, and everyone seemed to have enjoyed themselves. They had no pianist. Perhaps the *Vicomtesse* might consider obliging them on other evenings. There would be a fee, of course.

I called Maxim over from the bar.

"Jean-Maxime," I said. "What do you think? I have been offered a job, a paid job, for the first time in my life!"

Maxim smiled.

"I should take it, *Liebschen*. Such an opportunity may not occur again."

The patron called for silence,

"*Mein Herren und Damen*, the *Vicomtesse* de Langlade has said she will delight us with her playing on a regular basis. So I hope you will all come and hear her again tomorrow."

His audience applauded and cheered.

Accordingly, for a couple of hours every night, I provided the cabaret at the *Gasthube*. I would play for an hour, then there would be an interval, and then I would come back and play for another hour.

My early repertoire was usually dance tunes, to enable the younger ones to get up and dance, but inevitably there would be a call from the audience to play some of the songs from the war. I would usually play a couple before the interval, and then say, "Wait till the second half and then we can have a proper singsong."

I would also include a couple of jazz numbers, which was instructive, since the Führer was known to disapprove of jazz, and it was possible for Maxim, watching the faces of the audience, to pick out those who were politically correct, and expressed their disapproval of this 'Negro music'.

The interval was the occasion for the old men to gather at the bar, around Maxim, and some younger ones too.

A rather arrogant young man, with all the hallmarks of the new regime about him, said severely,

"Of course, there will be no war. The Führer said so, when signing the Munich Accord. I am impatient at all this nostalgia. We should be looking forward to the future, and the new world that we are creating."

A middle-aged woman beside me said in my ear,

"That von Arlen, he is not a gentleman. He is not entitled to his 'von'. He was a champagne, salesman like Ribbentrop." The dislike of the Nazis was apparent from her voice.

Von Arlen continued to play the party line, becoming aware that he was not exactly enthusing his audience,

"Well, I must go and have an early night. Early to bed, early to rise, that is the gospel of the serious skier. Franz," he said to his colleague, "do not stay too long. There is work to be done."

His colleague, at the table, was a more subtle performer. With his open, smiling face, he was clearly a listener, as we were. A more dangerous man.

When I resumed my seat at the piano, I was in a mischievous mood.

I turned to the Nazi and said,

"Herr Franz, your friend does not seem to like my choice of music. Is there anything I could play especially for you?"

He smiled guilelessly.

"*Vicomtesse*, I am afraid I am tone deaf. I cannot distinguish one tune from another. But you play so prettily, it does not matter."

"Tone deaf, Herr Franz? What a misfortune. But perhaps you are a great skier, in compensation."

"Oh, no," he said modestly. "My friend, he is a great skier. I am an indifferent skier, I am afraid."

"An indifferent skier and tone deaf? What are you doing in Switzerland, Herr Franz? Are you bringing in capital from Germany, like all the other Germans?"

It was a home thrust. He went white, and then red.

"Certainly not," he stammered. "The German Government is against the exporting of funds from Germany to Switzerland... Perhaps my friend is right, I should have an early night..." And with this he got up and hurriedly left the *Gasthube*. The other people in the audience seemed amused at his discomfiture.

I mused, as I broke into a gay waltz, how a party member in any gathering had the effect on the other folk of a vicar in a dog collar. Everyone watched their language, and altered their conversation into harmless channels. But I could not be unaware of how the Germans looked behind them, instinctively, when talking frankly to us.

After my playing, we gathered in the bar, and that evening we had an interesting conversation with a senior officer and his wife. It began inauspiciously. I had been playing some popular American music, and the General began.

"It is amazing how tuneful Jewish composers like Irving Berlin are."

'Here is a right anti-Semite,' I thought. I did not know then that, for aristocrats, Jews were a people quite apart. They were not necessarily hostile, more curious about this strange breed.

Maxim said lightly,

"But, General, can you think of a composer in Germany in the past century who wasn't Jewish, or part-Jewish. Mendelsohn, Mahler, Johann Strauss, Schubert, Brahms, the list is endless..."

"No, surely not. There is Mozart..."

"He was a freemason," said his wife.

"Hayden, Weber, Richard Strauss..." He pointedly did not mention Wagner. Wagner had been appropriated by the Nazi Party.

"You must not think I am anti-Jewish," he said hastily. "The shopkeepers, the bankers, the doctors, they are the natural supporters of a right wing government. I do not want these people, and the Jewish soldiers in my regiment in the last war, bracketed with the dangerous Jews, the Socialists and Communists, like Rosa Luxemburg and her crew!

"The Russian Communists, they are all Jews, Lenin, Trotsky, whose real name was Bronstein... I remember a girl from Russia making a joke that the USSR (CCCP) stood for *Suss, Suss, Suss, Russki*, three Jews to every one Russian.

"So I think the Government's policy of persecuting the Jews is wrong. It makes unnecessary enemies. Persecute the Jewish Communists, yes, but as Communists, not Jews. But Hitler is totally irrational about Jews. His mother died after being treated by a Jewish doctor, and Hitler has a personal vendetta against all Jews. His toadies in the government take their cue from him."

This was frank speaking with a vengeance, and his wife was looking about her apprehensively.

Maxim asked the direct question,

"Do you think the German Army would ever try to overthrow Hitler?"

Now it was the General's turn to look apprehensively about him.

"It is not impossible, but I do not think it likely. There are people in the Army who would like it to happen, but for most of us, who have taken our oath, we will stay loyal, however much we dislike the Nazis. But should there be a war, and it went badly, it might be a different story..."

Our discreet soundings over the next fortnight, confirmed this view. There were few fervent Nazis among the Germans. But a lot of the younger people felt that the Nazis were in favour of youth, giving the young people their say, and everyone agreed that the Nazis were an improvement on the Weimar Government. The Nazis had emancipated Germany from the rule of the Old Men.

The older generation were less happy; they feared another war, remembering the last one. The aristocrats profoundly disliked the arrogant Johnny-come-lately attitude of the Nazis and the younger indoctrinated officers. But of evidence of a concerted movement against the Nazis we found none.

At the end of the holiday, we returned to Zurich, and Maxim and I put down on paper all our impressions, and the conversations we had had. We put our report in the strong box in the bank, drew out some more money from Coppelius, and set off to Interlaken for the second phase of our mission.

Chapter Nine

The Listeners beside the Lake

The skiing holiday had been a dummy run, said Maxim, as we drove down to Interlaken. We had been lucky to get a few influential people there, and we had made useful friends. But the real top brass would be at Interlaken, and they might be more difficult to approach. We could not hope that the piano strategy would work twice.

Yet I was glad to be going to Interlaken. The boat would be there, and I knew how to sail. Maxim and I would be together more. In a way, it would be more like the George V, with the rich *Vicomte* and *Vicomtesse* making a splash. I should be able to wear the charming summer clothes I had bought in Paris.

Yet I did not despair that, even in this much more elevated company, my piano would fail to have its impact.

With a large bribe to the *mäitre d'hôtel*, I secured permission to play the piano in the restaurant foyer, with the guests in the dining room separated from me by a sort of transparent screen or trellis. I could be heard but not seen.

The *mäitre d'hotel* assured me that the grand piano was well-tuned.

"Often musicians play here, and the foyer becomes a dancing area." He said complacently, "If you play well, we shall be paying you to play for us."

"That offer was made to me, when I played on the ski slopes, at the resorts there. But my husband the *Vicomte* is rich, and I play only for my own pleasure. I hope you will find my playing is up to standard. I am conservatoire-trained, " I lied airily.

"I am sure it is. Do you wish me to introduce you, so the guests stop talking?" The German conversation from the dining room was a little bedlam of chatter.

"They will stop of their own accord when I start to play," I assured him nonchalantly, and dismissed him.

So this was the big one. This was going over the top, in the trenches, with a vengeance. I needed a violinist and a full orchestra, but my grand piano would have to serve. My friend in Paris had insisted the audience would hear the words, especially "Tomorrow will be too late!" repeated three times, at the end of each verse. Well, I knew my German, and had a carrying voice.

With a crash of chords I began the allegretto prelude and sang.

My musician in Paris had told me how the singers in the Vienna opera house, the Johann Strauss Theatre, because of the long run of the show, and because of the impact of this big number, would improvise variations of the words, to bring in different similes, for the various verses, which contained the same words in each of the three verses, "Don't you know our meeting has been ordained by Fate, for tomorrow may be too late..." "The old world charges on like a great bull at a gate, and tomorrow is far too late!" And so on, to enhance the impact of the message. Well, I could improvise too.

So I began and first sang the verse of Sylva, the broken-hearted heroine, for whom romance has gone awry, (the '*Spiel, Zigeuner*' verse):

> Play, Zigeuner, anything, but love songs are taboo,
> I have left my love behind, and don't know what to do,
> Play a lilting contrabass, so my aching pain will pass,
> Play so fierily, my inner fire will fade...

Then the music became pleading, rising in intensity,

> Weep, brothers, weep for me, I'm so much alone,
> Bombs, shells, elude me, for my heart's turned to stone,
> The old world charges on, like a great bull at the gate,
> *And tomorrow may be too late*!

Next I sang Feri's verse, the old boulevardier, trying to lighten my pain:

> Come, Zigeuner, take your bow and let your fiddle sing...

Ending with,

Don't you know our meeting here was ordained by Fate,
For tomorrow is far too late!

The third verse was that of Boni, the light comedian of the operetta, and I let the music speak for him.

But at the final chorus I pulled out all the stops, starting slowly and quietly and building up into a great fortissimo crescendo.

Jaj, Mamam, Bruderherz, ich kauf mir die Welt
[If I could sell off the whole world freehold]
Jaj, Mamam, was liegt mir um lumpigen geld?
[What should I do with those great mountains of gold?]
Weisst du wie lange noch der Globus sich dreht,
[The world's ticking on, like a great bomb at the gate,]
Ob es Morgen Nicht schön zu spät!
[Won't tomorrow be far too late!]

Then, with three thumping chords, I launched into the furioso presto of the coda to the song, a staccato *csárdás* of grieving and pain like the dancing of fiends at a witches' Sabbath. I played the last explosive notes and waited for the reaction.

I knew from listening to the reaction of the audience that I had moved them. The first verse had been heard in complete silence, as though a wave of nostalgia was sweeping through those middle-aged German officers, of the trenches, and the short, snatched leaves and rendezvous with pretty girls, before going back to the hell and the mud. In the second verse there had been whisperings, of reminiscences and the familiar words being repeated, and in the third verse, which I had played without words, I had heard the words coming, spoken not sung, from the audience.

But I had not reckoned on the sheer force of the reaction. It was as though a wall of people rose up as one from the dining room, and propelled themselves in my direction, some openly weeping, some laughing, and shouting to the middle-aged Fraus who accompanied them. The noise was uncontrolled as nostalgia swept over the company.

"Ach, do you remember, Ludovica, how after that show, I proposed to you..."

"*Gott in Himmel*, when I heard that music, I was back in the trenches, with the *Minnenwerfers* coming down..."

"Gustav, when I heard that music, I said, he can do anything with me, he liked, and then you asked me for my hand so formally..."

I was surrounded by middle-aged Germans, some with tears running down their faces, demanding who I was, and where I had learned that well-loved old song. I introduced Maxim, at my side as always to turn over my music, and the aristocratic title did not fail to have its effect. We spoke of our German cousins, the Von Bylandts, Dehms, Ezterhazys killed in the war. We exchanged cards. I was implored to play one of the old tunes. I remembered the catchphrase of the music hall comic, if his jokes were well-received, as I settled down to play again: "We're in, Meredith, we're in!"

There was only one discordant note. A serious-looking, bespectacled young officer, of the newer generation - his elders would have had to wear monocles, to counter their near-sightedness approached me portentously, with disapproval written all over his face.

"*Gnädige Frau...*"

Flushed with my triumph, I was in no mood to tolerate disapproval.

"*Ich bin Nicht eine Frau. Ich bin eine Vicomtesse und Franzozich.*"

He reddened and apologised.

"*Verzeihen mir, Vicomtesse.*" But he continued earnestly in German. "You played it wrong, *Vicomtesse*. You began with the second verse '*Spiel, Zigeuner.*' I know this song well, it was a favourite of my parents. We often sang it at home. It begins '*Nimm, Zigeuner, deine geige, lasst schön was du kanst...*'"

I would not be overborne. Reverting into French, I said,

"This is the way it was written down by my music publisher in Paris. If there is an error, it is his, not mine."

One of the German officers still round the piano broke in,

"You may be right. But consider, this is the line that the heroine Sylva sings in the Terzett. It is natural that if it is sung as a female solo, the singer will begin at the second verse, and sing the first verse second. I am sure that when I heard the *diseuse* Lottie Mannerheim singing it at a concert behind the lines in France, she too sang the second verse, '*Spiel, Zigeuner*, don't sing me a song of love...'"

Other offices joined in the debate. Yes, they agreed, it was possible to begin the song with either '*Nimm, Zigeuner*' or '*Spiel, Zigeuner*' as the singer wished. It was not important, and the

Vicomtesse had sung it most charmingly. Would she perhaps play and sing again?

The pedantic officer took himself off, and I played some more of my *limonades*, to rapturous applause. But after the war, I did have occasion to secure a copy of the Kalman score, and the pedantic officer was right. It does begin, "*Nimm, Zigeuner, deine geige.*"

But my friends and I have continued to begin with "*Spiel, Zigeuner*" and to be gloriously incorrect.

Thereafter our life was conducted on more formal lines. We took the yacht out on the lake, regularly each day, as I crewed for Maxim. We made the acquaintance of the yachting set and their wives. I continued to play the piano in the afternoons, ostensibly for my own pleasure, but usually to a little knot of wives and a few husbands, who expressed their pleasure at hearing me. There were no singsongs in the evenings; this was a more formal place.

As we settled into society, Maxim held dinner parties, at which he propounded his gospel that the gentlemen of Europe should unite, to prevent a second war happening.

"It is the nobility of France and Germany who will bear the brunt, if any war starts, as they did in the last war." He spoke of the casualties sustained by his family. His audience expressed assent, the Nazis among the party being most adamant that there would never be another war, while the soldiers, some of whom knew already where and when the next push would come, listening with certain cynicism to these protestations. Maxim gained the reputation of being a crackpot, with his heart in the right place, but a little naïve. This was just the impression that we wanted to convey.

Of course, we picked up titbits. I accompanied one Frau on a shopping expedition to buy winter clothes.

"But the Polish winters are not so severe?" I asked.

"The Finnish climate is said to be terrible in winter. One must make preparations..." And I was able to inform Carton that a German military mission was being sent to advise Marshal Mannerheim in Finland.

Other women spoke of having to make the most of their last holiday abroad, which indicated that the war would come later that year. From discreetly ascertaining when their husbands had to be back at their posts, we got a very clear idea of when the war was likely to start, around September.

All the indications were that the target would be Poland. This became apparent, a little later in the year, when the full propaganda blast of the media was directed against Poland. But in April, this had not started, and we were able to report our suspicions, and the conversations we had, back to Carton in London.

But still we could not find any evidence of any concerted conspiracy by the military against the German government. The German military hated the Nazis, that was clear, and the wives of the military usually did not talk to those of the Nazis.

"*Arrivistes*," women would murmur to me as a blonde and rather overdressed Aryan maiden came into the hotel, accompanied by her older, functionary husband.

Then we discovered all about the anti-Hitler conspirators. And it was nearly our undoing.

I was sitting, happily alone, in the hotel lounge when I heard a voice beside me say, "Mrs de Winter".

I froze. I had long rehearsed meeting a friend from the French part of Switzerland, and turned with a puzzled but pleasant smile to meet my locutor, who turned out to be an earnest young man in a slightly rumpled suit.

"Excuse me, I am the *Vicomtesse* de Langlade..."

"I know all about that. I have your name from Carton's office. I must speak to your husband."

My heart went cold. How could a leak have occurred in London?

I acted quickly.

"You will address me as the *Vicomtesse* de Langlade. My husband succeeded to the title a few months back. Do I make myself clear?"

He looked cowed.

"Yes, *Vicomtesse*.

"And we shall speak either French or German. I shall take you to my husband, the *Vicomte*."

Maxim was beside the boat. I said,

"Jean-Maxime, this is a friend or acquaintance of our friend Carton."

"Come on board," said Maxim succinctly. "Mélisande, you will steer."

We took the boat to the centre of the lake, where Maxim anchored.

"Come below," he said, "Mélisande, you too. Now Monsieur, what is your name?"

"Gerhard Frankenhayn," said the boy.

"Explain to me why you are here, and how you know my name."

It was a garbled tale that Gerhard told. He was a distant cousin of Helmuth von Moltke and had accompanied his cousin to London.

He had met Carton de Wiart. Carton had asked to be kept informed of any developments. Returning to the War Office before leaving London he had asked if there were any contacts in Germany, if he had urgent news to convey. Carton was not there, being in Poland, but an aide said there was a Mr and Mrs de Winter who would be staying at the main hotel in Interlaken. The hotel clerk at the hotel had said there was no Mrs de Winter, but there was a French lady, the *Vicomtesse* de Langlade. Gerhard had put two and two together, and had found me in the lounge.

Maxim's face had hardened at this breach of security. What was the vital information that he had to give? The young man blurted out the names of all the officers who had been involved in the aborted plot to overthrow Hitler just before Munich, from General Beck downwards, and all the influential civilians, like Mayor Goerdler, Adam von Trott, von Moltke, and so on, who were also active in the cause.

Surely it must be clear that there was a powerful anti-Nazi organisation that the British Government ought to support.

He finished and Maxim looked at him rumanitively.

"Young man," he said. "You are in possession of two dangerous secrets, that of your own organisation and of our mission. If I was sensible, I should drop you over the side, here and now, and let you drown! If you were to be picked up by the Gestapo, they would soon know all about your friends and you. However, now you are here, you will dine with us at the yacht club, and take the first train back to Germany in the morning. Lie low, and do not draw attention to yourself. We are grateful for your information, but do not be so trusting in future. We might well be allied to the Gestapo. Have you brought a dinner jacket? No? Very well, we shall dine early, informally. Mélisande, bring the yacht back to the mooring, if you please."

We dined at the yacht club, and Maxim introduced Gerhard to his friends as a cousin of Helmuth von Moltke, who had sent him to express the Graf's support for his gentlemen-of-Europe-against-war campaign. Some eyebrows were raised because Helmuth von Moltke was known as an anti-Nazi.

In fact, Gerhard's intrusion did us no harm. To be seen with a connection of Helmuth von Moltke, caused an elderly Prussian nobleman, now permanently resident in Switzerland, who expressed his antipathy to the Nazis by flying the flag of the old Imperial German Navy from his boat, to speak to us.

"Don't put any confidence in the anti-Nazi movement. All gas and wind and promises," he observed succinctly.

Maxim sought to dispel any suspicion by talking of his family's friendship with General Gamelin. If we were emissaries at all, it would be of the French military. Maxim also sought out the hotel clerk, and said the young man had made a mistake. Due to Maxim's father, the *Comte*, having the title of de Winter de Langlade, he had mistaken us for cousins of the same name.

We drove to Zurich the following day, and Maxim sent an abrasive note to Carton, saying that his department had blown our cover, and suggesting that we terminate the mission forthwith. Coppelius was to telephone Carton's reply to the hotel.

In Zurich, sitting in a café, the inevitable happened.

"Jeanne...Jeanne de Winter..."

It was two of my friends from our canton in Switzerland. I debated. The mission was virtually over. But let us remain in character to the end.

I turned with polite surprise toward them.

"Mesdames, I think you make a mistake, I am Mélisande de Langlade... Is there some way I can help you?"

I carried it off. They withdrew, full of apologies. It was my last small triumph.

Coppelius phoned the hotel.

"Carton agrees. Come home."

Our friends at the hotel were saddened by our departure.

They insisted I give a last concert, and surprisingly all the old officers joined in the songs. So we had a singsong as in Switzerland. The *pièce de résistance* was '*Spiel, Zigeuner*' which they insisted I encored. We exchanged addresses interminably, with the hopes that they could visit us at the Château de Langlade, or at their various *schlosses* and apartments in Germany. We did not know we had made so many friends.

At the end of the concert the Prussian nobleman came in.

"Have a last sail over the lake in my boat," he said, with a touch of urgency in his voice. Maxim agreed.

Down in the cabin of the Prussian's boat was a senior army officer. He handed over a portfolio.

"Give this to General Gamelin! If he can get the Americans and the Russians to combine with the French and the British, then Hitler may draw back. The terrible war we both fear may not happen."

We looked at the portfolio in the seclusion of our hotel. It was the complete battle plan of the invasion of Poland, dates and details.

We might have been better advised to have given this to General Gamelin. Our own War Office refused to believe in its authenticity, saying it was just a red herring. They filed it away, until on September 1st, it happened right according to plan.

We flew back to London from Geneva, Mr and Mrs de Winter once more. At the Savoy, Albert Robinson brought us our mail, forwarded by Madame Gossard from Switzerland. There was also a note from Carton.

"Well done. Come and see me at my Club, United Sports Club, Whitehall. 4.30 p.m. tomorrow."

Carton was sitting in the smoking room when we arrived in the club, at the corner of Whitehall Court. He rose to greet us.

"Will you take tea? No one here in the smoking room. We can talk."

Maxim said,

"Was it a value for money mission? I really must recompense you for Jeanne's wardrobe."

"Not at all," said Carton. "Compliments of His Majesty's Government. You were well within budget. I congratulate you. You also brought back a lot of very useful information. That battle plan was quite a coup. I only hope the War Office makes proper use of it. And as to your estimate of the anti-Nazi movement..."

"All gas and wind," said Maxim helpfully.

"They certainly seem to be as leaky as a sieve, and probably penetrated by the Gestapo as well. That Admiral Canaris, he's a man who plays both sides, if there ever was one..." He paused. "I owe you both an apology. That silly fellow in my office, he's gone. He had his just reward, I had him transferred to MI6. Now I suggest you take a well-earned break. You'll probably be called back to the colours in September or so."

We stayed in the Savoy until the ravages of my beauticians had worn off, my eyebrows had resumed their natural bushiness and my hair had resumed its unfashionable look.

Our friends in Switzerland were delighted to see us back.

"And do you know, Jeanne," one confided in me. "You have a double, in Zurich. We ran into her in Zurich a few weeks ago. We were sure it was you. But she looked much older, and made up to the nines. I think she said her name was de Langlade."

"Oh, that would be my French cousin," I said. "I've not met her, but we are said to be very much alike."

"Like peas in a pod. But you are much prettier than she was!"

As Burns once said:

"Ah, would that Fate the gift would gie us
To see ourselves as other see us."

Chapter Ten

In Which We Go to War

The summer of 1939 was the most beautiful in my memory. They tell me the summer of 1914 was beautiful also. But that was different because war came as a surprise. The killing of the Archduke Franz Ferdinand in Sarajevo in August 1914 could not have been foreseen, at least by most people.

But we were different. Because we had seen the German war plan for Poland we knew, almost to the day, almost to the hour, how much time we had left, and we lived every day to the full. We spent almost all me time on me water, or in it, sailing, swimming, sunbathing, till we became so tanned that Maxim said that when we returned to London, we should be asked from what part of the far flung Empire we came. It was absolute bliss to be alive.

We managed, by persistent letters and telephone calls, to get our agent Frank and his new young wife away from his beloved Manderley estate to spend a few weeks with us at the villa. Their white bodies contrasted with our tanned ones, and Frank was comically piebald.

His countryman's face and neck and his forearms as brown as ours, while the rest was virgin white. They joined in with our activities with gusto and were soon almost as brown as we were.

In the evenings Maxim told Frank and Phyllis a little of what we knew, and warned him to put the Manderley Estate on a war footing. In fact, Cornwall was one of the counties least affected by the war, and its hotels soon filled up with people escaping the Blitz, and with honeymooning military. As we owned several small hotels, this did the estate a lot of good.

We had time to put our affairs in order too. Mme Gossard became our agent for the villa, able to let it out on short lets to visitors, if she so chose, though we could not tell her when we should return.

So we had our bags already packed and ready, when Mr Chamberlain came on the radio that Sunday morning, September 3rd, to say that Britain was at war. And it was that day or just after it, that we received a phone call from Coppelius.

"Your suite is reserved at the Savoy."

Carton wanted us back. We caught the first available train and boat to London.

The next morning the faithful Albert Robinson brought us our orders. We were to meet Carton at the United Sports Club in Whitehall Court for lunch. The London clubs were not yet affected by the rationing.

"I have assignments for both of you," he said. "Same place, different headquarters.

"Maxim, I'm sorry I can't let you join your regiment yet. You're on the strength, have been for a year, but assigned to special duties. I'll let you have your real war later on.

"I need a really fluent French-speaking officer, assigned to the French headquarters, someone who understands the French and can work with them. You'll be given the temporary rank of Major."

"But, General, you forget I know nothing about soldiering. And how can I act as liaison with the British Army, if I don't know any of them?"

"You go to the nub, Maxim, as I expected. But you don't need this knowledge, initially, because you're damned intelligent, and you'll pick it up. You'll be under a Colonel Urquart, first rate soldier, very bright, but not a great linguist.

"Now we both know the French treat every negotiation, any cooperation, as though it were a crooked poker game. You seem to me to have the right temperament to be a good, cool poker player. There's always a great deal of hobnobbing of the bright ADCs in the corridors, as they explain what the real thing is that the French want. You'll be able to build bridges, to brief Urquart on any hidden agendas, smooth down any ruffled feathers. Things like that. Build up an atmosphere of mutual trust."

"You should be there with me. If anyone can build an atmosphere of trust in the British, you can," said Maxim sincerely.

Carton de Wiart smiled wintrily.

"There are those in the War Office who feel I'm too friendly with the French already. 'Half-a-Frog', that's how I've heard myself described, when they thought I wasn't listening. I shall come over from time to time..."

"And in the meantime you'd like me to keep you posted, on any significant infighting," Maxim concluded.

"Exactly!" said Carton de Wiart. "I like to have supplementary eyes and ears around. I have no private army any more, except you and Coppelius in Zurich. By the way, there are still some secret funds left in the Zurich accounts. I have had them transferred to the bank's Paris branch, which you will be able to access, in the name of the *Vicomte* and *Vicomtesse* de Langlade. I hope you still have your French papers, your *cartes d'identité*. You never know when you might need to use them. Jeanne might need to access the funds, as she is going to be a civilian officer/interpreter, with staff rank but unpaid, with headquarters of the British Expeditionary Forces in Paris."

"No more visits to the Paris salons, then?"

"Certainly not, Jeanne," said Carton de Wiart. "You are to revert to your mouse status, though with sufficient spirit to prevent yourself being trodden on by the top brass at headquarters. But you are going to be very useful to the war effort. There is no unified command and it is important to know which officer or department is the co-operative one in the French command – when it comes to transportation and other basic matters. Maxim will feed you this information. You will become indispensable to your superiors, for your breadth of contacts."

"Will we be based in Paris, then?" I asked.

"Initially, certainly. But if there is an advanced headquarters, should fighting begin in France, you may be posted there. But reckon on a stay in Paris for about six months at least."

"We should have stayed in Paris and avoided the cost of the hotel," said Maxim.

"Oh, no, you couldn't," said Carton de Wiart, smiling. "You are going to get yourself kitted out as a senior British officer, I shall give you a note to my military tailor, so as to dazzle the French high command. And you must go down, in civilian clothes, to pay your respects to the Colonel of the Duke of Cornwall's regiment. You're just a lieutenant there, remember, but you've been on the strength, as a ghost officer for about a year. Better go and reassure him you are still alive, able and willing. I must go, to an interminable meeting. I'll see you again before I go." And with that he rose, shook us warmly by the hand, and left us to make our pensive way back to the Savoy.

*

The Paris assignment was an unmixed triumph for Maxim but was more a bottom-of-the-bill act, for me, exposed to the boos of the impatient.

Maxim and his boss, Colonel Urquart, took to each other at once and were soon a perfectly synchronised military machine. Urquart was soon repeating, in his execrably accented French, the famous saying of Marshal Foch, "*Demandez à Weygand* (or in this case Maxim) *c'est la même chose*!" Urquart's French was perfectly serviceable, but appalling on the ear. He understood perfectly well what was being said, but so mangled the French language in his replies, that it was with perceptible relief the senior French officers heard him say, "*Maxim, dites!*" Maxim would switch into overdrive and commence smoothly, "*Le Colonel Urquart veut dire...*" and produce a seamless and elegant exposition of what the Colonel was attempting to say, taking on board the objections of previous speakers, and answering them point by point. At the end he would turn to Urquart and say, "C'est juste, mon Colonel?" "Just what I was going to say," Urquart would reply.

Maxim read a great deal at night and seemed able to assimilate and recall the exact French equivalent of every military expression of our army. He and Urquart had spent a lot of time together discussing military strategy and tactics. No one would think that he was a complete amateur and civilian when he entered on his assignment. His reading of Colonel Jack's war diaries had helped him considerably, he told me, and he probably knew the detail of the topography of the Western Front as well as those who had served there. He was even sometimes called in to adjudicate on arguments between veterans. "*Dites, Major, vous savez...*" He was soon an integral part of the French high command family.

My progress in the BEF military machine was less spectacular. In fact, it was an uphill struggle for recognition as a creature with a brain at all.

There was jealousy. Here was I, a mere civilian, and a rich and idle civilian since I took no salary, being pushed by personal influence in Whitehall to take a cherished post which others better deserved. There was the feeling that I was a protégé, and probably mistress of General Carton de Wiart, and likely a spy brought in to report on the shortcomings of the high command.

My fluency in French was grudgingly conceded, but I knew nothing about military matters.

At first I felt I was back at Manderley, being snubbed by everyone, particularly the ATS officers, the women officers who were more deadly and cliquey than the male.

But I was now resilient. Primed by Maxim each night, I did become a source of information. "Ask Jeanne who is the right French GHQ officer to speak to on this matter," and I would reply. If an irate French commander came on the line, complaining of this or that, Madame de Winter was called on to smooth him down, pencilled notes being passed to me surreptitiously by the Colonel in answer to my whispered enquiries. "He says, why hasn't this or that been done?" Then I would say in my most charming voice, "Mon Colonel veut dire..." I came to act as a buffer, with young French officers or stenographers phoning from French high command to say the equivalent of, "Jeanne, my General hasn't received, or he's lost, this or that report from the British! Will you tell your Colonel or whoever to do something about it quick, because he's going off his rocker..." Increasingly, they asked for me by name, unprompted by Maxim at their own HQ. In the early days of the war, the exchange of paper was more significant than the exchange of gunfire.

The moment when even the envious ones of GHQ realised that I had my uses was when a very senior French General arrived, unheralded and unannounced, at our headquarters with a major request for assistance which he had earlier asked for in vain. I took charge, charmed him, made phone calls, explained to a dozen different departments exactly what the General wanted, and was able to get the right information from the right people, in time to make a comprehensive presentation to the General.

In parting he paid me a rare compliment.

"Madame," he said. "I wish I had you on my staff." After that I became known in the building as 'Calamity Jeanne', to be called on in any state of intractable crisis.

After a few months, I began to understand the minutiae of running an army in a foreign country. I became absorbed in the physical, as well as in the contemplative sense, in the British war machine.

Carton de Wiart had indicated that life in headquarters was a light and easy existence. Perhaps in the first war, with the Generals far behind the lines in comfortable châteaux, it might have been. I found service in modern HQ rather more exacting. I arrived early, worked through the day, with my black coffee and my brochette taken at the desk, and staggered back to our apartment at about nine, ready only for my bed.

Maxim had a more luxurious existence at French headquarters, where gastronomy was regarded as a serious matter, not to be skimped, but he too worked long hours. We had no time for elegant cocktail parties and intimate dinners, designed to bring the French and the British officers together. It may have been going on, for all we knew. But we were too busy to be part of this beau monde.

Some large blocks of apartments had been requisitioned for the General Staff and their hangers-on, like Maxim and me. But they were not very satisfactory. We began to think seriously of buying or renting our own house, to give us more room. The outbreak of war had caused a number of rich families to leave their town houses for the country, fearing that Paris would be bombed to the ground. Prices and rents were low.

Maxim said that to buy a house might be a good speculation, and got Frank to transfer capital from London to our account in Paris, in the same Paris branch of the Zurich bank where was the de Langlade account was. But events moved so fast that no transaction was ever made.

So, in the months that we spent in Paris, I barely went out at all and saw nobody behind our English military circles. It was like being in the cantonments in Kabul. The whole city stretched out before us, but we contented ourselves with talking only with our own folk.

So, more by luck, and overwork, the paths of the opulent and idle *Vicomtesse* and the busy and dedicated Mrs De Winter never followed a similar pattern. That was to be helpful later on.

In the New Year, I went as part of Head of Army Intelligence's team to the forward headquarters in B. – as we were supposed to say. Maxim remained with the forward French HQ, increasingly restless at the French Army's over-reliance on the strength of the Maginot Line. He wanted to get back under British command, and put out diplomatic feelers to get transferred to the staff of General Alexander (the British Commander of the First Army, whom he had met and with whom he had developed a rapport). But the French high command, regarding him as a very useful and prestigious member of their 'court', were reluctant to change to a less *sympathetique* liaison officer.

"I have buttered them up too well," Maxim said in despair, as he visited HQ to press his cause.

"Gamelin's the best of the bunch. He's a cavalry man, and understands about mobile warfare. He appointed de Gaulle as a tank commander, very much against the wishes of his colleagues, who regard de Gaulle as obstinate and self-opinionated, which he is, but he's a damned good tank commander.

"But Gamelin isn't a strong enough man. As in every army there are rings; a ring round Weygand, who say he should be C-in-C; there's a ring round Pétain, supporting him. In the end, nothing positive gets done.

"I've met Gamelin and he sent his regards in an indirect way. He asked me if I was related to his old friend, the *Comte* de Winter. I said I was his English cousin. He said to send my regards to the *Comte*, and congratulate his son and daughter-in-law, the *Vicomte* and *Vicomtesse* de Langlade, on the excellent intelligence work in Switzerland, in which he was glad to play a small part. Carton must have passed on our reports and the German battle plan for Poland, though knowing the French command as I now do, they probably pigeonholed it - just as our War Office did. Gamelin maintained a poker face as he spoke to me, but I have the feeling he knew that I was the *Vicomte* and you the *Vicomtesse*. But I wish Gamelin were stronger and had better people to support him."

On April 8th, the war began in earnest, with Germany occupying Denmark and Norway. A month later, on May 10th, the Germans burst into Holland.

The day following, Maxim arrived on a motorbike, from French HQ. Looking like a French despatch rider, he marched into the offices where I was taking dictation from my Colonel.

"Colonel, the Germans are going through Holland like a knife through butter. Holland and Belgium will fall within a few weeks, and then the BEF will be cut off and isolated. Jeanne is a civilian and I want to take her away with me to Paris. The way things will be going, you won't need her. You'll be too busy looking after yourselves."

The Colonel bowed to the implacable will of his junior officer.

"I can't hold you, Jeanne..." he began, and Maxim cut in.

"I'll be back in a day and I'll help you all I can. Alexander has said he'll take me on his staff. But I must get Jeanne away. The roads will be a shambles as soon as the people know the Germans are coming. If we leave now, we can get through. Jeanne, do you have all your papers with you?" I nodded. They were sewn into the lining of my jacket, a precaution we'd fixed many months ago, back in Paris. Maxim had said we must always be ready to move, at a moment's notice.

Pausing only to commandeer a soldier's greatcoat and a crash helmet for me from the despatch riders' pool, we mounted and rode away. It was a breakneck but exhilarating ride through the French countryside, riding pillion behind Maxim, my arms round his waist, as the great motorbike ate up the miles, hour after hour.

In Paris, Maxim reported to the Paris HQ of the British forces while I went to the bank to draw out funds for the journey, and to buy sufficient clothing and supplies for the journey into Switzerland.

The panic had not yet begun; I was able to book a first class sleeper on the night train to Bern. I went to a small hotel we knew to book into a room, where I packed my newly bought case with clothes for the voyage, and unpicked my lining to retrieve my Swiss papers. I was again a Swiss citizen, Jeanne de Winter.

Maxim joined me at the hotel and after celebrating, as he put it, the last rites of our marriage, we went out and had a last dinner together. Alas, the time did not allow us to go to Montmartre and have our last meal together in Florians.

At dinner Maxim said,

"If things go as badly as I anticipate, and they were pretty glum at HQ, we may have to evacuate the army to England. I may have to go with them. We may be separated for some years. So look after yourself, love."

Such British understatement. I had to smile.

"I wish you could come with me, Maxim, I shall be so lonely by myself in Switzerland. Perhaps Madame Gossard and I shall form a knitting circle."

He smiled.

"Practise your piano and I may come back to Switzerland to find you are a famous concert pianist." Then the reserve broke down.

"Oh my God, I'm going to miss you, Jeanne."

"Me too, Maxim."

We rode through the Paris streets, with a very slight shower making the pavements gleam under the night lights. Paris was never a wholly blacked out city, as London was. It was nice to hold Maxim still, round the waist.

We parted at the station. To conceal any emotion I said,

"Be careful to return the greatcoat and the crash helmet to whomever you got them from. They may miss them."

He grinned.

"Meticulous as ever, Jeanne. If everything goes as I fear it may, there will be an awful lot of Army equipment that will go missing before we get the troops back to England."

We parted with almost a casual embrace, fearing to show too much of the emotion we felt. Maxim saluted me as he drove the motorcycle off, I waved back.

I showed my ticket to the railway official and my Swiss passport to the gendarme on the platform. I climbed on to the train and found my first class sleeper, carrying my single small suitcase with me. At least, I thought irrelevantly, I shall have no trouble with the Customs.

I did not weep. I lit a cigarette, the first I had had for many months.

I had bought a large packet of cigarettes as part of my purchases, knowing I should need them on the voyage.

What were my feelings then? Many years later I heard Adlai Stevenson say, after his presidential defeat, that he felt like the little boy who said he was too old to cry, but it hurt too much to laugh. I realised that encapsulated exactly my feelings as the train moved out of the station, that night in May 1940, with me on board, and Maxim somewhere out there in France.

So I returned to Switzerland and the villa, alone.

Chapter Eleven

Waiting For Maxim

I arrived back in Switzerland to wait for Maxim. From May 15, I waited for a call from him. Even if the worst happened, and he had to be evacuated with the British Expeditionary Force back to England, I was sure that by some means, through Carton, Coppelius, or by some means, he would get a message through to me. That he might not send me word did not enter my mind.

I resumed my residence at the villa. I called on Madame Gossard to take back my keys. After a six month absence she seemed delighted, but not surprised.

"Always I knew, sooner or later, you would come back."

She said I should find the villa spick and span and ready for my immediate use. She, and latterly her great-niece Rose, had gone in every day to dust and clean the place. Rose, a student, was using M. Maxim's study to revise for her examinations. This was in order, was it not? I said I was delighted.

Mention of M. Maxim's room led her to ask about Maxim. Why was he not with you? Would he be returning later? I said I fervently hoped so. He was in England, I hoped, and he would shortly be in touch with me. We had become separated, in the war in France...

She did not press me. Returning to the subject of Rose, she said darkly,

"*Prenez garde à Rose! Elle est etudiante, et barbare...*"

I was musing, as I entered the villa, on what sort of barbarities Student Rose the Barbarian indulged in. I was soon to discover.

The French windows that led on to the terrace were partly open, and I opened them wider, with a creak, to enter on to the terrace. I saw two figures lying on mattresses on the terrace, both of whom turned to look towards me.

I saw a pert, dark-haired girl about seventeen, and a fair-haired boy about the same age. Both were totally naked, with never a stitch between them.

The boy evinced some embarrassment, hastily pulling on his trunks. The girl remained totally composed and smiled up at me. She was Rose Blanchisseur, she said, and this was her friend, Claud-Aymon.

I smiled.

"You are Madame Gossard's great niece, I think. She calls you *La Barbare*, the Barbarian. I think now I can understand why."

Unhurriedly she rose and shook my hand. *Tante* Mathilde, she explained earnestly, was too old fashioned, too stuffy. Why, one even had to wear shoes when one was in her villa. How foolish it was in this hot weather encumbered with clothes. She had to study, and how could one concentrate when one was hot and sticky and one's clothes clung to one? Once free, one could work.

I could see this situation called for delicate negotiation, so that les *regles-du-jeu* could be established. In life it is necessary to compromise, I said. I was broad-minded and a woman of the world, and it was not my concern how much or how little clothing Rose chose to wear, if she wore any at all. But the rules of propriety in my house dictated that she should receive young men *chez-moi* in at least a swimsuit and the young men should be similarly dressed. I appealed to the young man. Was this not a reasonable request? He solemnly concurred that it was.

Rose was compliant, if regretful. A young man's body revealed his character, she said, and *embrassement au naturel* was a very agreeable sensation.

"*Embrasse moi, donc, Claud Aymon. C'est pour le dernier fois, comme ça.*"

Smiling broadly, Claud Aymon obliged and a little after went off. Rose remarked that her clothes were in Monsieur's workroom and ran gracefully up the stairs. But I did not think she evinced any great enthusiasm to put them on.

Dear Rose. Her cheerfulness and her outrageousness helped divert my mind at a very tense time, as days, weeks, and even months passed without a message of any kind from Maxim.

I tried not to think about it, tried to be patient. I had been to the nearest big town, and had bought the most advanced radio that they had. Nightly, and at different times in the day, I scanned the wireless, seeking to pick up the British Services. Strange, that for two and a half years, Maxim and I had sought to banish English speech and English voices from our lives. Now I was greedy for any scrap of English to discover what was going on. I even listened to 'Germany Calling' and the self-satisfied voice of William Joyce.

I knew only what everybody knew, that the British Army, from the 30th May, had been evacuated from the Dunkirk Beaches. On the 8th June, I heard reports of Churchill's great speech in the Commons of a few days before, how for days and nights a little armada of boats, small and large, had ferried the British troops across the Channel, bringing back 335,000 men, though 30,000 were left behind, dead or prisoners. It was only then I had a *frisson* of fear that Maxim might have been among the dead. But he was invincible...

During these tense days, the outrageous barbarian Rose proved a diversion.

I would hear her enter, hear the noise as she kicked off her shoes, and then hear her humming a merry tune as she busied herself with the cleaning.

"*Bonjour, Rose...*" I would call from wherever I was.

"*Bonjour, Jeanne. Comment ça va?*" she would reply. Then after the housework was done, she would go up the stairs to Maxim's workroom to continue her studies.

For a time there would be silence and then there would come the inevitable cry, "*J'etouffe*, I am stifling..." then a little later, the stentorian "*On... Doit... CONCENTRER...*" at which point a skirt or shorts, a blouse, and other intimate garments would describe a graceful parabola down the stairwell to the floor below. There would be a cry of "*Ah, c'est mieux*" and then silence again.

Often as I played my piano, I would become aware of a naked cherub, the white papers in her hand, contrasting with the brown of her skin, squatting on the stairs and silently listening to me. Or when I was working at my desk, I would hear a patter of bare feet down the stairs, and an insistent cry of, "*Jeanne, Jeanne, aidez-moi, s'il vous plaît*" as she sought my wisdom on some intractable problem of study.

We got on pretty well, and Madame Gossard congratulated me on how well I had tamed *La Barbare* Rose. I insisted she kept a robe close at hand, wherever she was, so as to slip it on should *Tante*

Mathilde pay an unexpected call. *Tante* Mathilde, when she called, said,

"So you have not been able to discipline *La Barbare* Rose. Always she goes barefoot!"

I did not tell of Rose's other barenesses.

I resisted Rose's daily indoctrinations as to how delightful it was to go *au natural.*

"*But Rose, je suis une serieuse femme mariée...*" Only on the hottest days would I compromise with Rose's revolutionary views, to put on a swimsuit. "*Oh, vous êtes belle,*" she would say. "*Quelle dommage...*" But I would not be persuaded.

But the weeks of waiting began to take their toll. I finally drove to Zurich and begged Coppelius to do everything he could, to get word from London; what had happened to Maxim, and any message from him. He said he would do what he could, but he might have to pursue a roundabout route, and it would take time. He promised to phone me if he got any news, it was some weeks after that, that the telephone message came. Rose, fully clothed, unusually, was in the room and took the call, handing it to me. It was Coppelius.

"Jeanne, I am so sorry. I have news of Maxim. He was reported missing, presumed killed, at Dunkirk. Let me know if there is anything, anything, I can do..."

Rose, looking at me with concern, said "*Monsieur est-il mort?*"

I said, "I don't know..." And suddenly the tears came. I wept on Rose's sympathetic shoulder, and she wept for me.

For the next weeks I went around in a daze. Rose, no longer outrageous, gave me silent sympathy, and did all she could for me without words. She was a great comfort.

Then all of a sudden I came to a decision. I would go to France and find Maxim. That night, I took Rose and went out in Maxim's boat on the lake. We swam naked from the boat, as I had done with Maxim.

Afterwards we sat in the boat in the warm night and silently looked at the stars. I had stripped off all the inessentials of my life; I was beyond grief, beyond pain, a glowing naked spirit of resolution.

"Rose," I said. "I am going back to France, to find Maxim."

She squeezed my hand.

"I am glad," she said. "I have felt for you in your pain, all these last days,"

"You were right, Rose," I said. "*ON DOIT CONCENTRER...*"

She laughed, and the tension lifted.

The following day I drove again to Zurich, and had a long meeting, in a soundproof office, with Coppelius. I explained to him my resolve. I should put on my disguise of the *Vicomtesse* de Langlade, and set up house in Paris. I should use my friendships made among the Germans of the ski slopes and of Interlaken to find out exactly what had happened to Maxim, and if he was still alive. If I could become a listening post in Paris for Carton, as I had been in Interlaken, that would suit me fine. I wanted to rejoin the private army, in whatever way I could, consonant with my desire to find where Maxim lay, dead or alive. He promised to pass on this to Carton, through the established channels. I should hear from him.

I returned to the villa, and in our bedroom laid out my old finery as the *Vicomtesse*. Rose came from the nearby workroom to marvel at it.

"What beautiful clothes..." she breathed in awe.

I smiled at the naked cherub.

"I thought you detested all clothes, Rose."

One must be practical, she, retorted. For the villa in summertime nakedness was best. But in the real world clothes were important, and these were clothes of such chic and elegance. I invited her to choose anything that took her fancy for herself, and she proved to have a remarkably good eye for colour and for cut, kissing me warmly in gratitude as she bore away her spoils.

In due course, I had a note from the bank, bidding me come in and test the key of my deposit box. It was normal security procedure.

I went in and opened my deposit box. I found a return ticket from Geneva Airport to Lisbon, a reservation for a room for Madame de Winter in the Hotel Lisboa, and some Portuguese currency. There was a now, "You will be contacted there. C." I did not know if the C stood for Coppelius or Carton.

At the Hotel Lisboa, I discreetly asked if there was a Mr Carton staying there. The flight from Geneva had been uneventful, with most of my fellow passengers Swiss businessmen acting for overseas interests.

International business had to go on, despite the war, and flights were tacitly allowed by all warring parties, Axis and Allied alike, between the various neutral capitals, Stockholm, Madrid, Lisbon, and

New York. Swiss Air was one of the international carriers that carried this traffic.

The hotel clerk could find no Englishman of that name, but did mention that there was a South African diamond buyer, Mr Adrian den Bloem, in the hotel. He was the only English speaking gentleman he had seen.

Adrian was Carton's Christian name, and he had lived in Bloemfontein. It was just possible. I sat in my hotel room and waited for a call. It came. Mr den Bloem was on the line, with so thick an Afrikaans accent I could barely understand him. He said he thought we had mutual friends, that he was alone in Lisbon, and could we perhaps have dinner together.

"Mr den Bloem," I asked. "Do you know London well?"

Mr den Bloem knew all the capitals of Europe, especially Amsterdam, the centre of the diamond trade, where he could not go now, because of the damned war. He knew London, but did not like it much.

"I always think of how the British persecuted my people in the South African war, with their concentration camps and their maxim guns."

Maxim? It was a clear hint.

"Are you perhaps a member of the United Sports Club?"

He admitted he was, a place where he could get away from the *verdammt* English. I agreed to the dinner invitation. He had one last shot in his locker.

"And may I call you by your schoolday nickname, 'Smelly Mellie'?"

"Certainly not," I said. "Sidonie de Savoie, my aunt, would not like it."

He laughed and rang off. Assuredly it was Carton in disguise.

I should not have known Carton again. There were superficial differences to his appearance, the moustache more luxuriant and Zapata-like, glasses with one lens misted to conceal his blind eye, instead of the pirate king black eyepatch, rather loud and opulent clothes. But it was the interior of the man that had wholly altered. He had gone back to his Boer farmer persona of the South African War, or rather the made-good financier son of that Boer farmer.

His personality was overwhelming. Bar acquaintances would sing out to him, "How's the diamond market been today, Mr den Bloem?" and he would reply,

"Boys, my knowledge of the diamond market is my stock-in-trade. You think I shall give that to you for nothing? But I tell you, you can't go wrong in buying diamonds or diamond shares, whatever the market is doing. You'll recoup your money, believe me."

"Monsieur den Bloem," I said in slightly accented English. "Do we speak French or English, tonight?"

"My God, my darling, it's years since I spoke French. Let's speak in English, if you please. You Swiss speak it better than we do"

"Better than he does, at any rate, Miss," said someone at the bar. We kept up our pretence over dinner, which was very good. We only exchanged pleasantries. At the end he said,

"And, now, my darling, I am going to show you the beautiful city of Lisbon, by moonlight..."

"Watch him, Miss," said the irreverent bar colleague.

"What, do you think I'd take advantage of a pretty Swiss lady, on her first night in Lisbon?"

"Yes," they all chorused.

Later we sat in a small deserted garden near the hotel, and dropped the masquerade.

"You'll be wanting to know about Maxim. So was I, when I heard that one of my family was missing. I spoke to Alexander and the people who last saw him alive and well, and I'm very much of the opinion that he may be still alive. He was wounded, certainly, but they never found his body. There is a good chance that with his command of French, he may have been sheltered and concealed, and that in the fullness of time, he may come marching home."

My heart missed a beat. Maxim alive?

"Do you truly think this?"

"Truly," he said and began to explain how Maxim had come to be wounded. Alexander, in charge of the defensive bridgehead, was concerned that the route of some of the troops, the Leicesters, still in good battle order, was going to be down a road which was being subjected to air attack. From his map it seemed there might be a cross country alternative.

Maxim, with his command of French, was sent back to talk to people in a local village, to see if they knew a way and could direct the troops. A boy in the village said he knew such a track. Maxim made contact with the advancing Leicesters, and with the boy led them on this track, leading them first in his staff car, and when the going became too rough, left the car and went with the Leicesters on foot. When he saw they were almost there to the Dunkirk beaches, he went back along the route, to take the boy in his car back to his parents. The car was sighted by an enemy aircraft and strafed.

"Alexander says that when they found the car, it was upside down in a ditch with the driver dead at the wheel. There was a lot of blood over the back seats. But of Maxim and the boy there was no sign. Alexander thinks they might have got away wounded. He was sorry to lose Maxim, who was one of his best staff officers. He sends his commiserations."

"So if I go to France, as the *Vicomtesse*, I might find him."

"Or he may find you. Listen, Jeanne, I don't want to risk you, but your going to Paris might provide us with a golden chance to set up a safe house, and a communications centre, right in the middle of Paris. If you become the *Vicomtesse Collaboratrice*, the friend of the Germans, as you were in Interlaken, you could provide just the front we need. If you could win their confidence, and become a friend of the military, and get information of what they were thinking and saying, that would be the jam on the cake. But basically we want you as a respectable Paris householder, whose activities no one will suspect"

"So I go to the château in the Auvergne, and go from there to Paris?"

"Exactly. It's in the unoccupied zone of France, so you can use your Swiss passport to get there, and you'll make your formal application for a Paris residence permit from there. You'll have to find an why excuse why the *Vicomte* isn't with you. Either he's not well, or the *Comte* isn't well, more likely, heart probably, and he can't leave him."

"How can I make enquiries about Maxim? Even if I say he is a cousin, that will tie me up with the British connection, which you won't want."

"I don't think that matters. Most of the aristocratic German officers have British cousins, or connections, so that could be part of your cover. You told them you had German cousins, so why not British too? I think you have to imply, a little delicately, that cousin John de Winter, Major in the Duke of Cornwall's regiment, was a little more than a cousin, almost a lover. That also will fit in with your French stereotype."

"Carton," I said reproachfully. "You're making me out to be a loose woman."

"That's what the German officers are going to hope, Jeanne. A beautiful married woman, living apart from her husband in Paris, enough to excite their chivalry. Of course, you will be faithful to your husband, and you will be particularly kind to officers' wives. And, of course, you will play your piano. It might be a good idea to arrive in Paris in time for the Christmas season, when there will be a lot of parties, and the *Vicomtesse au piano* will be much in demand."

"Carton you are trying to compromise me. Once upon the schnapps, and the girl is mine."

"Not at all, Jeanne. You will be a *Fiordiligi* of fidelity to Maxim. When you get to Paris, you'll find all your orders in the safe deposit box in the Paris branch of the Zurich Bank. And enough money to sustain you in your grass widowhood in Paris."

"Carton," I asked. "How long will I be in Paris?"

He was serious, for the first time.

"I don't know, Jeanne. I honestly don't know. As long as it takes."

As it happened, I was to be there for almost until the end of the war.

I flew back from Lisbon the following day. I did not see Carton again. He was busy setting up some listening posts in Lisbon, the meeting point of very many interests, Allied and Axis. Oil was going to be the lifeblood of this war, he said. Whoever got the oil, and debarred the other side from getting it, would win the war, he told me. And Lisbon was an important part of the international oil network.

When I got back to the villa, Rose was waiting for me.

"They think Maxim is still alive," I told her and we embraced again. I told her to use the villa for her studies in vacations. She would use the villa to invite her friends down to study parties, but they must be discreet. "Not too many midnight bathing parties..."

She perfectly understood.

"*Soyons sage!* Of course you can rely on me, Jeanne." She was like a little Eve before the Fall, armoured in innocence. We have remained good friends since. She had a very successful legal career before marrying. She now complains to me of the liberties young people, and her daughters in particular, seem to expect.

I left Madame Gossard my keys and said I was going back into France to find my husband, missing after Dunkirk. She bade me Godspeed and said she would pray for me. However long it took, the villa would be there waiting for me, ready for my return. And four years later, when we returned, it was, spick and span and welcoming. You can rely upon the Swiss.

Chapter Twelve

From the Château to the Capital

After my meeting with Carton I flew back to Switzerland. I went to see Coppelius in Zurich, and discussed with him what visas I should need to travel into unoccupied France. The same arrangements would apply in the bank in Paris as in Zurich, he said. I should go to them and funds from the standing account would be transferred into a special account in the name of the *Vicomte* and *Vicomtesse* de Langlade. I should have my sealed orders within my deposit security box.

I went back to the villa and made my last preparations. I told Madame Gossard that I was going into France to find my missing husband, and might be away for some years. If I did not return, I would leave instructions with my bank that the villa would be hers.

She was full of praise for my heroism, and said that I was sure to return, the *Bon Dieu* and his angels would protect me, and she would keep the villa spick and span for my return, however long it might be. I gathered together all my *Vicomtesse* finery and packed it into the old car. I missed the *Hispano Suiza* tourer but the *Vicomtesse*, like the rest of France, had fallen on bad times.

I stopped off, as before in Vichy, now the seat of government, had a meal and telephoned the château. Gabrielle-Pauline answered, squealed with delight at hearing from me, and said I must instantly come on to the château and stay for a long time. She had a wonderful surprise to show me.

As I drove into the château's courtyard, a little weary from a long drive, Gabrielle-Pauline came running down the steps to greet me. She was different, impetuous still, but more at peace within herself. Gabrielle-Pauline had realised her full beauty and maturity. I sensed that some man was behind it.

"Jeanne, what do you think? I am married!"

I embraced her and congratulated her. She chattered on, in French.

"Just imagine! I had always thought I would be an old maid. Oh, Jeanne you must meet my 'Mr Butter'. He is so funny. I am sure you will like him."

She continued in full flow, as she led me into the house. Mr Butter was so clever, so intellectual. She could not have imagined he would be attracted by a country girl like herself. But then he had been brought up in the country, and was a splendid horseman, though *Grandpère* thought he had too lazy a seat on a horse.

At the head of the stairs, was the *Comte*, looking spry and alert. Mr Butter, whoever he was, and whether this name was an alias I did not know - nobody could bear such a ridiculous name – had obviously had a good effect on his father-in-law.

"Jeanne," he said with obvious pleasure. "Welcome back into our house. But where is Maxim? Why is he not with you?"

I hated to spoil Gabrielle-Pauline's happy mood, but it had to come out.

"Maxim was reported missing presumed killed at Dunkirk. I have come to France to find him, or where he has been buried."

His face became sad, and Gabrielle-Pauline squeezed my hand in sympathy, her eyes filling with tears.

"And I have been running on about my new happiness. Poor Jeanne. It must be terrible for you."

The *Comte* said,

"It is more than six months since Dunkirk. The country has been stable for some time now. If he was dead, the Germans would have reported it. Give them their due, they are punctilious about such matters. There must be a good chance that Maxim, with his command of French, may be hiding up somewhere, first to recover from his wounds, then to seek the chance to escape back to England. There is still hope."

His matter-of-fact tone reassured me, as Carton had been unable to do.

With an effort I switched the conversation back to Gabrielle-Pauline's Mr Butter. The *Comte* laughed,

"Oh he is a character, an original. He is a *professeur*. He works all day in the library, only coming out to trumpet some new find or other. He is cataloguing our library, and the family correspondence, so long just thrust away into drawers and he calls it his Aladdin's

Cave. Even I may not go into my own library while he works. But you will see him at dinner time. Come, let Gabrielle-Pauline show you to your old room. We will talk later on how you can go about finding Maxim."

We went down to the entrance where the old servant was taking my luggage out of the car.

"So many bags, Madame," he said admiringly. "You travel as the gentry used to do, in the good old days."

Between us we got the bags into the house, and carried them, in relays up to my room, the old servant protesting the while that the mademoiselles should not strain themselves with carrying too much weight. As the mademoiselles were quite as strong as he was, this caused us both to giggle.

Just before dinner Gabrielle-Pauline came conspiratorially into my room.

"Are you dressed? Oh, what a pretty dress! If you come with me, you can see my Mr Butter. It is so funny! "

I followed her down to the hall, where she concealed herself and me behind pillars. Across the hall was the entrance to the library. She explained,

"We always ring the dinner gong twice. The first time, fifteen minutes before, is for my Mr Butter. See. Louis is just going to sound the gong."

The elderly retainer approached the door of the library with majestic tread. Pausing for a moment, he beat vigorously on the dinner gong he carried, and departed in the same measured tread. There was a pause, and then the door of the library was thrown violently open. A lean, gangling man in shirt sleeves shot out like a white rabbit out of its bolthole and shot up the stairs at full tilt, saying, "Oh, my goodness, oh, my goodness," and disappeared precipitately into his room.

Gabrielle-Pauline turned to me, her eyes full of laughter.

"You see, Jeanne, my Mr Butter. Is he not droll?"

A little later, when the second gong sounded, and we foregathered in the hall for the pre-dinner sherry, I was able see Mr Butter in all his glory.

Down the stairs, with a more dignified gait, came a lean, gangling, bespectacled young man, in a dinner jacket, his wild hair sleeked down, looking a little like the film actor James Stewart, with the same awkward guileless expression.

"Mike!" said Gabrielle-Pauline and went to him, to embrace him.

"Hi, honey," he said, giving her a big kiss.

"Jeanne de Winter," said the *Comte* formally, with a twinkle in his eye. "Allow me to present to you my new son-in-law."

He shook my hand warmly.

"Glad to meet you, Ma'am. Benedict Michael Burr, BURR [he spelled it out], very much at your service."

Burr, so that was why Gabrielle-Pauline, speaking in French, had called him Mr Butter.

The *Comte* said, speaking in English.

"Jeanne's husband is Maxim, whose father wrote the war diaries. Mike's eyes brightened.

"Is that so? Fascinating stuff, Ma'am. Makes you feel you were right there, with the old man. Real contemporary archives. We must get them printed some day."

At dinner, the *Comte* explained how he had managed to acquire so unlikely a son-in-law. After our visit he had decided that if war came, he might need to leave France, and was concerned also that if war came into central France, that the family archives might be damaged or destroyed.

Accordingly, he had written to his remarried daughter-in-law, Caroline, now a formidable New England matron, asking her to enquire if any American university might be interested to purchase the Voltaire correspondence with the Jacobin. The University of Virginia had expressed not only interest, but eagerness, to acquire this treasure.

They sent over a young professor, expert at authenticating ancient documents, to see the letters and authenticate them. That professor was Benedict Michael Burr. Mr Burr had fallen in love with the château, the archives, and lastly with Gabrielle-Pauline. After carrying out his task for the university, he had resigned his faculty, married Gabrielle-Pauline, and settled down happily to what he hoped would be his life's work.

"For an archivist, this place is a goldmine," Mike said. "That old Jacobin, he filed his letters in drawers for each year, but never elaborated on what letters there were. I've only been through a few years, but I've found letters from Robespierre, Danton, Carnot, and virtually all the important members of the *Comité-de-Salut-Publique*." His French was good, if accented with the Mid-West.

"I think when I've gone through them all, we shall have a totally different picture of those revolutionary heroes, or villains, dependent on your point of view."

Mike had been able to resign because his father, a builder of skyscrapers in New York and elsewhere, had given him a generous allowance.

"I was a bit scared of telling my dad that I was marrying the daughter of a French Count, because he had been driven out of Poland by the Czar's pogroms, but the old man was very good about it and said I must pursue my life's work. Very good of the old man. But then he has my younger brother to carry on the family business, so he reckons I'm expendable. Or perhaps I'm his revenge on the aristocracy," he concluded drolly.

I thought of Coppelius né Czytarowski in Zurich.

"Mike," I asked. "How did you come to get the name of Benedict Michael Burr?"

His face darkened.

"Some practical joker taking advantage of my father's ignorance of American history. My Dad arrived at the immigration desk, and the clerk had some difficulties with spelling my Dad's old name Bor-Komorowski. He suggested my Dad should take an American name, like Burke. At that some Paddy who was in the room called out, "Don't call him Burke. Everyone will think he's an Irishman." Well, says the clerk, "what about Burr, good old New York name?" So my father agrees and gets his American papers with the name Victor Burr on them.

"The same thing happens when I'm born. They're looking round for a good American Christian name for me. Some other joker suggests Benedict. Luckily they put Michael in as well, because my grandfather was called Misha or something like that.

"So I grew up in America and at school I find I've been given the names of the *two chief baddies* in American history: Aaron Burr, who was accused of treason by Jefferson and put on trial, and who killed Alexander Hamilton in a duel, and General Benedict Arnold, who went over to the British in the War of Independence. You can imagine what my schooldays were like, and how my school fellows ragged me.

"Never mind, Mike," I said. "You're not the only one to suffer. I was christened Mélisande Yolande. You were never jeered at as 'Smelly Mellie' in the playground."

" I guess we both had crosses to bear," he said glumly.

"But Mike," said the *Comte*, "you said your father left Poland because of the Czar's pogroms. But you are not a Jew."

"My father lived in Vilna, a very Jewish town. I reckon he just got scooped up with the rest. You remember the joke in Russia at the time of the *putsch* of 1936. There are a whole army of rabbits who come up to the Polish frontier, seeking political asylum. The frontier guard asks why, and the chief rabbit says that Marshal Stalin has declared all giraffes to be anti-Party and must be eliminated. The frontier guard says, 'But, rabbit, you're not a giraffe!' The rabbit replies, 'We know that. But you try explaining that to the Secret Police!'"

We all laughed at the joke and Mike said,

"I reckon it must have been something like that with my dad. But it worked out okay. He was a good builder and he arrived in the US about the time the first skyscrapers were going up. He never looked back."

The *Comte* held a family conference the next day, at which we all attended, in the great library. Mike had been told, firmly, that he must take a day's holiday from his research and make the library available for a family conference. He gracefully assented.

We sat round the one large table not covered by Mike's papers. Mike and Gabrielle-Pauline sat on one side; covertly holding hands, and I sat opposite them. The *Comte* presided at the head of the table.

"My children," he said, "I want you to listen carefully to what I say and give me your opinions. No one person can think of everything, and you must adopt a hostile attitude and see if you can pick holes in my ideas.

"Jeanne wishes to go to Paris, to seek news of Maxim, to find him if alive, or his resting place if he is dead. She also wants to revenge herself on the Boches, by insinuating herself into their counsels.

"Let us take first things first. We have to find a reason for Jeanne to go to Paris, which is in the occupied zone, as she therefore requires a sheaf of permits, certainly from the French authorities and perhaps from the Germans too.

"Jeanne wants to find her husband. But she cannot say this, a least initially. She is going to Paris as the *Vicomtesse* de Langlade, and the man she is seeking is an English officer, Major John de Winter, whom no one knows is the *Vicomte* de Langlade, save the *Maire* and the officials here.

"But education goes on, and academic research, even under the German Occupation. I had first thought she might plead that she must go to Paris to continue her musical career, but some bureaucrat or Boche might tell her that she could as well do that in Lyons, or elsewhere in the unoccupied zone. But if she says she is writing a book, on the life of the Jacobin, *Citoyen* de Winter, *ci-devant Vicomte* de Langlade, why she must visit his house in Paris, read the original documents of the debates of the National Assembly and the Convention during the Revolution, study original material. For that she must be in Paris.

"Let us go further and bait the academic hook. Let us write to a professor of history at Paris University, and say that you have certain manuscript letters, from Voltaire, from Robespierre, from Carnot, and would like to bring them to the professor for authentication, you will get an immediate invitation from the professor to bring them up to Paris. You can make a forgery from the original letters, can you not, Mike? They do not need to be very convincing."

"I surely could," said Mike. "And I think I know the professor to send it to, likewise."

Gabrielle-Pauline said,

"Should we reveal our hand so much? If some Boche pig of an official reads it, will he not realise we have a goldmine here, and find some excuse to come and pillage it. We do not want to draw attention to the château, *Grandpère*."

"That is a very sensible observation, Gabrielle-Pauline. We must change our tactics, but the strategy is still valid, I think."

Mike said,

"I think I can write a letter to the professor I have in mind, perhaps citing Professor BM Burr of Virginia University, which would secure Jeanne – *Vicomtesse* de Langlade, we should be calling her – an invitation to visit him in Paris. That's what we want. Any reference to original source material will be to the Voltaire correspondence, which is now at Virginia University, and the presumption will be that any other source material would be there as well."

"That seems an acceptable compromise," remarked the *Comte*. "In addition we can suggest that my young sister, Honorine, who is widowed and lives in an apartment in the Avenue Victor Hugo requests a young companion to stay with her. Honorine did indeed write to us that she was bored out of her mind, and hoped Gabrielle-

Pauline would come and stay. I could write and suggest it. It would be quite convincing for a married woman to leave her husband for a time, to nurse an ailing relative.

"That would get you into Paris, and then you can make your own arrangements, as your General Carton shall determine. And if you have this research project, that would give you an excuse to stay in Paris, to work on your book. How does that strike you as a proposition?"

"It sounds perfect," I said. "I can contact Carton and his people in Paris through the bank, and I can use my money, or the secret funds, to live while I am in Paris."

"When you are established in Paris, then you can approach the German authorities, to see what their records show. If you make friends there - and perhaps some of the Boches you met in Switzerland may be there, Paris is a soft posting - you can ingratiate them by bringing delicacies for their table, produced here in the Auvergne, truffles, our good local wine, things like that. I grudge the Boches our delicacies, but it is surely the way to their hearts, through their stomachs, and it will give you a good excuse to come back here to us, from time to time."

"You think of everything, *Comte*," I said admiringly.

"I have after all been a French staff officer. Now I will see the *Maire*, and write to my sister Honorine, and we shall see."

The wheels of French and Germany bureaucracy grind slowly, but someone in the *Maire's* office happened to have a cousin in the appropriate office in Paris, which helped.

Honorine wrote much more quickly to agree with her brother's excellent idea that her dear niece Mélisande should pay her an extended visit. She delighted in young company and Mélisande could help walk the dog. She said that she had never received a photograph of dear Mélisande, and begged her dear brother to have one taken, outside the château, so she could get it framed and placed with the other family pictures on the piano. She was glad Mélisande played the piano; she would get hers tuned. She missed the Auvergne and all its delicacies. With compliments to all the family, Honorine.

Within the letter was a second letter, for the authorities. Its tone was very different.

Madame de Bracieux was an old lady living alone in Paris, in poor health and with failing sight. She needed her relative, the

Vicomtesse de Langlade, to stay with her, and to remain in Paris, to be able to come to her assistance, should she be taken ill.

It struck just the right tone.

"What a shrewd old bird the *Comte's* sister must be," said Mike admiringly. "She wants a picture for sentimental reasons, she says. But she's damned certain she won't let any stranger into the apartment on the Avenue Victor Hugo, until she has an authenticating picture, by the château, with the *Comte*. You're welcome, but you must make damn sure you bring some wine and truffles with you. Great old girl, and how piteous she makes her situation sound. The authorities won't be able to resist."

Nor did they.

Mike's professor wrote, answering the letter Mike had drafted, but I had signed. The professor was most interested in the *Vicomtesse*'s research, and her discoveries, and if she came to Paris, he would put all facilities at her disposal, and co-operate with her over her research into *Citoyen* de Winter, that little known figure of the French Revolution. All the permits came through in due course, including one to own and drive a car in Paris. It had taken several weeks but it was worth it.

I left to drive to Paris. Gabrielle-Pauline said she would visit me in Paris, with Mr Butter, even if it meant enduring a visit to *Tante* Honorine. The *Comte* said no, Mike must stay in the château, to make outsiders think that Maxim was living there. We all embraced, and Mike took photographs, to supplement the rather forbidding picture of the *Comte* and me, taken earlier in front of the château, a copy of which I bore in my handbag, to authenticate my identity with Honorine. The *Vicomtesse* was on the road again.

Chapter Thirteen

The *Vicomtesse* Sets up Residence in Paris

I arrived in Paris on December 2nd, 1940, and I could not have chosen a better time if I had planned it. Get to Paris in time for the Christmas festivities, Carton had advised. But even he could not have imagined that 1940 would be the best and most carefree season of celebrations that the German Army was to know, in the whole period of the war.

The German Army was in a mood of euphoria and self-congratulation. Whatever the shortcomings of the other services, the German Army had triumphantly achieved everything it had set out to do. Holland, Belgium and France had fallen to its advance, the British had been bundled out of Europe. Casualties had been slight, and at the end of 1940, the French and other European resistance movements had not yet raised their heads. Victory had been total, and it had been achieved without the interference of Hitler. The Old Guard, the Green Freemasonry of regular officers, had done it all, and the Army was immune from the sniping of the Nazis and the Gestapo, because of its success. Life was very sweet.

If there had been setbacks, they were not of the Army's making.

The Luftwaffe had failed to knock the RAF out of the air, and had lost 2,000 planes between July and October. That would prevent them from being too cocky, said the Army. Though it was not openly expressed, there was the feeling that if Hitler had not himself altered the battle plan, in fury at the British raid on Berlin, the Luftwaffe would have wiped out the RAF on the ground, and rendered their airfields unusable. Well, that was what happened when you let a mere Corporal interfere in your strategy.

The Italians had attempted two major offensives, in Egypt and in Greece, and had got a bloody nose in each. Well, they were bad soldiers and uncertain allies. Serve them right. In the New Year, the hero of the French campaign blitzkrieg, Rommel, would go to North Africa with his newly formed Afrika corps, and would put all to rights, and the German Army would come in and clear up the mess in Greece, and probably wipe up Yugoslavia in the process. Trust the German Army, if it was allowed to do its job. In the meantime, *prosit* and have a Merry Christmas.

I found the apartment in the Avenue Victor Hugo and introduced myself to Madame de Bracieux, the *Comte's* sister. There was a cascade of barking, and authoritarian cries of "Down, Mimi!" and Madame herself opened the door to me. She was short and stout and wore black, with a double row of expensive pearls round her neck. Her eyes were sharp and alert. Some three small dogs rapturously leapt up round me, giving loud and cheerful welcomes and were rebuked and shooed away by Madame.

She made me welcome and offered me tea in a silver teapot. So I was Mélisande. Henri-Xavier had told her all about me. I was welcome to stay here for as long as I liked, though she understood I should be finding my own place as soon as possible. Had I liked her letter to the authorities? It was droll, was it not, and so piteous. All lies, of course. She had not had a day's illness in her life, though, *bien sûr*, she was not as active as she had been, and could not get round and see her friends as much as she liked. Since I had a car, we could go round and pay visits, though most of her old friends were dead or as creaky as she was. She was bored, *mon Dieu*, and she was sure I could amuse her. I played the piano, did I not? Well, there was a piano here, though the bon Dieu only knew what state it was in. She would get a man in to tune it, if I wanted. It would be pleasant to hear music in the apartment again. We could exercise the dogs together, though with so many Boche soldiers on the streets, walking in Paris was no longer the pleasure it had been before the war. And all this was directed at me, in sharp little barks, not unlike those of her dogs. I began to like Madame de Bracieux.

So I settled down to a comfortable routine. Madame had enthused over the gifts from the château, the truffles, the cheese, and the great side of ham. What a considerate girl I was to bring all these delicacies to her. I pointed out that the *Comte* was the giver of the gifts, and myself just the carrier. Dear Henri-Xavier was a generous brother, though he was getting on, and the cheese was not as mature as it ought to be. She would write him a letter of thanks.

As soon as I could get away, I went to the Paris branch of the Zurich bank.

In the safe deposit box I found francs and a letter. It was from a Paris estate agent. He thought that an oldish house in the Rue de Varenne, to let furnished on a long lease, might well suit my requirement. There was a hand-written note at the bottom that the building might need rewiring, and that a good electrician, M. Léon Tomas, was the man they recommended for this work. His address was enclosed.

With Madame de Bracieux and the dogs, I visited the house on the Rue de Varenne. It belonged to a Jewish businessman who had thought it prudent to relocate to the provinces when the Germans entered Paris, leaving his house in the care of his advocate who was waiting for us at the mansion.

Madame was highly critical of the furnishings, so old fashioned it was bizarre, and why should I want a great barn of a place to live in by myself? What I needed was a small, smart apartment.

But Carton wanted me to live there, and that was enough for me. I needed space to carry on my historical research, I said. There was a music room and a piano. And I was accustomed to big houses, however run down. I had seen that the house was in a quiet street, and had a big enough courtyard to take my car, and any others that might want to stay there overnight, with a big gate that concealed them from prying eyes. Carton's people had chosen well.

The rent was not high, because property prices in Paris were depressed, because everyone feared air raids, and there was a lot of empty houses which sensible people had vacated. I persuaded Madame de Bracieux that it was a great bargain and just what I wanted. She grudgingly conceded that it was not expensive, and that if I wanted to live in a barn, that was my concern. I placated her by saying that it was near enough to the Avenue Victor Hugo for me to visit her often, and exercise the dogs, who were at that moment expressing a loud desire to be gone. I arranged to come to the lawyer's office to sign the deeds.

I had then to get the electrical wiring of my new house to be attended to. I wrote a civil letter to M. Tomas, asking him to come and see me, and give me an estimate on what needed to be done and to bring references with him. He wrote back the next day, fixing a time when he should call on me at the house.

M. Tomas came to see me at the house and we carried out a little comedy to establish our mutual bona fides. I asked him for references, and as expected he produced two glowing ones: one from M. Albert Carton, referring to a job successfully carried out for him by M. Tomas at his house in Marne-le-Vallée, just outside Paris; and a second reference from Madame Sidonie de Savoie, extolling the rewiring work carried out by M. Tomas at her villa in Casablanca.

I raised my eyebrows.

"Casablanca?"

M. Tomas explained in French that bore a strong North African accent, that he had worked for some years in North Africa, doing the electrical installation work for the leading North African hotels, in Casablanca, Oran, Tunis even. His work was well-known in the top international hotel trade. He could get references from them, but it would take time. I assured him that there would be no need.

He took me round the house, with which he was already seemingly well acquainted, pointing out the deficiencies of the existing installation. He was a short, and stocky man, with very black hair, and it occurred to me that in build and mien he was a little like the old tin miners that I recalled from my days in Cornwall, as mistress of Manderley.

He assured me he was not North African, but came from La Barrée, in the Loire Valley.

This was going to be a very big job, he said wearily. He would give me an estimate, but before he went to the trouble of this, he would like to be sure in his mind that the *Vicomtesse* had sufficient resources.

I gave him the number of my bank account in Paris, and of my strong box number. If he wanted a personal reference for me, I said haughtily, he should write to Herr Coppelius, in the bank in Zurich, Switzerland.

The name of Coppelius seemed to give him reassurance and he relaxed visibly. But I was not expecting the flow of words that followed.

"Thank God, we've got that over," he said in the pure Welsh tones of the valleys. "I've not had the chance to speak English for ever so long. The name is not Leon Tomas, Ma'am, it's Llewellyn

Thomas. And I'm not from La Barrée, in the Loire, I'm from Barry in South Wales!

A Welshman from North Africa? That was a new one for my collection, to go with my South African half-Belgian, and my Swiss Pole, Coppelius.

"How do you come to be in Paris, Llew?" I asked. "And how did you get that strong North African accent?"

It was a long story, he said. He'd been brought up in Barry, and got a job in the nearest pit as a miner, though his great interest was in all things electrical. He had joined up in 1914, see, and had become an electrical craftsman in the Army. Then in 1917 he had been badly gassed, one lung quite useless you see, Ma'am, and he had been demobilised with a pension. Couldn't go down the mine, then, after the war, but had done electrical jobs in Barry. Then the Depression came, and he found himself out of a job. But he had his pension, see, and he'd decided to go and live in the sun, where living was cheap.

He'd chosen Gibraltar, because they spoke English there, and he'd lived quite well there, getting, some electrical work from the Navy. Then the Americans began building big hotels in North Africa, and a mate who was a builder came back to Gibraltar and said there was good money to be made there, because there was a great shortage of skilled craftsmen. You'd need to join the local trade union, *Le Syndic*, but that was no problem, he was told.

So he'd gone over to North Africa, and worked as an electrician for the Americans, and they were delighted to find someone who spoke their language, and knew their standards. So he'd done pretty well, and when the hotel contracts ended he'd started his own business in Casablanca with a local partner. When he came to get his union card, the official couldn't cope with Llewellyn, and compromised by calling him Léon, which was the nearest the official could get to Llewellyn. He'd misspelled his surname too, as Tomas, but you know what the French Moorish officials were like, Ma'am.

He'd settled down in Casablanca and learned the language.

"I married a local girl, see, and that helped." But Marie-Claude, his wife, had died in childbirth, "Poor little mite," and he'd not wanted to marry again. He devoted himself to his work, which included installing burglar alarms and security devices.

"Well, the war came, and I was called in to the Consulate in Oran, to install burglar alarms and security devices. They asked me if I could fix up a transmitter, and that was no problem. They were glad that I was Welsh, and so could keep my tongue. Then after I'd done it, the top security man there asked me if I'd set up business in Paris, and put in some secret transmitters there. Well, I wanted to help my country, so I said yes. Had no ties left in Morocco, and I'd trained my people well, so they could go on quite well without me. General electrical work, no security apart from burglar alarms. Security had been my speciality."

He had met Carton de Wiart and become one of his private army, trained in everything connected with the installation of transmitters.

"That was right at the start of the war, mind you, when nobody except the General thought the Germans would break through like they did. The General arranged for me to buy an electrical business in Paris from an old Jew who wanted out, and no wonder. I have his son-in-law, whose father was a good Catholic, working for me now, and another very good boy who's half Jewish, but you'd never know it. So they don't like the Germans any more than we do. So, we've got a good business, very respectable, and we have our transmitters as a sideline"

Carton and Llew had discussed their operations in the days of the Phoney War. The district where the business was wasn't ideal; too many people knew it had been a Jewish firm. So Carton's idea was that, as soon as convenient, they would move the business to a safer area.

"Having you here is ideal, Ma'am. This rewiring job is going to take a very long time, doing it from top to bottom of the house. We're going to be here for months, years even. So what would be more logical that I should rent your ground floor, and carry on my other business from there? I'd keep my vans in your courtyard, and actually live in the servants, quarters. My boy Louis has a wife who will cook for us, and do cleaning for you. And after a time no one will think it strange that me and my boys go out in the vans to do jobs around Paris."

I said it seemed a splendid idea.

"We may take on extra labour from time to time, painters to do the restoration after we've done the job, plumbers and what have you. They'll stay in the house while the job is being done, and go out with us on the job. So if someone wants to stay in the house for a few days, he'll be one of the extra workmen, with no questions asked.

"And in the meantime, Ma'am, you're going to get friendly with the Germans, so your house will be above suspicion. I think it will work out very well for all of us. We'll just be doing our jobs, you included, and nobody will get in anyone else's way. You'll use the front door, we'll use the servants' entrance in the yard, and you won't know we're there at all."

We shook hands on the deal, and reverted to French, with many expressions of "*Je suis d'accord, M. Tomas*", and "*Parfaitement compris*" or "*Bien compris, Madame la Vicomtesse*", a pretence we kept up until Llew wanted to speak English again, in the confidence of my sitting room.

I began my campaign of getting to know the Germans. The Paris HQ was a soft posting, Carton had told me in Lisbon, staffed by the older members of the Wehrmacht, seasoned campaigners, while the young and ambitious officers were seeking appointments in Rommel's Afrika Corps, or in the armies that would shortly sweep through Yugoslavia and Greece. Paris was for the old reliables, probably pre-war officers, who were determined it would remain anti-Nazi, so that everyone would have a quiet life. It was just the place where the Green Freemasonry, the old aristocrats, would be strongest. It was a near certainty that one of my old friends from Interlaken or the Swiss slopes would be based there.

And so it proved. I had barely come into the foyer of the HQ, and filled in my form to speak to the duty officer, when I was hailed cheerfully.

"*Vicomtesse*, what are you doing in Paris? Have you come to see your old friends? We have quite a nice little family of officers here whom you will remember..."

It was Major von Ahremburg.

Chapter Fourteen

The German Headquarters in Paris

Von Ahremburg went to the duty clerk and got back my carefully composed note to the duty officer. He would take care of the *Vicomtesse*. He proceeded to take me on a grand tour of the German headquarters. On every floor officers came out of offices to greet me, to tell me about the news of their families and to ask about the *Vicomte*. I replied that he was well, but with his ailing father, the *Comte*, in the Auvergne. I was in Paris to work upon a book. All hoped I would come and play for them at their Christmas parties. It was a very relaxed atmosphere. But then, who could stand up to the might of the German Army?

After I had been taken up to the very highest level – one of my Swiss friends proved to be a senior General – I asked Major von Ahremburg if I might speak to him alone.

He was all sympathy, and led me into a small private office. There I confessed, dabbing periodically at my eyes. I had not told the entire truth, I said earnestly. The *Vicomte* and I had had some disagreement, which was why we had decided to separate for a time.

I told movingly the story of my shame. In the early part of 1940, I said, we had been visited in the château in the Auvergne by a distant English cousin, a soldier, Major John de Winter.

Major John de Winter and I had become very…friendly. My husband, Jean-Maxime, had become very jealous and had banished Major John de Winter from the château. Things had been a little difficult between us, I confessed.

But worse was to follow. Major John de Winter had gone back to the war, and he had been reported missing, presumed dead, at Dunkirk.

I had come to Paris in the hope that I might find my cousin and, let me say it, my lover, to find where he was buried, and to weep upon his grave. And if by chance he was still alive, I would walk barefoot through fire and water to find him... All of this must remain wholly confidential...no one here must know, here in this place. But if Major von Ahremburg could ask someone to look through the records, he would have my undying gratitude.

Maxim always said I should have been an actress, and this was one of my best performances, helped by the fact that it was almost true.

Major von Ahremburg was deeply affected, blew his nose, and promised me that he would personally attend to it. No one else would ever know my secret (they did) and my story would go no further (it did) and the Germans were known for the efficiency of their records (that at least was true). If necessary, he would get research done in Berlin.

I asked, tremulously, if he thought the worse of me for having given myself, in a moment of passion, to an Englishman, an enemy of the German Reich. He assured me not. All good German families had English relatives, he assured me. The war was virtually over and soon the German aristocrats, the French and the English could be friends again. With heavy German gallantry he wished that it had been to him I had turned to, rather than this Englishman.

I was suitably confused. I had never been unfaithful to my dear husband the *Vicomte* before, I said tremulously, and I never would again. But if Major von Ahremburg were to bring me news of Major de Winter, oh, he would be my true friend! Considering that this whole conversation was conducted in German with a Swiss accent, I felt it had been a bravura performance.

He escorted me down to the entrance of the German HQ, his arm virtually around my shoulders. I should come in a week or ten days, he said, and ask personally for Major von Ahremburg. And any time I wanted to ring up, this was his extension.

All in all, I felt, as I made my way back to the house in the Rue de Varenne to report my progress to Llewellyn Thomas, the morning had not been wholly unprofitable.

*

I duly visited the accommodating and gallant Major von Ahremburg at the headquarters, as he bade me, and phoned up in the interim. I became, in time, so well known that the security guards would let me through on the nod.

As Christmas approached, the invitations rolled in, and I took my place at the piano to acclaim. There might be other and more talented pianists, but in due course there would be a cry, "*Vicomtesse*, play for us," and I would modestly take my place at the keyboard. Champagne flowed and my efforts would be roaringly applauded.

I began to have slight qualms about my mission. My friends were kind, so gallant, so hardworking on my behalf. Von Ahremburg had himself driven me to the very spot where the wrecked staff car had been found on the outskirts of Dunkirk, and I had seen the cross put up over the body of his driver.

"We are making *exhaustive* enquiries, *Vicomtesse*," he would say ponderously.

It was amazing though to be singled out, to be made to feel special. There were Frenchmen and Frenchwomen at these parties, the big official parties, businessmen-on-the-make, and people anxious to ingratiate themselves with the Germans, who treated them with condescension.

"These French people are only here to use us," a General confided to me, as we stood together, and watched the French smiling and milling around, buttonholing the influential.

"But, General, I am a Frenchwoman."

He gave a great laugh.

"You are different, *Vicomtesse*. The others, they are parasites. But you are one of us, *Vicomtesse*! One of the alliance of the gentry of Europe, as your husband would say."

Yet here was I, seeking all means to betray these people, these friendly folk who had taken, and were taking, so much trouble on my behalf. I felt a Judas for accepting their friendship, their hospitality.

But then something happened at the New Year's party. Everyone was in tremendous spirits. I played the Radetsky March, and the rhythmical clapping was deafening.

There were toasts to the new Afrika Corps and Rommel, as several bright-looking young officers, who were there smiling and happy, their wives and sweethearts, saying farewell to the HQ before being posted to this crack part of the Army.

Von Ahremburg slyly suggested that I play '*Spiel, Zigeuner*' for them, which the older officers joined in, singing uproariously. But I was interested to observe that the line, "*Morgen ist viel zu spät*," had the same effect on the younger officers as it had on their elders. Of course, it was different from the trenches. Of course they were going to a whirlwind victory, as in France. Nevertheless...I saw the hands of the officers reaching out to squeeze those of their girlfriends. The old magic, the old invitation, did not fail to have its effect.

Just before midnight, the most senior General took his place on the dais, thanking everyone for coming, thanking in particular the *Vicomtesse* for performing on the piano.

"This headquarters needs *Kultur*..." he bellowed! "I am going to suggest that the *Vicomtesse* comes every week to the officers' mess, and gives us a concert. The war is total but we need to take our minds off it, for an hour, and remember the great composers, artists and writers that have given us the heritage for which we are fighting." There was tumultuous applause, and I bowed modestly, thanking the General, and saying I would do what I could.

The General had not finished.

"And now, as 1940 comes to an end, let us salute the glorious victories of the year, to which every German soldier has contributed, has played a glorious part."

There was more tumultuous applause.

"Our victories continue. I can tell you that yesterday our glorious Luftwaffe, which only a week or so ago destroyed the might of Britain's motor industry in Coventry, have done it again. In a great raid, they have laid waste the City of London, the great Square Mile, as they call it, of the core of London's international financial centre. We have created a second Great Fire of London!"

The applause was deafening.

I sat there frozen, a false smile still stuck to my lips. All those landmarks I knew so well, St Paul's, the Royal Exchange, the Mansion House, all blazing and soon to be just blackened shells.

The General was going on, hailing greater successes in the New Year, and calling on me to play '*Deutschland uber Alles*', which I did, almost like an automaton. The faces had changed in my eyes. My nice kind German friends were cheering the death and mutilation of Londoners, my people. The jolly Afrika Corps boys were going to the desert to kill British soldiers. I was surrounded by ravening wolves. I was never to feel sentimental about betraying my German friends again.

Chapter Fifteen

Establishing a Good Collaboration Routine

In the New Year of 1941, I began work on my book, telling the story of the Jacobin, the *Vicomte* de Langlade of the French Revolution. It was nearly to prove my undoing.

For me this was just a front, an excuse to be in Paris. But, unfortunately, I was taken seriously. The main part of the Jacobin's work during the French Revolution had been as Agent-General overseeing the procurement of supplies for the French Revolutionary armies, and later the armies of the Consulate and Empire, commanded by Napoleon.

This was of minimal interest to me, but it was of the greatest interest to the intellectual officers of the German HQ. Bespectacled earnest officers would buttonhole me in the corridors, saying how fascinating my research was, and did I know they had written a doctoral thesis on the provisioning of the armies of Frederick the Great in the Seven Years War, and would I like to read it?

One intellectual officer actually suggested we work on a joint research project, contrasting the methods of procurement, and the corruption involved, in the French Revolutionary Wars, the German armies in 1914-1918, and the methods of procurement of the modern German armies of today.

This put me into something of a panic. Clearly a detailed review on how the modern German Army was provisioned would be of the greatest interest to Carton, and to the RAF, who might want to interrupt such supplies if they could. But how was I to undertake my side of the work?

I obtained leave to go down to the Auvergne, and put the matter before the expert, Mike. He came up with the ingenious solution. I was to tell my professor in Paris of the German Army's interest in my research into this aspect of the Jacobin's career, which would put the wind up the professor, as it had done me. I was to suggest that professional researchers look into this specialised subject, which I could later incorporate into my main definitive book on the life of the Jacobin.

This was done, and I realised for the first time the beauties of delegation.

Until this little contretemps came along, which did not happen until the end of 1941, my relations with the professor of the university in Paris were cordial, and I was given great help in finding my source documentation. I became very interested in the Jacobin, and what had started as a front became my serious study, to which I devoted part of every morning.

Carton had stressed the importance of establishing a strict routine, as a result of which I should become virtually invisible, since I was where everyone expected me to be, and therefore accepted as part of the scenery.

I had a fiery confrontation with a neighbour, a retired accountant, who claimed that letting of my basement to Léon Tomas was lowering the tone of the neighbourhood. I retorted that not everyone was as rich as M. Dutard the accountant, and that letting out my empty ground floor and basement to the very respectable M. Tomas helped to pay my rent, and meant that I got my rewiring on the cheap. I had very little trouble after that.

After a few months it was normal to see M. Tomas's vans going to do servicing work across Paris. (These vans had transmitters built into them, because Llew said it was dangerous to transmit too often from one location.) I only saw Llew when he had something to discuss with me, or I had some titbit of information or gossip to relay back to Carton, of conversations I had overheard or about troop movements to different sectors.

I also established a fixed routine with the German HQ, coming in to give my weekly piano recital, and making myself available as a friendly adviser to any new officer wives posted to Paris, to assist them with their shopping or in general familiarisation with the Paris scene.

It was the conviction of most officer wives posted to Paris that the shopkeepers would try and fleece them, because they were German. So they liked me to be around while they made their first contacts, or let me, the knowledgeable and *mondaine Vicomtesse*, be their spokeswoman. My title never failed to make a deep impression on the ladies.

I might have done well, had I so chosen. The shrewd-faced mesdames that ran the boutiques I patronised sometimes suggested that they pay me commission whenever I brought German ladies into their shops. I professed to be indignant, and to avoid their shop altogether if such a suggestion were made again. Everything about any visitors I brought had to be of the utmost discretion. Their sales assistants must appear to be unaware that their visitors were German, though a German speaking girl should be on hand in case of any difficulties.

"There may come a time, Madame, when we both may wish to minimise or conceal the services that we performed for the Germans," I said prophetically.

I added rather grandly that if Madame wanted to give me pleasure, and gratify my German clients, she should offer them a discount, for being a friend of the *Vicomtesse*. She agreed to do this.

It was a fatal mistake. Years afterwards, I met the friendly head of an *haute couture* house who insisted on showing me the wartime ledgers. Against every transaction with the German military, were the initials PLV, which he laughingly told me was shorthand for: '*Pour l'amie de la Vicomtesse*'. He further said that even today, when an important overseas customer asked for special treatment for a friend, the subsequent discount was known as a '*Vicomtesse*'. Unwittingly I had entered the French language, or at least the argot of the Parisian fashion houses.

I also refused any suggestion of a fee for my recitals in the German HQ.

"I do it merely to give pleasure to my friends, General. When I cease to give pleasure, then it will be time to go."

But I did suggest that as a *douceur*, which would give me greatest pleasure, I might be able to get my petrol from the supplies reserved for the German officers. As a result, I never went short of petrol while I was in Paris.

I also visited the Auvergne from time to time, armed with the most impressive of passes, personally signed by the Office Commanding, Paris Garrison Forces, which had me rushed through checkpoints in no time at all. When I returned from the Auvergne, I brought with me food and delicacies, and wine, to the delight of the officers at HQ.

After a time I was so well known that my car was not even searched or my documents examined, which was very convenient when I discovered, on my return once, that I had left behind my important official pass at the château.

With such devotion to routine, the year passed quickly. I was doing my job, Llew was doing his, and we never interfered with each other. If strangers came and stayed in my house, and Llew showed me with pride a veritable priest's hole he had created, over a false ceiling, for emergencies, I did not know of it. I provided a highly respectable, if collaborationist front. He did what he had to do behind it.

Of Maxim, there was still no sign. It was as though the earth had opened and swallowed him up. I no longer had my gallant Major von Ahremburg to canvass the Berlin records on my behalf. He was now somewhere in Yugoslavia, coping with the Yugoslav partisans as best he could.

It was a muted Christmas at German HQ. It had not been a bad year, all agreed. Rommel had done well in North Africa. Yugoslavia, Greece and Crete had fallen. But the Russian invasion had begun in June, and though it had carried all before it, by December the Army was still at the gates of Moscow, held up by the fierceness of the Russian resistance.

And in December the Japanese had launched their attack on Pearl Harbour, bringing the United States into the war. There were dark forebodings by the armchair strategists in the Paris HQ that the German Army might be overstretched.

But there was some good news for the Germans. Just before Christmas came the news that *The Prince of Wales* and *The Repulse*, famous British capital ships, had been sunk. On Christmas Day, Hong Kong surrendered.

So at the New Year's Eve party, the German Officer Commanding for the Paris garrison was able to make a barnstorming speech, promising new successes in 1942, and we toasted "A Final Victory in 1942".

I played the Radetsky March, and all the familiar tunes, including a new one, the haunting 'Lilli Marlene'. An earnest, elderly officer assured me that 'Lilli Marlene' was not a prostitute, as some people said. She was just a simple girl, waiting around in the hope of seeing her boyfriend, who had been posted overseas.

There were sufficient veterans around to call for me to play '*Spiel, Zigeuner*' which we old hands all sang with gusto. But I thought the song had got back some of the foreboding of the First World War trenches. We all felt that death was very near, for all of us. But it was a jolly party that went on into the early hours, and ushered us into 1942.

Chapter Sixteen

The Hinge of Fate

Winston Churchill called 1942 the Hinge of Fate, when the balance of the war began to shift in the Allies' favour. It was certainly so with me.

There was a cold start to the year, in more ways than one. It was as though the carefree days were over and security was much tighter. Even when I went in for my weekly recital at HQ, a guard who knew me perfectly well said gruffly, "Remember to get a pass from the office before you come out, *Vicomtesse*, or I won't be able to let you in next week."

The days when I could leave my travel authorisation behind in the Auvergne, and be waved through on my return to Paris, were clearly over and would never return.

The reason for this increased security was the activities of the SOE, the Special Operations Executive in London, who during the previous year had managed to get a number of operatives into Unoccupied France. There was considerable satisfaction when the principal operative, Georges Bégué, and a dozen of his colleagues were captured by the French police in October. This turned to fury when, at the start of 1942, the elusive Bégué managed to escape from a concentration camp in the Dordogne, and took his fellow prisoners with him. Though it was thought that they had got away to Spain, which proved to be the case, there was a general concern that he might be loose again in France, possibly even in Paris. So the Army and the Gestapo were in a state of nervous vigilance.

Llew knew all about Bégué and his activities, and loudly deplored the lack of professionalism that led to the network being broken up.

"There's this colleague of Georges', he arrives in France, and doesn't try to get in touch with Georges, no. For some mad reason, he tries to contact the local resistance, and of course he gets picked up in Limoges. And the silly fellow doesn't even have the gumption to destroy his papers.

"So they find the address of a garage in Châteauroux. They arrest the proprietor and stake it out, and pick up some more SOE men, one of whom has on him the address of a safe house in Marseilles. So the whole thing unravels like a piece of string."

He hoped no one from the SOE decided to make use of our safe house.

"That would really spoil our nice little set-up."

Llew had his own picked contacts among the French Resistance in Paris, who made use of our house in the Rue de Varenne as a safe house, and were taken on as additional workers, and stayed in the empty rooms of the house.

"Don't fret about what I'm doing, Ma'am," he used to say. "It's better you don't know who comes up the back staircase. You concentrate on your job, and I'll do mine."

His caution paid off. No one ever discovered our safe house, and when trouble came, it was from a quite unexpected quarter.

I continued to be an accepted figure in German HQ. Officers talked quite freely in front of me, though obviously not on matters of strategical importance, which I had to pick up by hints and unguarded references. My recitals were an excuse for private conversations, under the cloak of the music, and I was amused that sometimes for greater security they spoke in English. They little realised that it was my native tongue, and that the figure forgotten on the piano stool had a very keen sense of hearing, and total recall.

Morale veered upwards and downwards during the start of the year. Of course there was satisfaction at German HQ when Singapore and Burma fell to the Japanese, and jubilation when the two German capital ships, *The Scharnhorst* and *The Gneisnau*, with *The Prince Eugen*, managed to break out of Cherbourg Harbour, and despite all that was thrown at them managed to escape into German waters. The champagne came out that night.

But morale veered downward when the RAF began to make heavy raids on the German homeland cities. Bremen, an old wooden city, burned like a torch when attacked by the British bombers, and this was followed by even heavier attacks on Hamburg and Cologne. Many officers had family in these cities.

"It is contrary to all the tenets of civilised warfare," a one-armed officer from the Afrika Corps told me. "The British are no better than the SS," he said with contempt. "At least our war with the Eighth Army was conducted as a war between gentlemen."

It was amazing how the old regular officers still attached importance to gentlemanly conduct. After the war I met a British prisoner of war who said you could always get some harsh edict revoked by saying that no British officer or gentleman would do such a thing!

That the regular officers in the Paris HQ were anti-Nazi to a man, I already knew. But it was not until much later that I learned how wide-ranging was the network of anti-Hitler intrigue that permeated the Paris HQ, which became even stronger as the Army became bogged down on almost all the areas of operation.

I remember how I had made my first gaffe. I was talking about my husband, the *Vicomte*, when people asked after him, as they often did, and I pretended that he was still in the Auvergne, and that a reconciliation between us was looking ever likelier.

"The *Vicomte* said to me recently, 'Jeanne' he said..."

They picked up the gaffe at once.

"But *Vicomtesse*, your name is Mélisande. Why does your husband call you Jeanne?"

I had to think fast.

"My husband calls me Jeanne," I said "...after Jeanne d'Arc."

I had to be outrageous to divert attention.

"He nicknamed me Jeanne d'Arc, or Jeanne for short, because just before the war I had said that, to stop the terrible war happening, I should be ready to go to Berlin, and shoot Hitler through the head!"

I thought I should shock them with my boldness. But the senior officers, after a pause, began to laugh, uproariously.

"Oh Jeanne d'Arc," one grizzled officer chortled. "You would never get near Hitler, the queue would be too long!"

I was amazed at their responses. Another officer said,

"Helmuth here and his friends have been trying to bump Hitler off for years, haven't you Helmuth?"

And a very serious younger officer said, petulantly,

"You should not jest about such matters. We have our network in place, and when the time is ripe..."

They only laughed at him the more. But in 1944, an officer called Claus Schwenk von Stauffenburg did in fact put a bomb under the table at Hitler's headquarters. Only chance protected Hitler. The stout oaken table absorbed much of the blast and, because it was such a fine day, the conference for which the bomb was intended was held, not in Hitler's bunker, but in a hut nearby. But for that, Helmuth's friends could have carried out the deed.

I spoke much of my husband the *Vicomte* in the early part of 1942, because I was now certain he was dead, and liked to recall his memory.

Then one April day, Llew came up to my sitting room and said,

"Jeanne, I'm thinking of taking on an extra painter. I'd like you to have a look at him first."

"Oh, Llew, I wouldn't interfere with your business. The less I know about it the better."

Then I thought it might be an emissary of Carton, telling us to wind up the mission, and that I should see him.

"Tell him to come up then."

The telephone rang and I went to take it. It was one of my German friends. A new officer had been posted to HQ, and his wife wanted to be given the tour of the shops. While I was talking, Llew's new painter came in. I had the impression he was tall, and very gaunt and bearded and dressed in shabby overalls, with down-at-heel boots. Ulrike was chatting away, ten to the dozen, and I motioned him to sit down, which he did. It took some time to get Ulrike to cease her chattering, but finally it was done, and I said to the man,

"Well, Monsieur, have you anything to say to me?"

The worker shuffled, embarrassed at my imperious tone.

"Only that you are looking in fine beauty, my love. Being a Mata Hari seems to become you."

I had not known him until he spoke, he was so altered. In an instant I was in Maxim's arms, embracing him and kissing him, asking him where he had been, and how he had changed his appearance so that I did not know him. Had he been wounded? Was he better? How thin and gaunt he was. I must have gone on like a very Ulrike.

He fielded all my questions, and answered the more essential ones, as he led me to the sofa, and got out a not very impressive handkerchief to wipe my eyes, which were overflowing with tears, entirely without my volition, because sadness and grief were the very last things I was feeling now.

"Yes, I am well, though I've lost about ninety pounds. It took me quite a time to heal my wounds. I had four bullets in me, I may say, including one that grazed my skull, and getting better took time. When we go to bed, which I hope won't be too long away, you can have a full inventory of all my impressive scars."

"How did you take so long to come back to me?"

"It wasn't easy, my love. First, I had to recover, which took more months than I'd thought possible. Then when I was well, the Germans began to take a very great interest in the whereabouts of one Major John Maxim de Winter, and I had to lie very low indeed, to avoid detection."

I put my hand to my mouth.

"Oh, Maxim, that was my fault. I went to the German HQ, and found some of our old friends, and asked them if they would look for you, or your body. I am so sorry."

"Not at all, my love. From what Llew told me below, and I'd have never guessed he was a Taffy – his North African accents are most convincing – it got you your entrée into German headquarters, where you've been doing sterling stuff, in reporting on their activities."

We exchanged kisses and information on the sofa, rather more of the former than the latter, but we had been a long time apart.

Finally, I wanted to know how he had found me.

"Pure chance, and a husband's homing instinct. Actually, it was through our bank, the Zurich Bank in Paris. And that was high comedy, I can tell you."

"You didn't know I had come to Paris to find you?"

"Not a word. That was very courageous of you, my dear. I thought you'd be waiting in the villa in Switzerland, as I'd told you."

"I had to find out if you were alive or dead. And if you were dead, I wanted to avenge you. Does that sound very melodramatic?"

"Very melodramatic, but very you. You have all the heroic character I lack. I just wanted to survive."

"You can laugh at me, but if you were dead, I didn't want to go on living. But I wanted to go out with a last dramatic gesture."

"An actress to the end," he said, but he was moved, and squeezed my hand.

He soon recovered his urbanity and bantering tone.

"And thanks to my wife being a Mata Hari, tonight I shall have a luxurious bath, a change of linen – if Llew has anything in my size –

a sumptuous dinner, and if Llew lets me, I can shave off this terrible beard. You'll ask him to dine with us, I hope."

The girl, Marie, laid on a very wonderful dinner, and afterwards Maxim made us laugh as he described his visit to the bank.

"The place where I was staying got in touch somehow with the French Resistance about smuggling me out of France and into Spain. They said they would be willing to try, but it would cost money, to get the documents and to oil a few palms. I said if they could get me to Paris, I had ample resources on which I could draw. So they smuggled me into Paris on a lorry.

"I hadn't thought about my appearance until I got there. I was just dressed as a worker, as you see, and that was a good disguise for not attracting notice in the street.

"And then I realised that I should have to go into a great bank in the most fashionable quarter of Paris, where I should stand out like a sore thumb.

"But there was nothing to do but to brazen it out. I'd hoped I'd chosen a time when the bank wasn't busy, but it seemed to be full, with businessmen in their expensive suits, and all the ladies in their best fur coats. I could see them turn and look at this ragamuffin as I made my way through the banking hall, and the security guards looked at each other, debating whether to throw me out.

"I got to the counter at last, feeling myself the battery of questioning, disdainful eyes, and I asked the counter clerk if I could see the manager. He asked me my name.

"I said, 'The *Vicomte* de Langlade'. I saw his eyes dilate. He clearly thought I was a madman, and I saw his hand go towards his alarm button.

"So I realised action was needed and fast. I drew myself up to my full height.

"*'Erwarten Sie!'* I rasped in my best officer German, which carried right round the hall. *'Ich bin ein Offizier von der Wehrmacht. Intelligenz! Ich muss sofort ihren Manager sehen, mit ihnen sprechen. Bestimmt!'* And out of the corner of my eye I could see everyone in the bank look away and become extremely interested in their own business. *'Im Privat!'* I rasped to complete the clerk's discomfiture.

"Now, the French and the Swiss don't cringe in the way that the Germans do, but he looked distinctively apprehensive as he called the manager, and I stood there scowling.

"It was an under-manager with an intelligent face who ushered me through to a private office. I explained that I was the *Vicomte* de Langlade, in disguise, and that I had two accounts in the bank, one in the name of the *Vicomte*, the other in the name of Maxim de Winter, and that I should need to draw out some funds.

"He was perfectly understanding. Was the de Langlade account authorised from Zurich? I said it was, from a Herr Coppelius. He asked whether this was this being done on anyone else's authorisation. I mentioned a M. Carton and a Madame Sidonie de Savoie.

"'In that case, Major de Winter,' he said, 'welcome back into the land of the living. I am sure we can arrange for you to have funds to restore you a little more to your normal appearance.'

"And then he told me you were in Paris, and gave me your address.

"Then he took me back through the banking hall, talking German all the while, myself severe, him servile, and showed me out of the bank, with everyone in the bank contriving not to catch my eye."

Llew slapped his knee and roared with laughter as Maxim concluded his tale.

"The beauty of it is that if you were traced or followed to this address everyone would think that we were part of a German intelligence operation and leave us well alone."

I was puzzled.

"But surely the Germans know who their own intelligence people are?"

Llew chortled.

"Not they! There are networks within networks, and many of them spend their time spying on each other. Maxim, you've done well, and I could almost let you shave off your beard as a reward!"

"Do you mean that?" asked Maxim hopefully.

"Sorry, boyo, this is a respectable electrical firm that only moonlights on military intelligence on the side. Any man that joins us with a beard, has to stick with it, or the police might get curious."

"I was afraid you'd say that," said Maxim sadly.

*

Later that night, curled up beside a bathed, well-fed and contented, if still whiskery Maxim, I asked him,

"Where have you been, this last year and more?"

"You may be amazed to hear it, but I've been in a lunatic asylum most of the time. I've been Jean the farmer's son, the house painter, who was shot through the head and doesn't remember who he is and where he came from, and has lost his papers. A most effective disguise, when you want to lie low and recover from your wounds."

Maxim was adorned in a capacious night shirt, borrowed from Llew, which concealed the ugly scars that pitted his body.

"But did you actually lose your memory?"

"Never for a moment. But the doctor in the village who patched me up suggested the idea, and arranged for me to be transferred to the asylum. Clever man, that doctor, in more ways than one."

"But a lunatic asylum..."

I remembered the simpleton who had haunted the grounds at Manderley, and his terror at being taken away to an asylum.

"Exactly, my love, it makes you shudder. And it has the same effect on the German troops looking for fugitives. Their visits to the asylum were very perfunctory and they accepted, without question, that someone with a hole in his head and a totally impaired memory was a genuine case. So I was left in peace to recover from my wounds and the loss of blood."

"How did you come to get to the asylum, after you were wounded?"

So Maxim told me the whole story.

*

He had just sent the Leicesters on their way, thanks to the guidance of the shepherd boy, and had got back in the staff car, to give the boy a lift back to his village.

"We'd have been wiser to go on foot, but it meant a walk of about five miles, and I was anxious to get back to Alexander. We'd driven for about ten minutes down the track when we saw a *Stuka*, coming towards us at hedge-hopping height, and with his machine guns ablaze.

"We didn't stand a chance. Boyce, my driver, was killed and the staff car went out of control. At the same time a machine gun bullet ploughed through my scalp, and another bullet smashed through the fleshy part of my arm and another through my thigh, fortunately missing the bone and any vital organ. The scalp wound stunned me, so I don't remember anything until I woke a few minutes later, beside the overturned car, with the boy, who had been thrown clear and had not even a scratch.

"There was nothing to do but to leg it back to the village, like two village drunks, lurching from side to side, supporting each other.

"Luckily the boy, Philippe, was about fourteen, and a big, strong lad for his age. He almost carried me the distance, because I was weak from loss of blood, and my wounds were beginning to hurt damnably, particularly the wound in my thigh that made walking difficult.

"Philippe kept urging me on, '*Courage, mon capitaine*, not far now.' (I shall always remember that phrase. When I die, and the recording angel comes to get me, I'd like to think he'll say, '*Courage, mon capitaine*, not long now.') Somehow, I don't know how, we got to the village, and the boy's mother helped me in and put me on the boy's bed. The boy ran off to get the local doctor.

"I was lying there when the doctor came in, a good horse doctor, who knew all about wounds, and treated the people and the animals indiscriminately.

"I remember his first words, *'Vous parlez Français, mon capitaine?'* I was just able to say, *'Oui, parfaitement, et sans accent. J'ai demeuré trois ans en Suisse.'* He said, *'Bon,'* and then I passed out, which was just as well, as he dug around inside me and got out the bullets.

"When I came to, I was bandaged up, and he was looking down at me *'Bien,* Monsieur, we have a choice,' he said, coming straight to the point. 'We can hand you over to the Germans, and they will take you to their hospital and treat you until you are better. Or we can conceal you until you are well enough to escape back to England.'

"'Conceal me, if you can,' I said. 'Provided it does not get you into trouble.'

"'That is our worry,' he said. *'Regardez*, Monsieur, you have a head wound. It is trifling, but we could make out that it is worse than it is, and that you have lost your memory. We dress you in peasant's clothes, and we send you to the local lunatic asylum, about twenty miles away. They are good people and friends of mine, and they will hide you. What was your father?'

"'A rentier, a landowner.'

"'There are not many of those round here. You could be a farmer or a son of a farmer, but your hands are not those of a farmer. Is there anything else you can do?'

"'I can paint,' I said, remembering how I had personally restored the big room at Manderley,

"'That is good. You will be a housepainter, the son of a farmer. But remember, you know nothing of what you have been. You are just Jean, the man with no memory, except that you think you were once a housepainter.'

"So that was what we decided, and he put me in the back of his car, and drove me to the asylum. And that's where I stayed, until I was well."

"Was it very terrible there?" I asked.

"Pitiful, more than terrible. So many people with broken spirits. There were people who couldn't cope with the world, who had retired into themselves, silent and withdrawn. Then there were people whom the world had made angry, who whipped themselves into a frenzy when they thought about it. Then there were the misfits, whom the world had rejected, the old people who had become senile, and whom their relatives had packed off to the asylum, in order to enjoy the things for which they'd worked all their lives, the farm, the little fortune carefully accumulated. And variations on the whole theme of misery and rejection.

"After a year and more in that place I'm not going to pass judgement on anyone. The nurses coped, gave kindness where they could. And the housepainter called Jean, the man with no memory, looked on and tried to think of you, and how you would have given silent or vocal sympathy to these wrecked lives, and broken people. I also painted the walls, ceilings and floors of the place from end to end, so I made my little contribution.

"When I was well enough, I spoke to the head of the asylum about getting out, and getting back to England. I said I had ample funds in Paris, and would pay him for his hospitality, which he refused, and was able to make a contribution to my escape route costs.

"Then the men of the Resistance came, and we negotiated a price. They got me forged papers, and finally came in a van, and drove me all the way to Paris. They gave me an address, a café on the Left Bank, where I was to come with the money."

But Llew, when he heard about it, was sceptical. This was a cowboy outfit, he said, the kind that takes your money and then turns you in. But Maxim said he owed the men for the false papers and the lift to Paris, and Llew said one of his people would take some money there, to pay what Maxim felt he owed, and sound out the land. The man reported unfavourably, and anyway the café was raided by the police shortly after and the escape network cowboys were taken away.

Maxim had only one thought, how to get back to the war, and if possible how to take me with him back to England. But Llew and I argued that our work was not done yet, that it would become even more important as the Second Front approached. We reckoned that the invasion of Europe would happen in 1943, and the Dieppe Raid that year had made Paris feel for the first time that it was in a war zone.

I wanted Maxim to stay in Paris with me, resume his role of the *Vicomte* de Langlade, and help us in the work. Llew thought this dangerous, and wanted Maxim to go back to the château in the Auvergne, to await the time our network would have completed its work. But Maxim wanted only to get back to England and the war, and wanted to take me out of the front line.

We finally decided that Maxim would go and I should stay. It was a painful decision. But in the end, Maxim and I had more than sixteen weeks together, before we were parted.

The problem for me was how not to let my happiness at having Maxim with me become too apparent to the Germans. Everyone commented on how radiant I was looking, and how absent-minded I had become. They thought I was in love, which indeed I was. I told those who knew both of us, there were still one or two left in headquarters, that my husband and I had reconciled to each other, and that I should soon join him at the château. I tried to conceal my happiness as much as possible, because there was not too much to smile about at German headquarters at that time.

Llew knew of a woman lawyer, Mâitre Dumoutier, who was connected to various escape routes for airmen and other fugitives.

Llew, and I then staged a great quarrel, regarding his men working unseasonable hours in violation of his lease, and to my discomfort. The *Vicomtesse* and M. Tomas decided to go to law to settle their differences. And while we were volubly arguing our rights, and Llew's violation of my privacy, in front of Mâitre Dumoutier, in her chambers, we were passing notes between each other on how Major de Winter, escaped prisoner, with independent means and Swiss papers, could get out of Paris and into England.

Mâitre Dumoutier wrote down a contact name, which Llew wrote in his list of customers, and told us not to be silly. She decided in my favour, but effected a reconciliation. We paid her a very fat fee, part of which went to oil the wheels of Maxim's escape.

Madame Dumoutier was finally betrayed to the Germans, went to the notorious Fresnes Prison and on to a concentration camp. But that was not until 1943, some six months later. She was a real heroine of the Resistance, and I was glad to hear that she survived.

So Maxim went out of my life again, and I was left to play my listening role. It was in my arms that my Afrika Corps veteran wept, when the news of the El Alamein victory (or defeat, as far as we were concerned) came through. I had got to the state where I almost identified with the German Army, and the HQ officers certainly thought of me as one of them.

I played at the Christmas parties at the end of 1942, though they were a bit muted in their celebrations, with 'Lilli Marlene' much asked for, and '*Spiel, Zigeuner*' not at all. We were all too much concerned at what new ill tidings tomorrow might bring.

Chapter Seventeen

Stalingrad and After: the Anti-Nazis Emerge

With Maxim back in England, and pursuing his war, I was free to continue with my work, my book and my music. Paradoxically, the knowledge that he was alive and well, and barring the fortunes of war making him a casualty, would be waiting for my return at the end of me war, which we confidently expected would be by the end of 1943, actually inhibited my work. When I thought Maxim dead, I did not care what happened to me. With Maxim alive, I wanted to live, to survive this nightmare and get back to normality. Never had I pined so much for the Swiss villa, and our untroubled pre-war existence.

I began to think of cutting down my social life with the German military, the more so when, with the Parisians expressing their anti-German feeling more openly, I returned to the Rue de Varenne one night to find "*Collaboratrice*" painted across my door. (Llew had it removed the following day, and the word passed round that the *Vicomtesse* should be left alone. There was an interim after that, then "BOF." was scrawled on my door.)

This accusation that I was a black market profiteer puzzled me. BOF. stood for *boeuf* or *buerre*, *oeufs* and *fromage* (beef or butter, eggs and cheese), and was commonly used to describe those who trafficked in them, and traded with the enemy. Apart from bringing back a few delicacies for the officers' mess on my return from the Auvergne, I had never traded in comestibles on the black market. Well, somebody had made a mistake, it seemed. But when Llew had treated this latest attempt at graffiti, I thought no more about it.

Before I could even begin to voice my feelings, came the shattering news of Stalingrad. The Paris HQ was of course aware that a titanic struggle was going on, but even they were overwhelmed by the extent of the defeat. The surrender or annihilation of an army of 330,000 headed by Field Marshal von Paulus and fifteen other Generals, was deeply felt by the Paris HQ, since it meant the loss of so many friends and comrades.

I went and offered my condolences to the General Officer Commanding, which were genuine and heartfelt, because I knew some of the officers posted dead, missing or prisoners, for many of them had spent time in the Paris HQ. I suggested that in these terrible times perhaps my recitals were inappropriate.

He clasped my hand.

"No, do not leave us, *Vicomtesse*. At this terrible time of misfortune, we need all our good friends to stand by us. Continue your recitals, I beg you, and continue to favour us with your presence and your moral support. We need you around, so we know what the real Parisians feel."

I told him how my house had been daubed with graffiti, and he was very shocked, and even suggested that there should be a guard on my house, which I politely declined.

"You are not a collaborator, *Vicomtesse*, you are a friend. That is very different. Perhaps like many French people, you would like to see the war ended, and the Germans defeated. I do not know. But you are a true friend, not afraid to voice your views, and that we cherish and esteem. God knows all of us would like to see this terrible war end."

So I continued to give my recitals, and be invited to social occasions. The very fact that I had been threatened yet still came in to play, counted very much in my favour. I was truly one of them, and they did not scruple to speak frankly in front of me.

After Stalingrad the mood in the headquarters, always covertly anti-Nazi, was now openly hostile to Hitler. The plotting against the Nazis began in earnest, and the opinion was openly canvassed that the Nazi Government, which had brought nothing but disaster to the Army, should be replaced, and open peace negotiations should be commenced with the Western Allies. The British and the Americans had been barbarous in the bombing of German cities, but they were open to reason.

As one German wife said,

"They have committed atrocities, but then so have we. It should not stand in the way of negotiation."

I was surprised that anyone would admit that the Germans had committed atrocities, though most of them were attributed, by the army, to the hated SS.

"Their only merit is that they are efficient," said one officer. "But they too will turn against Hitler in the end."

He told me the grim joke about one SS regiment, angry at being told to attack again and again, in Russia, regardless of losses, had put a severed hand of one of their comrades in a chamber pot, and sent it to their Führer, as a token of their anger and contempt. Everyone regarded the Russians as subhuman monsters, the direct descendants of the Golden Horde of Ghengis Khan. As more Soviet victories filtered through, like the great tank battle at Kursk, the officers at headquarters became even more bitter and apprehensive. Nothing could halt the Russian steamroller, and Hitler must sue for peace with the West, and if he would not, he must be replaced and someone else must do it. I was surprised that the Second Front was welcomed. They would fight bravely, of course, if France was invaded, but it would hasten the end. There was the universal feeling that the war could not be won.

The appointment of Rommel and Field Marshal von Kluge to the Western Wall raised morale. Rommel was still regarded as invincible. It was the lack of oil that had defeated Rommel, not the British and the other Allies. And von Kluge, Kluger Hans, the army called him, was a clever fox of a soldier as his nickname, 'Kluger (or Clever) Hans' suggested.

But the hatred for the Nazis was not diminished. Rommel had been called a Nazi General, but he was not one any more, I was assured. He was just the man to negotiate peace terms with the Allies, who respected him.

The sheer loathing of the officer corps for Hitler was epitomised in an exchange I overheard. A German engineering officer came into the mess when I was there, and said he was charged with building the launching pads, he said, for Hitler's secret weapon.

A Colonel said,

"Don't call it Hitler's secret weapon, for God's sake. If Hitler has anything to do with it, it'll probably blow up in our faces, like all Hitler's other bright ideas."

There was general laughter at this.

I asked the officer, idly, if he knew what the weapon was. Poisoned gas, or something like that. I was supremely disinterested.

"Don't ask me, Gnädige Frau," he replied. "I'm just responsible for the launching pads. I think it is something terribly complicated, concerned with rocketry, I think, that they are hatching up in Peenemunde. None of us are allowed to know what it is."

I got Llew to send a message to Carton, summarising this conversation. It was the first we knew of the V1 and V2 rockets, which were launched on Britain the following year. The RAF bombed Peenemunde.

I felt I was beginning to be useful to Carton, and justified my separation from Maxim. But I missed him very much.

So in June I was surprised to be told when I returned from attending to my research (yes, I was continuing to work on my book on the Jacobin, which Maxim was later to complete, after the war), to be told by Llew that the *Vicomte* de Langlade had arrived and was waiting for me in the drawing room.

I ran up the stairs in great confusion. Could Maxim have decided to come back into France, perhaps parachuted in by the SOE, to take me out of France at this juncture, or to join me in my work?

But it was not Maxim who was waiting for me in the drawing room. There just as gangling and smiling as ever, was the man I had last seen running up the stairs of the château in the Auvergne, crying out, "Oh, my goodness, oh, my goodness..."

It was Gabrielle-Pauline's husband, the American Benedict Michael Burr.

Chapter Eighteen

The Second *Vicomte*

I looked at Mike in amazement. He was better dressed than I had seen him last, with a hat and a fur coat, and looked every inch the successful French businessman. But underneath, it was the same Mike.

"Mike," I said a little breathlessly. "What are you doing here? I thought Maxim had come back for me. What are you doing, masquerading as the *Vicomte* de Langlade?"

"No masquerade, Jeanne," he said. "Behold the authentic *Vicomte*, mark two. And I've come to chide you, for turning an honest-to-goodness American professor and researcher into a criminal forger and a crook."

"Let's have some tea," I said weakly. "Then you can tell me the whole story."

*

"It all began," said Mike, "when you left behind your authorisation to travel from the General Officer Commanding, Paris Region, on one of your visits to the château! It was a most impressive document, authorising everyone to give you free passage, and to admit any produce you might bring back, for the GOC Paris region, and the officers' mess. Very impressive.

"My job is authenticating documents, and doing any running repairs on them. In other words, I'm a licensed forger. So I took this document to see if I could forge it. And I did a very good job, in all modesty.

"Now, the *Comte* is involved in the Resistance, as an adviser, though he can't be a combatant any more, at his age. He was very interested in this talent of mine, and sought to use it in a good cause.

So I've become the principal source of forged papers in all Central France.

"The *Comte* was concerned to hear of Maxim's assumed death in action, and was glad to hear from you, on your last visit, that Maxim had escaped to England. But that left a vacancy in the line of De Winter de Langlade, and at the same time I was masquerading as Maxim down in the Auvergne, in case any Germans come nosing around, to see if the *Vicomte* was really there, as you said he was.

"So the *Comte* decided to regularise things. He had adopted Maxim as his son and heir, but Maxim was now officially dead. So he went through the same procedure, though not with the same ceremony as before, and made his son-in-law his heir, so that the de Winter line could go on. No problems, and I was able to forge an authentic set of papers for me as the *Vicomte* de Langlade. There was a little matter that there were now two *Vicomtesse*s, one in Paris and one in the country, but the *Comte* assured me that this was not unusual. So I became the bigamous *Vicomte*.

"Then there was an occasion when we needed to get a Resistance agent out of Paris, and another Resistance worker in... So the *Comte*, and Gaby and me, we put our heads together, and came up with a most ingenious idea. We'd use that authorisation, and any fakes I could make from it, to join the black market. You were authorised to bring in produce for Germans. We'd do the same.

"Now I remembered how you'd said that your lot, the regular army, never spoke to the SS, who had a separate HQ in Paris. What we'd do was to make contact with the SS, using the authorisation your people had given you. So Gaby and I we went to Paris, and we made contact with the messing officer of the SS. Gaby explained that her sister-in-law, you, with whom she never spoke now, and whom she regarded as an upstart, "my husband's ex-wife", was doing some black market dealings with the GOC, Paris District.

"She proposed to do the same on a regular basis with the SS, and brought a list of produce. She could regularly supply the SS HQ with meat, wine, and other delicacies. Of course they were delighted, as it would be one-in-the-eye for the Green Freemasonry. Gaby, who put on a magnificent performance, I may say, said that in order to give the SS a really competitive price, she'd also have to bring in produce for the French black market, and they were quite agreeable to this.

"As a result, Jeanne, we have an authorised little convoy of two vans, coming every eight weeks, with me, two drivers and two drivers' mates, straight into Paris from the Auvergne, with documents from the SS.

"The drivers are always the same, but the drivers' mates change with a different one on the return trip than on the outward one. Me and the drivers, we're well known; and no one pays much attention to the drivers' mates. So with SS papers, we're getting men into Paris, and out again, and we've become a regular escape route for Resistance men. And we're making a nice little number in black market goods. What do you think of that?"

*

"Mike, it's brilliant," I said. "That accounts for the graffiti on my wall, BOF. But why have you come to me now?"

"The *Comte* thought it would add authenticity to your story if your husband visited you from time to time. And I'd like to have a base in Paris, where I can stay for a few days at a time, to carry on my forgery activities. There's more demand in Paris for forged papers than there is in the country. So if you were willing, I'd like to take a room in the Rue de Varenne, and set up a place to carry out my forgeries, when I'm in town."

I gratefully acceded to his request. It would help my cover. There was nobody now at HQ who remembered Maxim from our Swiss days. I called in Llew and he was enthusiastic. His people needed false papers from time to time. He set to work, and built a false bookshelf that revolved, and had a desk on the reverse side, which could contain all the materials that Mike needed for his work. It as an admirable arrangement, and it meant that from time to time I should have Mike's company in the house, which would mitigate my loneliness. Llew was good company, but our activities were very different, and we tended to live very separate lives.

All went smoothly until the first weeks of 1944. Mike was staying in the house when there was an air raid on Paris.

Paris was a comparatively soft target, and we had not endured many air raids during the years of the war. Bomber Harris's heavy bombing raids were ten being directed at the German mainland cities like Hamburg, in the Gomorrah Offensive, and at the Mohne Dam, which had been breached, and caused serious flooding in the Ruhr. But we in Paris had not become accustomed to bombing in they way that the people of London had become.

This too was a very special and audacious raid. A small squadron of Mosquito bombers had been briefed to take out the Gestapo headquarters in the centre of Paris, in the Avenue Foch, flying in low under the radar screens in a surprise dawn attack, at about five in the morning. The only snag, as far as I was concerned, was that the Gestapo headquarters being attacked was only a few streets away.

I was asleep in bed when without warning all hell broke loose! I was awakened by the noise of bombs exploding, in the next street, it seemed, and then every anti-aircraft gun in Paris seemed to open up.

I was absolutely scared out of my wits. I leapt out of my bed and ran barefoot into Mike's room, screaming and whimpering with sheer terror.

He was up, looking out of the window, which even as I ran to him, cracked right across from the force of the blast, which only added to my terror.

Mike did his best to comfort me as I wept hysterically and clung to him. Then, like the weaver in the Benjamin Britten ballad, he did the only thing possible. He put me into bed, and covered up my head, if not to save me from the foggy, foggy dew, at least from the terror of the bedlam of the guns and bombs of the air raid.

Simultaneously, we felt a flame of desire go through us. So I made no objection when he tenderly helped me off with my nightdress, soaked in sweat from my terror. I wanted to cling as close as I could to him, to become part of him, to feel him in me, to feel cosseted and protected. After a while the guns grew silent and we slept.

When I woke next morning, Mike was already up and partly dressed.

"Oh, my goodness," he said in distress. "We shouldn't have done that..."

I sat up in the bed, as naked and as unashamed as any Rose.

"What's done is done. We couldn't help ourselves."

I felt strangely at peace.

"But we have helped ourselves, and pretty generously too." Strange that at a moment like this he should be quoting Gilbert and Sullivan. "I've never been unfaithful to Gaby before."

"Nor I to Maxim, but isn't there a kind of dispensation, for people in the fighting line, as we have been? I'm sure Maxim will understand, and I hope Gabrielle-Pauline will as well."

"I hope so," he said miserably. He turned his eyes to me on the bed. "Honey, could you find something to put on. The way you are, I can barely restrain myself from putting my hands on you..."

I found my crumpled nightdress and put it on. I wanted nothing else. Still in my nightdress and barefoot, I rooted around and made coffee for Mike and found some croissants. We breakfasted in silence, Mike still acutely embarrassed. I found his feet under the table and put my bare feet on them.

"It's all right, Mike, really it is. No harm done. No one need know."

He tried to smile.

We carried out our social duties, separately and politely. I went to the university to continue my research, and Mike praised what I had done so far, saying it was going to be a great book. Mike went out to see his people with his forgeries, concealed in the false bottom of his suitcase. I had no need to visit headquarters, and no shopping trips to arrange. It was an ordinary day, like any other. We dined together, cordially.

But as night fell, I knew that I could not spend the night alone. If necessary, I would go naked into his room and climb into bed beside him. But it was not necessary. After we had kissed goodnight, he followed me without speaking into my room and I welcomed him into my bed as a lover.

Mike stayed for a week, and we parted as good friends and comrades. I never slept with him again, or with any other man.

But a few months later I discovered I was pregnant.

Chapter Nineteen

The Year It All Blew Up

Everyone knew that 1944 would be the year of the invasion of France, though no one knew where, and the Allies managed to deceive the Germans right up to the moment of invasion. A wretched year for weather helped in the deception, but we knew that a strip from the Wash to Land's End was designated the invasion zone. It had to come.

The news was all bad. The Russians had pushed the armies back, until their forces had actually invaded the lands beyond Russian soil, Romania and Poland. Kiev had fallen in November of the previous year. Even the Japanese were being dislodged from New Guinea.

In Italy, the Allies, having taken Sicily, were doggedly pushing their way northwards up Italy. But our troops – I almost identified with the German Armies now – were fighting strongly, and making them pay for every advance the Allies made.

Strangely enough, this was a very busy time socially. Rommel was constantly at the Atlantic Wall, talking to the ordinary soldiers, and at his HQ at Roche Guyon, near Paris, but he and his deputy von Kluge needed to get to know as many of his officers personally as they could. So there were a series of drinks parties at headquarters, to most of which I was invited.

The usual practice was to gather the officers. Then I would play *'Deutschland uber Alles'*, which got the officers on their feet, at the end of which Rommel or von Kluge would make their appearance, to applause. There would be a short speech, then the drinks would be brought, and Rommel and von Kluge would circulate. I never spoke at length to either war hero. I would probably have been presented, then after a complimentary remark, "Ach, *Vicomtesse*, you play well.

You must come and entertain our soldiers in the Front Line," the hero would have been off on his rounds. I was not important.

The mess was much more united now. No cracks against Hitler or the SS. We were in it together, and though the SS were perfect swine, as everyone knew, at least they could fight like tigers.

All this social drinking was bad for me. I found I often woke with a hangover and a feeling of nausea. But it passed, and I began to regard it as an occupational hazard. It also made me feel I was putting on weight. I resolved to eat and drink less.

All that spring we waited for the invasion. When the invasion came, Llew and I would wind up our operations and softly steal away. Llew had sent two of the vans to another location. But he stayed with me, because the graffiti merchants had come back, and "*Collaboratrice*" was daubed on my wall again. On one occasion some windows were broken.

But I still went to German headquarters as I had always done. There were still titbits to be picked up and relayed back to London.

Then on June 6, as I was playing, the General Officer Commanding came in and called for silence. I expected him to announce the fall of Rome of which we had been hearing unconfirmed rumours for some days. But what he said was more dramatic.

"Gentlemen," he said, "we have just heard that the Invasion has begun in Normandy. Everyone to his posts!"

It had come at last. Our work was over, and we could pack up and go. I felt elation, then dizziness, and I collapsed off the piano stool in a dead faint.

*

When I came round, I was lying on a sofa, my clothes loosened, and the medical officer attached to the HQ was fussing over me.

"Ah, *Vicomtesse*, you have recovered consciousness. You must go home and rest. Take things easy. One never knows what complications may occur, if you go rocketing round."

"But am I ill?" I asked.

He gave a fat laugh.

"No, no, not according to my diagnosis. But you must consult your own doctor. He will know if anything is wrong. But I think you are doing well, very well indeed."

"But, *Herr Doktor*, I must know. What is the matter with me?"

"Do you not know? The symptoms are quite clear. You are four months pregnant. But nothing to worry about. Your first?"

"My first" I said weakly. I now knew what legacy Benedict Michael Burr had left with me. And I had no one to blame but myself. One night might have been enough. But I had been greedy, and had seven days. And that was more than enough.

I thought how I had anguished with Maxim, about being unable to bear his child. Now I was with child, and the father could not be Maxim. How ironic life is, I thought weakly.

Llew was glad of the news of the invasion, but concerned about me.

"It may be a bit difficult, you being in the condition you are. But I'll make all preparations to get us away, quietly like, so they don't realise we've gone."

They referred to the graffiti merchants, who came back again and again. The French police did nothing. Disorder was beginning to break out in some of the working class suburbs. One major breakthrough by the Allies, and the whole city might erupt.

I continued my routine. I felt I would be given brownie points by the Germans, if I continued to come in, despite being pregnant.

It was getting extremely interesting at German headquarters. Von Kluge was holding the British at Caen, the Americans had suffered casualties at Omaha Beach. Perhaps the line could hold. It was not until a little later that they began to talk about the Falaise Gap, the encircling pincer movement that so nearly succeeded.

It was July now, and Llew was beseeching me to cut and run. But I made excuses. But on July 20, all our worlds were turned upside down. A one-armed, one-eyed Panzer Colonel, with an eye patch just like Carton's, tried to blow up Hitler, by planting a bomb in a meeting of the General Staff over which Hitler was presiding.

Chapter Twenty

The *Vicomtesse* Becomes a Fugitive

On July 20, von Stauffenburg attempted to kill Hitler, and all our lives were changed.

Since the Invasion, everyone's lives at HQ were so fraught that it was mutually decided that afternoon that concerts were inappropriate. But I was asked to play, instead, during the lunchtime period, between 12.30 and 1.30, so that officers could snatch a moment to eat and relax, listening to my playing.

On that morning, my concert was interrupted by the General Officer Commanding coming in to the mess, calling for silence, and saying dramatically:

"I have just, an hour ago, received a phone call from the War Office, the Bendlerstrasse. Hitler was assassinated in his bunker. They say it was an SS plot, though I have my doubts. Anyway, our instructions are clear. We are to arrest all the SS and Gestapo units in Paris!

"You have your orders on what to do in this eventuality. These must be carried out. I would ask everyone to take up their battle stations as agreed!"

There was a general movement towards the door, and the General approached me.

"*Vicomtesse*, I am sorry to have interrupted your music, but there is likely to be fighting in the streets. I suggest you go home at once and make your preparations to leave for the Auvergne. Until this matter is resolved, nobody in Paris will be safe."

We spoke for a little while, and he thanked me for all that I had done, my music most of all.

"You have been a true friend of the German Army, *Vicomtesse*. If they call you a collaborator, that will not be true. The real collaborators, from Pierre Laval downwards, they have used us for their own ends. You, alone, have done what you have done out of pure friendship, and that will be remembered."

Our conversation was interrupted by a signals officer running in, calling,

"General, General!"

He came up to the General, saluted and said:

"We have received another message from the Bendlerstrasse, General. It purports to come direct from the Führer's bunker. It says Hitler is alive, that there has been a plot to kill him by the Generals, and that every unit must stay loyal to the Führer. We have been receiving these conflicting signals at regular intervals."

The General swore, and then apologised to me.

"The fools at Bendlerstrasse! They have not bothered to supervise the telephone switchboard, and the clerks are sending out messages from them and from Hitler. I suppose they have to cover themselves, in case one side or the other wins. But what fools! I can see them, sitting in their offices, making grandiloquent phone calls, and not bothering to find out if their own HQ is secure. But we must do our duty, according to the plan. Warn our troops and officers to expect resistance. We have got to move fast, and take the SS by surprise. Put all units on full alert, and get them moving."

He turned to me.

"*Vicomtesse*, this is going to be very tricky. Get home at once."

I did not wait to be told twice. I made all speed to get back to the Rue de Varenne, and went straight to Llew.

"Llew, there is a military coup taking place in Paris. We must wind up the operation immediately, and go into hiding. If the Nazis win, God knows what may happen."

"I'll get the boyos out immediately. But we must get a message out. Carton will want to know. But you and I, we'll stay here as long as we can. The *Vicomte* Mike is somewhere in Paris. Maybe he'll be able to get you out to the Auvergne."

It was the first that I knew that Mike was here. It gave me comfort. We waited for forty-eight hours. I was desperate to know what was going on. We heard of troop movements, and tanks being deployed in the streets. But which side was going to win?

Then I decided I would wait no more. It was the supreme act of madness, but I would do it. It was the day of my afternoon recital. I would go into the German headquarters as usual, and find out what was going on.

I passed Llew in the corridor. He lived with me in the house now, and we cooked for each other. All the other workmen were safe in their hideouts.

Llew saw the music in my hand and frowned. He did not immediately realise its implication.

I passed him and went on down the stairs.

"Llew," I said, "I'm going to the HQ, to find out what has happened. I may not come back. Take care of yourself, and thank you for everything."

He followed me down the stairs, expostulating, his Welsh voice going even higher in his passion. I was out of my mind. I was throwing my life away. The operation was over, no sense in putting my head into a noose.

He was still expostulating as I got into the car.

"Well, don't expect me to be here when you get back," he said. "I'm quitting. You're out of your mind. And you're on your own now, girl, I warn you."

Llew was right, I thought. I'm on my own, now, and I'm going to my death. But I had to discover what had happened to my German friends. I had been their betrayer, I know, but I was concerned about their fate. That I might be making their lives more dangerous did not occur to me. I had to know. Perhaps my pregnancy had made me mad.

I parked in my usual place, and went by the usual sentries, who did not ask for my pass. That should have alerted me.

There was an officer I did not know in the hall. My foreboding were realised.

"I am the *Vicomtesse* de Langlade, and I have come to give my afternoon concert," I said.

He was polite and apologetic. Due to the recent disruption at headquarters, he was afraid that all concerts had had to be suspended. He hoped their discontinuance would not be of long duration.

"Then I will go home," I said. "You know my address in the Rue de Varenne. You can send for me when things are normal again."

He coughed. He did not wish to inconvenience the *Vicomtesse*, but there was a gentleman who wished to have a word, purely routine. He might be able to enlighten the *Vicomtesse* as to what had been going on.

It was all so polite, so menacingly polite. I shrugged my shoulders and followed the officer down corridors to the office until recently occupied by the General Officer Commanding. A well-dressed, pleasant-looking man was sitting at the desk. He rose politely when I entered, and motioned me to a chair, resuming his seat as I did so. He offered me a cigarette from a silver box, which I refused politely, saying that I did not smoke. He regretted the pernicious habit, congratulated me in my resolution, and after seeking my permission, lit a cigarette himself.

I was a little taken aback at this courtesy. I had expected the head of the Gestapo to be a ranting brute like Himmler and his entourage. This Gestapo officer was in a different league.

He regretted that my recital was postponed because he was very fond of music, and would have dearly liked to hear me play.

"You heard, I expect, of the regrettable little contretemps here recently." His French was faultless.

"Yes, I was present in the headquarters when my friend the General Officer Commanding came into the mess to tell us that Herr Hitler had been assassinated in a plot by the SS, and he had instructions from the Bendlerstrasse in Berlin to arrest the SS units in Paris."

"So he told me. But the Bendlerstrasse people were not being wholly truthful. It was one of their number, Colonel von Stauffenburg, who put the bomb in Hitler's headquarters, and the plot was in fact hatched by those superannuated Generals at the War Office in the Bendlerstrasse.

"They were all shot by an over-zealous officer who remained loyal to the Führer, and he himself was, rather regrettably in the circumstances, shot on the Führer's orders, for failing to keep them alive for interrogation. The other conspirators were strangled slowly by piano wire, and their death agonies were filmed, so the Führer could watch them himself. You must not repeat this outside these walls, but I fear our Führer is not quite a gentleman. But he was deeply provoked."

I was aghast at these descriptions.

"And my friends, have they been killed in the same way?"

"Good heavens, no," he said deprecatingly. "We do things in a more civilised way, here in Paris. You would have been amused.

Your General came to arrest me. I pointed out that the battle was not yet decided, and he must not be too premature. I suggested we went to a nearby restaurant to dine, and when the result of the battle was known, I should be his prisoner or he would be mine.

"He agreed and we enjoyed an excellent dinner. Everything hinged on whose reinforcements got there first. The SS, who are very efficient, even if a bit crude, got their reinforcements into Paris first, and so your friend became my prisoner. That is the way gentlemen should behave."

Despite my peril, I could not help but laugh.

He smiled.

"So you understand my desire is to clear this up, with the minimum of trouble. There is a war going on, and good officers are scarce. There will have to be sacrifices. I very much regret that Marshal von Kluge has committed suicide, and Marshal Rommel too. He is a great loss, and we shall put out that he has died from his wounds."

"But what is all this to do with me? I am French. I have never meddled in politics. Anyone will tell you."

He smiled, so pleasantly.

"Forgive me, dear lady. But there is a file on you in headquarters. We Germans love making files. And this file states that you approached Major von Ahremburg, whom you met in Switzerland before the war, and asked him, in 1940, to enquire about an English cousin of yours, Major John de Winter of the Duke of Cornwall's regiment, who was reported missing at Dunkirk. The gallant Major carried out exhaustive enquiries on your behalf, which are all recorded."

"But many French people, and many Germans too, have English cousins."

"I do not," he said simply.

I did not reply. I began to see the drift of his reasoning.

"I am under pressure to bring serious charges against your friend the General and his colleagues. Suppose it was suggested that these same officers harboured in German headquarters a lady with English relatives, who might well have been spying for the British, then their case might be perilous indeed."

"But you know it is quite untrue. My friendship with the Germans goes back over several years."

"I do not know if it is true or untrue. I gather that you told someone that your title is relatively recent, and that you were in fact adopted, or rather your husband was, by the *Comte* de Winter et de Langlade, and that in fact your husband is only a cousin of the *Comte*. Could he perhaps be an English cousin?"

"A Swiss cousin. My husband and I are natives of Switzerland."

"A Swiss cousin? With an English cousin? The relationship becomes ever more international..."

"This conversation is pointless. I will not assist you in creating a pure fiction to blacken my wholly innocent friends."

"Not wholly innocent, mistaken we hope. They did try to carry out a military coup in Paris, whether they were deluded by the Bendlerstrasse or not..."

I got up.

"I presume you wish to arrest me. I hope you will allow me the usual courtesy of being allowed to go home and pack a suitcase?"

He raised a deprecating hand.

"You are not under arrest, *Vicomtesse*. I am making certain enquiries, here and in the Auvergne. I do not want your friends kept behind bars, but fighting for their country. We need good officers. They may have to change their theatre of war, but I want them out, truly. If I can get them amnestied I will. But if I am under pressure to make a case against them, then your role cannot be ignored.

"I shall be happy that you stay in the Rue de Varenne until I need to talk to you again. I hope we can still observe all the courtesies even in these trying times."

I got up to go. He rose courteously. I could not resist asking,

"Was it a piece of folly then to come to these headquarters?"

"Not at all. It must have taken courage to come here, not knowing how things stood, and I admire courage. Comfort yourself with the reflection that if you had not come to me, I should have called on you. Goodbye, and I hope that when we next meet it will be under more pleasant circumstances."

I could not fault his manners. He even had a parting shot.

"Oh, *Vicomtesse*, I hope you will not be so unwise as to try to escape, to disappear into Paris. You live in the Rue de Varenne, a very significant name. Remember that the French royal family attempted to escape along the road to Varenne. They were recaptured and both died under the guillotine. Any flight is always taken as a presumption of guilt."

He came to the door to open it for me.

"Goodbye, once again, dear *Vicomtesse.*"

He took my hand as though to kiss it, German style, then changed his mind and instead shook it warmly.

"Let us shake hands the English way. After all, you have English cousins..."

Not to be outdone, I smiled and said,

"*Herzlicher Gruss.*"

It was a mistake, and his rapier wit flashed out again.

"How well you speak German. You must have a gift for languages. German, French, English perhaps..."

Then he went back into the office.

I went out of the headquarters with my head held high. I got into my car and drove away. My network was unravelling like a piece of string, as Llew would have said. All I could do was to go home and wait. Perhaps I could get a message somehow to the château. Why had I not left Paris when Llew first suggested it?

I hoped that Llew had kept to his resolve to quit the house, even if it would be lonely without him in the big house. Ah well, no use repining. Better go home and face the consequences. But I never got home.

In a narrow intersection, a van had stalled, bringing all traffic to a halt. Horns hooted, people swore. I braked the car to wait.

Then my door was pulled open, and I was half dragged from the driving seat. A voice in my ear said,

"This way, *Vicomtesse*," and a girl, it was Marie, took my place at the wheel, letting out a piercing double hoot. The van miraculously discovered its momentum and moved off and the traffic cleared.

The man who held me – he was Llew's assistant and the husband of Marie – said urgently,

"Come this way, *Vicomtesse*. Mike, he is waiting for you, a few streets from here, with a man of the Resistance who will guide you out of Paris."

"Will Marie be all right?"

"Oh yes, she will drive your car a few streets and abandon it. Your car is hot, *Vicomtesse.*"

"Don't call me *Vicomte*sse, call me Jeanne."

"Okay Jeanne, but we must hurry."

We hurried through the back streets, and I put on his raincoat to look less conspicuous. My friend, I never remember his name, came to an old house with a basement down some steps.

He whistled, and a corresponding whistle came from the basement.

"Mike is there. Go down and meet him, Jeanne."

I almost tumbled down the steps and into Mike's arms.

Mike's chin was bristly, and his clothes were rough. He looked more like a homespun farmer, the rustic *Vicomte* up from his estates, but his welcome was characteristic.

"Easy, honey, easy. Remember you're carrying junior. The little rascal just kicked me, in protest."

I couldn't help smiling.

"Why, Mr Benedict Michael Burr, I do declare you're getting quite paternal."

"I should be," he said, "I'm a double father. Gabrielle-Pauline is pregnant too.

"My word, you do get around."

"A human sperm bank, me," he said with pride.

I became aware of our circumstances. The basement, devoid of any furniture, suddenly seemed menacing, claustrophobic. I wanted m be gone.

"Mike, where is the Resistance man who was going to help us escape?"

"He just went out to see if the coast is clear. He'll be back directly. Listen. I think I hear him coming down the stairs now."

But down the stairs came half a dozen of the most unprepossessing young street Arabs I had ever seen. Congreve or one of the Restoration dramatists would have probably categorised them as 'slovenly bullies' or 'rude boys of the town'. These petty crooks and spivs of Paris had attached themselves to the Paris Resistance, and did their dirty work, evening up old scores and grievances.

I thought at first that they were going to rob us, and had my purse ready to hand over to them. But I soon realised that worse was in store.

The leader paused and looked at me familiarly.

"Why, if it isn't the *Vicomtesse Collaboratrice*, the bosom buddy of the German military! And without her officer protectors. How funny! We're going to have some fun, aren't we boys?"

I looked at Mike. Mike looked at me. There was six of them, all tooled up with knives, probably guns.

The leader swaggered forward.

"Yes *Vicomtesse*," he said, "if we catch women collaborators, we cut their hair off, strip them, and throw them out on the street, for the police to pick them up. But for really bad mistresses of Germans, we rough them up a bit, and spoil their beauty. For you, I reckon we kick you around like a football, and kick in the head of that little German bastard you're carrying in your womb!"

Chapter Twenty-One

The Ordeal of the *Vicomtesse Collaboratrice*

Attack was the only method of defence. I thought of British Beatrice, Maxim's sister, and my course was clear.

"How *dare* you threaten me?" I said in crisply accented, aristocratic English. "I am an Englishwoman and a British intelligence agent! I have been spying on the Germans, not collaborating with them. Ask this gentleman. He had been working with me and he is an American!"

"Sure thing," said Mike. "I'm an American intelligence officer."

The thug paused.

"I do not believe you. This bitch says she's an English spy. I think she's bluffing. I reckon we go ahead," he said to his colleagues, who snarled their agreement.

"Touche moi, ou ce monsieur, et quand les soldats Anglais et Americains arrivent à Paris, dans quelques semaines, tu seras pendu!"

The talk of hanging seemed to infuriate him.

"The Americans and the British will not come for months. And when they do, what? There will be two naked, unidentified bodies in the morgue, in the meantime we shall have our fun and have done justice on you. Grab the man, two of you."

Mike tried to fight, but was quickly overpowered. He was to watch my violation.

The leader drew a knife and advanced on me. With his free hand he tore my dress down the front, and then grasped my hair, forcing me to my knees.

"What a pretty face," he said mockingly. "What a pity to have to scar it."

I did not flinch. In seconds my cheek would be sliced open, and then my humiliation would begin.

There was a single shot, and the leader leapt in the air, releasing me, as the bullet hit the ground by his foot.

Llew said,

"The next bullet goes up your arse. So back off, boy!"

I scrambled to my feet. Avid to watch and participate in my humiliation, the thugs had crowded round me, and had not heard Llew Thomas come down the stairs into the basement. There he stood, blocking their exit, with a machine gun cradled very professionally in his arms.

Llew said, his North African accent strong and menacing,

"Que tu m'emmerdes! Espace de cons, all of you! What kind of Resistance fighters are you, half a dozen, and not one of you bothering to protect your rear? But I know you, pimps and cowards that you are, you make war on women. Now don't try anything silly. This MKI6 is on automatic, and I can cut you all to bits if you make one false move. Just release the American, and drop your weapons on the floor. Move!" He raised his machine gun menacingly.

A cascade of knives, knuckledusters, live preservers and a couple of pistols fell to the floor. Llew looked at the knives.

"Knife fighters, are you? I should call down my Algerian *copains*, and then you'd really see knife play. Any of you fancy taking them on? No, then get out, you little gutter rats, and keep moving. You won't see my Algerian *copains*, but if I whistle, they'll find you, quick enough. No, not you, King Sewer Rat, you stay behind. I've something to say to you."

The man tried to brazen it out.

"I suppose you will say you are an English agent too," he said in quite passable Americanised English.

"No, boyo, Welsh! Remember us? We kick the pants off you at Parc-au-Prince and Cardiff Arms Park. I've something to say to you with this!" And he brought up the barrel of the gun and cracked the thug on the point of the jaw. He went down as if poleaxed, but presently crawled to his feet, holding his face and saying his jaw was broken.

"Oh, I do hope so, boyo, I really do! It'll be something to remember me by, when you next think of laying hands on a lady. Now get up those stairs, and don't linger. If my Algerian boys get you, they'll slit your throat and cut off your balls. They cut the balls off first, see, so you know all about it, and then they slit your throat. Old Algerian custom. So get moving and don't stop!"

The thug did not wait to be told twice.

"Oh, Llew," I said shakily, trying to pin up my torn dress with safety pins. "You were wonderful. Was it a bluff?"

Not entirely, love. There's Marie and her husband Louis up there, posing as courting couples in a doorway. But if I'd whistled, they'd have got their knives out and been among those thugs like lightning. Element of surprise, see. You don't expect courting couples to pull a knife, do you?

"Marie's deadly, so's her husband, but Marie is the greatest. Got roughed up when she first came to Paris – they called her a *pied-noir* – and she's carried a knife ever since. She's lightning, you should see her. Must be all the cutting up of meat she does in the kitchen."

I thought of placid even stupid Marie opening the door, and serving tea to my German officer wives. What would they think, to know she was a knife fighter? Life was full of surprises.

"Well, you saved me from death, and from a fate worse than death before that. And you arranged for me to be snatched too. That was best."

"Just routine," he said. "A forward tail in front of you, a rearward tail behind you. I got on the radio to the boys, as soon as you set off, and as my vans are now stored with Mike's black market lorries, and as he'd arrived with a consignment that very day, we roped him in too. I fixed the place of assignment, where we should meet up. Didn't know about the thugs. Sorry about that, and the tear in your dress."

"An accident of war, Llew. But would they really have stripped me, as well as cutting off my hair? I'm fairly easy about my body, as Mike knows, but I do feel it should be for private delectation and not for public entertainment."

Mike said,

"Jeanne, you're wonderful. You go through all this, and can still quote Oscar Wilde at the end of it."

"It wasn't Oscar Wilde," I said pedantically. "It was the last line of a Chinese play, *Lady Precious Stream*, which I played in at school. Because of my height I had to play the male lead, the gardener, Sher Ping Qui. It's a lovely play with two successful Generals in it, General Su, who knows he knows nothing, and so listens to the experts; and General Wu, who is so ignorant that he doesn't even realise he knows nothing, and wins his battles by bravado and luck."

I was talking for the sake of talking, to cool my nerves. The others humoured me.

Llew said,

"Good Lord, I knew Generals of both types in the First War. When was it written, that play?"

"I think it was a modern version of a play that goes back centuries. There is this recurring riddle. I say, 'If I say your lover is far, far away,' and Lady Precious Stream says, 'He is a thousand miles away...' (I made an outward circling movement with my hands). Then I say, 'And if I say he is near, very near,' (an inward circling movement), 'He is before me!' And again, 'If I say it is long, very long time away', 'It is a thousand days before you must go away', 'And if I say it is short, very short', 'It is tonight!'" We laughed.

"Well, all I can say is, I wish we were a thousand miles away at this moment, and if you don't leave tonight, I don't think you'll leave at all. Where is that Resistance man, Mike?"

At that point the Resistance man, who looked like a bespectacled copying clerk, came in. He was very nervous and shaking, and as unlike a hero of the Maquis as I could imagine. He was a contact man, not a combatant.

"*Mon Dieu*, *messieurs*, I heard a shot and thought the Gestapo was here! So I hid in a *tabac* and watched, then six men came out, running as though the devil was at their heels, and I was sure the Gestapo were here. What was going on?"

"A little disagreement with some Apaches, who muscled their way in. Nothing to worry about," said Llew comfortingly.

"And this is the lady and gentlemen you want me to shelter. *Oh, merde*!" he said, and the expletive sounded so strange from those prim lips. He was so white I thought he would faint.

"While I was in the *tabac*, I bought an evening paper, to justify my being there. *Regardez!*" He thrust the paper in our direction.

My Gestapo friend had not wasted time. It was less than a couple of hours since I had been snatched, but he had phoned the papers and made them hold the front page, while he rushed a picture and story over to them. I think he must have expected me to try to escape, and had the copy pre-prepared. Once he knew that this had happened the wheels rolled into action.

On the front page of the paper was a picture of me in my best dress, champagne glass in hand, smiling and talking to (the late) Field Marshal von Kluge, who was smiling back. (Actually it was the occasion when he had told me, "You should be playing for my front line troops..." a very palpable rebuke. Someone must have photographed me unawares.)

The headline read "New Mata Hari Sought", and the article below said that the police were seeking the *Vicomtesse* de Langlade, known as *La Vicomtesse Collaboratrice*, who had been an intimate friend of many of the German officers accused of the plot to assassinate Herr Hitler. It continued that further research had indicated that the playful *Vicomtesse* was a double spy, working for the British, and relaying table talk and bed talk to them. It also stated that the *Vicomtesse Collaboratrice* was thought to be making for the family château in the Auvergne. The police were offering a substantial reward for her arrest, the article concluded.

The little man's teeth seemed almost to be chattering in his agitation.

"Everyone will have seen the picture...the reward too...if we were to shelter the *Vicomtesse*, our own network might be endangered –"

Llew said sardonically, his North African accent very pronounced,

"Of course we understand, boy. We didn't worry about our own security, when the *Vicomtesse* and I sheltered your Resistance friends in our safe house in the Rue de Varenne, but I can see things are very different now."

The little man grimaced.

"I shall have to report back to my people. It is a new situation. Obviously, if we are able to help, we will."

"What sort of man are you, when you're not running errands for the Resistance? What's your name, so I can remember you in my prayers?"

"I am a senior bank clerk," said the man with an attempt at dignity. "My name is Monsieur Toppin." He looked nervously around, fearful that somebody should have overheard his name.

"Toppin, eh?" said Llew brutally. "I know your type, Toppin. A little terror to the junior clerks, and never doing anything that isn't according to the book, and authorised by headquarters. Well, have a topping day, Toppin, and tell your friends we will be able to do without their services. Run along, little man, or you may get contaminated by contact with us rough folk."

The little man sped away.

"You were a little hard on him, Llew. There was some truth in what he said. With my picture everywhere, it might have been dangerous to shelter me," I protested.

"It's his type I can't stand. And the Froggies, they always look after their own backs, and are never there when you want them," Llew said contemptuously.

"What now then?" asked Mike.

"You'll get in your van, boyo, and go hell for leather for the Auvergne. You've all your authorisations to get you out of Paris, and if you go fast, you can get ahead of the Gestapo, before they can circulate Jeanne's picture. I'll meet you at the van in fifteen minutes. Just got to get Marie to find a change of clothes for Jeanne, and then you can be away." He stumped off and left us.

So in half an hour we were on the road. Marie brought some nondescript dowdy clothes and I changed in the back of the van.

With a scarf around my head, spectacles on my nose, and some shapeless peasant clothing on, I hoped I looked very different from the elegant *Vicomtesse* of the portrait. Llew advised the driver to halt just before the checkpoints, and approach on foot to see if my portrait was there. Then he embraced me and we were away.

The three of us so in the front of the van, and I was told to duck down if we paved any other vehicle. The road was fairly empty since petrol was so short that most people now used bicycles.

We passed the first checkpoint, the bored soldiers recognising our van and only glancing cursorily at the papers with their official seal. The second check point was negotiated, and we began to relax. Then we were overtaken by an Army despatch rider, and a little later the same rider came back past us. We shrunk down but his eye was on the road.

Then at me ran checkpoint, we stopped just at a bend in the road, out of sight of the checkpoint. The driver went forward to gossip with the guards, asking for a match. He returned, with a serious expression.

"Your picture, *Vicomtesse*, it is there. And the guards, they asked me if I had seen you on the road. They know your name: the *Vicomtesse* de Langlade."

Mike cursed.

"My papers are in the name of the *Vicomte* de Langlade. Even if you were to hide in the back of the van, they'd be sure to see it, and ask questions. Turn the van round, Marcel, and let's try a different route."

But the despatch rider had been before us. At each reconnoitre by the driver before the checkpoint, the driver returned with the same bad news. My picture was at every checkpoint, and the troops were alert. We must have zigzagged across the outskirts of Paris, from road to road. At every juncture, there was my picture.

With all that they had to do, with Patten and the other forces making all speed to reach Paris, you would have thought that the Gestapo had better things to do. But that is to underestimate the German mind, the Teutonic persistence. The Führer wanted the German officers punished. I was the living evidence of their treachery and disloyalty. I had to be recaptured.

Finally, at the umpteenth attempt, Mike gave up.

"It's no good. All exits are covered. You'd better take the van, Marcel, and go back your normal route. Your papers are in order, you're clean. Warn the *Comte* and Gabrielle-Pauline that the Germans may come after them. Say that Jeanne and I are taking the scenic route and may be some time."

We watched the van drive away. We were on our own, and the Auvergne was four hundred kilometres away to the South.

Chapter Twenty-Two

The Long Way Home

Mike and I have always promised each other that one day we will get out a large scale map of France, and find out exactly where we wandered, that uncertain and treacherous August of 1944.

Issoire is about four hundred kilometres from Paris, a journey of perhaps five hours. We took a little over a fortnight to make our painful way in fits and starts back to our home country.

My pregnancy, the strain, the effort of walking long distances, and possibly a touch of fever, meant that for much of the time I was light-headed and barely aware of my surroundings. It was Mike who had to be my guide, my support and our organiser for much of the journey.

We had three advantages. We had money, I was in an advanced state of pregnancy, and Mike was very persistent.

From the moment that the van left us on our own, Mike took over. We walked until we found a farmhouse, where Mike told the farmer's wife that our car had crashed, we had been given a lift as far as the road outside, and that his wife was seven months pregnant but wanted to go back to her family home in the Auvergne to give birth to our child. We were overwhelmed with kindness.

I was given the best chair in the kitchen and told not to over-exert myself. Later I was ensconced in the best bed, and told to lie there until I felt stronger.

"*Bien sûr*, Madame will not wish to risk the life of her baby..."

I was content to be idle. In the morning, the network of neighbours and relatives will be called in for a noisy think tank. Which one was going into market? Would the poor pregnant Madame and her husband be able to get a lift on their produce conveyance, usually a horse and cart. I was directed to some friend or relative in that town, who would look after me. I had never known such kindness, not just from one person, but successive people in different towns and in different homes. Being pregnant certainly seemed to bring out the best in country people, normally a bit stand-offish and suspicious of strangers.

We travelled on the back of farm carts, in old fashioned governess carts, and endured being bumped around on interminable journeys in local buses. These were powered, Mike informed me, by fuel oil or spirit distilled from chicken dung. This made me smile. Since the French word for fuel is 'essence' the idea of essence de chicken dung conjured up in my mind the vision of some diabolical Dior perfume.

Between these forms of country transport, we walked. I kept up as well as I could, though I was frequently overcome with such weariness that I had to sit down forthwith by the side of the road and let the world go by. My ankles also were a bit swollen, and often at the end of the day I had such agonising back pains that I began to think that I was going into labour. It was my nightmare that my contractions would start while we were walking along a country lane, miles from anywhere, and that Mike's baby would be born under a bush, with only Mike to be midwife.

We occasionally travelled by local trains, from small stations, but I always felt terribly exposed sitting on the station platform, or surrounded by strangers.

I shall never forget having a friendly conversation with a young seminarian returning to his seminary after a retreat in Paris. Whatever was going on in the country, the life of the Church continued.

We talked a little of Paris and we said we had been there recently staying with our aunt, Madame de Boissy. We did not give our aunt's real name.

The seminarian asked if our aunt was devout. We said, very, a daily attender at Mass.

"The old families they are the backbone of religious life in France." (Clearly this was no worker priest.) He went on to ask if we too were members of the old ruling class.

Incautiously I said,

"We are from the de Langlade family, and there is a family château in the Auvergne."

Perhaps my pregnancy had made me stupid. Mike flashed a warning glance.

The seminarian pricked up his ears.

"De Langlade? How curious. I am sure I saw that name in a newspaper when I was in Paris." He pondered. "No, I can't remember what it was about. Doubtless it will come to me later."

We devoutly prayed that it would not.

He began to chatter on about the interlinking of the Church and the old families, from the Crusades onward. We relaxed. He was not dangerous, just a student of history, and a snob.

But thereafter, travelling on trains became a nightmare of mine. It had to be done, and I never complained. Mike was in charge of transport, and what he said went as far as I was concerned. But I was much happier in more rustic, if slower forms of transportation.

We made our slow way. One morning, getting up out of bed in a small hotel in a small town, we heard cheering. We dressed and went down to see what the rejoicing was about. A man shouted to me,

"The French Resistance has taken Paris! They have driven the Germans out!"

I could not join in the rejoicings. I could only think of the good time girls and the girls who had genuinely formed friendships with the German soldiers, being dragged through the streets of Paris by exultant men and hard-faced women, having their heads shorn, perhaps stripped, abused and violated, as I had so nearly been. I thought of a forlorn, shaven-headed, French Lilli Marlene, waiting under the lamplight, for her German boy who was being forced to leave her and to leave Paris.

We were getting nearer to the château now, and we began to see parties of refugees on the roads. A huge battle had been raging now for weeks, between the Maquis, and the German divisions in the South, including the crack Reich Panzer division stationed in Toulouse, and trying to fight their way back to help their comrades in Normandy.

It spread over a hundred mile area, from Châteauroux to Sussac, and the most deadly conflict was along the two main road links, the road from Toulouse to Normandy, and the road from Bordeaux to Normandy, and the various rail lines from the south. The Germans retaliated with massacres as at Oradour, and with the burning down of homesteads and sometimes even small villages, to deprive the Maquis of their supplies and as a warning to people not to support the Maquis.

The displaced people were making their way to the Auvergne, where there was little fighting, as yet. But we did not know if the Germans had reached the château.

I was tired beyond belief. A cart had brought us to within five miles of the château. He stopped at a large barn.

"The refugees are in there," he said, and left us.

There was a group of about twenty people in the barn, old men, weather-beaten women, children, and young women, though very few young men. They were with the Maquis. They looked up at us with suspicion, which turned to concern as I slumped down on the ground. One of the women came and brought a pillow to go under my head and asked how I was.

"My back is aching, low down," I said. "It is painful."

"That probably means that you will soon go into labour," she said comfortingly. Job's comforter!

Mike said:

"Look honey, I think I shall go and reconnoitre round the château. If the Germans are there, I shall know. I'll go and talk to one of the gardeners, whose cottage is sufficiently far from the house, so that the Germans wouldn't notice it. He'll tell me what is going on at the château."

"If Llew got his message through to London, and London put it on the radio, the *Comte* and Gabrielle-Pauline will have left the château and gone to ground. You may find it quite deserted."

"Maybe," Mike said. "If the Germans have been there, I hope they haven't tampered with my archives."

Oh, you...pedant!" I said laughing. "I think you care more about your precious archives than about Gabrielle-Pauline."

"That's not fair," Mike said reproachfully. "Gaby has her father and the whole household, including me, to look after her. But my archives have only me."

Mike's droll ways had been the greatest comfort to me in the last weeks. We had long since ceased to be lovers, but we were comrades, which was much better. Even though in our wanderings we had often had to share a bed, he never touched me, nor did I ever turn to him for comfort. We had got so we did not need to speak, to understand each other's minds.

"Well, go and reconnoitre the château, Mike," I said. "If you get offered a bed or a bath, take it. Come back to me in the morning, squeaky clean and smelling of roses. If you see the *Comte*, give him my devoted respect. I'll be all right, with these people to look after me. I couldn't stir a step myself."

"If you think it is all right to leave you...?" he asked anxiously.

"Perfectly all right. Get yourself a comfortable night."

He went off reluctantly.

The refugees had listened to us talking in English, with some puzzlement.

An old man said,

"Did I hear you talk about the *Comte*, Madame? Do you know him? "

"He is my father-in-law. My adopted father-in-law," I explained.

"I used to work for the *Comte*, many years ago. Before I got my own farm near Châteauroux. Burned down now by the Boches. But I said to myself, 'The *Comte* will look after us, me and my wife.' So I have travelled over here, me, my family and some neighbours. I wish only to see the *Comte*, and he will set us up in small holdings on his estate, all of us, so that we do not starve. The *Comtes* de Langlade always look after their own people."

This was pure feudalism, I thought. The lord of the manor may have powers of life and death over his people, but he also had absolute obligations, which he would never refuse, never think of refusing, to look after his people if they were ever in trouble. There was something to be said for feudalism.

I missed Mike during that night, the comfort of his presence. When I awoke in the morning, I was sure I was going into labour, with the contractions beginning. Oh, Mike, where are you? I hope I shall not give birth to your baby, in this stable, without you around to hold my hand. Giving birth in a stable, what biblical associations, but I really had no wish to emulate the Holy Family.

All this was going through my mind, when there was a distant rumbling and the old man cried out,

"Listen! There is something coming up the road!"

We were all awake, and silent as we listened.

The noise of the vehicles got louder.

"It is the tanks," hissed the old man. "The Germans are here! Please God they will pass us by!"

The vehicles came nearer, tanks, lorries, we did not dare to look out. There were several of them, lumbering by. Then ominously, they stopped, just outside the barn.

A woman's voice shrilled,

"It is the Boches. They have come for us. Holy Mother of God, have mercy on us!"

I stumbled to my feet. Let the Germans shoot me, I did not care. But I could talk to them, and perhaps they would take me to a hospital, and I could have my baby. After that, I did not mind what happened.

I staggered out into the street, momentarily dazzled by the sunshine after the dark barn. There was a military scout car, a couple of military lorries, soldiers...

Then I blinked. The steel helmets of the troops were not those of Germans. There was the familiar khaki. With overwhelming surprise I realised that these were not Germans but British.

A cheerful face looked out at me from the scout car.

"Bon-jour, Madame," he said in execrable French. "Is there anyone here wot speaks English?"

"I do," I said, feeling I did not know whether to laugh or cry. "I am English."

"Well, what a coincidence. First person I speak to, and she's as English as meself. You can be of great help to me, Missus.

"The Brigadier, he heard there were refugees hiding in this barn. So he sent us along to bring them back to the château, so they'll be a bit more comfortable. So could you come with me, Missus, and explain to the Frogs, and we can get them loaded on to the lorries. Can't stay too long. We're a flying column and we got to be on our way before long."

"Of course I can" I said? "But could you take my arm? I think I'm going to have a baby."

"Oh, my Gawd," he said and got out of the scout car, to support me. "We'd better make it quick then. Then you can get in my spare seat, and I'll get you back to the château of Langladdy in no time at all"

"Langlade," I said faintly in correction. "I come from there. I was trying to get there to have my baby."

"Well, lickety split, we'll get you there, Missus. Just tell those Frogs wot's going on, and then we'll get you there, never fear."

My explanation to the refugees did not take long. I explained succinctly that *les soldats Anglais* had come to help them, and they must all climb on to the lorries and be taken to the château, where they would be well looked after. The refugees seemed reassured, if still apprehensive. On the way back to the scout car, the Sergeant said admiringly,

"My word, you do speak French well, Missus. You surely told them."

"I've spoken nothing but French for the last four years," I said. "I'm a British agent."

On the way back, reclining in the scout car, and feeling more relaxed, my contraction having stopped, I asked the Sergeant what his regiment was and how he came to be there.

"First battalion, Duke of Cornwall's Mounted Infantry, Missus. We're part of Maxcol, a flying column what's belting down the roads of France, to link up with the forces that have landed in the south of France."

The penny dropped. He was a member of Maxim's regiment.

"My husband was a member of your regiment. Do you know him? He was Major John de Winter."

He nearly lost control of the steering wheel, so great was his surprise.

"Gawd Almighty, I've got the Brigadier's lady on board! You better not have your baby in this scout car, Lady, or Brigadier Max will have my guts for garters. We're called Maxcol, Lady, because it's Brigadier Max de Winter's flying column. He's the boss, see. And he's up there at the château this very minute."

Then it was my turn to faint.

Chapter Twenty-Three

The Second Maximilian

I was still semi-conscious when we finally drove into the courtyard of the château, though I was aware of a great concentration of vehicles within the courtyard, and in the roads approaching the château. Maxcol was clearly a formidable mobile force. The Sergeant carried me in his arms into the château and up the stairs to the bedroom where the lady members of the château took over my recumbent body.

I remember trying to thank the Sergeant for all his kindness, but I was in such a daze, and the words seem to come from me drunkenly and with difficulty.

The Sergeant told me afterwards, when I was properly able to express my gratitude, that I had tried to thank him over and over again.

"But the words came out like you were right pissed, if you'll pardon the expression, Ma'am."

All I remember was utter weariness and I went to sleep in my comfortable bed for more than twenty-four hours.

When I awoke it was evening, and Gabrielle-Pauline, not as evidently pregnant as I had been, but in great beauty from her pregnancy, was sitting by my bed.

"Gabrielle-Pauline..." I was at a loss for words, and all I could blurt out finally was, "... Forgive me."

She gave a conspiratorial smile.

"Hush," she said. "Let us not talk of that. I have spoken to dear Mike, and he has explained everything. You were frightened, you turned to Mike. It was natural. And you continued to fear to be alone. It was a misfortune of war, not to be repeated."

"Never. Mike is my *bon camerade*, my *chevalier* in shining armour, but nothing more. Without him I should certainly not be here."

"But without him you would not have had such an uncomfortable journey. I hope you will not have anything going between you, or I shall set my cap at your Maxim. He looks so handsome in his uniform. Mike is nothing compared to him. But we came through all right, and we kept it in the family."

"Where is Maxim?"

"I thought you would never ask. He is waiting to see you, chérié, so impatiently. Brigadiers must not be kept waiting. You must have your baby quickly, as soon as you are strong enough. Maxcol has to be back on the road in forty-eight hours, and the war will not wait on your convenience. I'll go find him."

She paused at the door, with a ripple of laughter.

"I must tell you about Mike. It is droll. He was spotted by Maxim's advance guard, sneaking round the château. The soldiers could not believe that Mike was an American, when the papers said he was the *Vicomte* de Langlade. They locked him in the guardroom all night, and it was only the next morning, when Maxim arrived, and I came over from the Montmorins, that he was let out! I had been sheltering with the Montmorins after I heard your Paris friend's message over the BBC: 'Gabrielle-Pauline and Henri-Xavier, Jeanne is detained in Paris.' I knew you had been arrested then, it was terrible. 'Make all necessary arrangements.'

"So I knew than I had to leave the château at once in case the Germans came. But Mike said it was the last straw, and he has been sulking ever since. You must talk to him. Maxim had already sent the lorries to pick up the refugees when they let Mike out. Poor Mike! Everything happens to him, he says."

So I was still laughing when Maxim came into the room. Gabrielle-Pauline was right. Maxim did look magnificent in his uniform, and much younger and fitter than I had seen him last. I noted that he had got rid of his terrible beard. How stupid, I thought, Army Brigadiers don't wear beards. All I could think of was how awful and ugly I looked, after my nightmare journey, and with the terrible burden of guilt I carried, in my womb.

"Maxim," I began and tears began to trickle down my face. "What can I say to you, looking like death warmed up, and carrying a child that isn't yours?"

His smile broadened.

"Well, 'Good evening' might be a start, and 'How nice to see you'." He dropped his bantering manner and took my hand, saying with emotion,

"Oh, my dearest little girl, you're here, you're alive, you've come back to me. You're safe, and your war is over. Mine isn't yet but it won't be long. We're going to be together again. Nothing else matters except that."

"But it must matter. I was unfaithful to you. I can never forget that."

He resumed his bantering tone.

"Since Gabrielle-Pauline and I are not worried, why should you be? I've spoken to Mike, who is quite as guilt ridden as you are. From what he tells me, it was a pure act of God. You were frightened, you went to Mike. You continued to be frightened, you stayed with Mike. That was probably unwise, as we see now. But it was totally understandable, and totally forgivable. Added to which you've given our house an heir. If Gabrielle-Pauline has a girl, he will be the sole male heir."

"Mine may be a girl."

"No, the midwife visited you, while you were unconscious, and she says the way the baby is lying, she's sure it is a boy. So don't look miserable, be happy. We should be celebrating. Another little de Winter. The line goes on."

I began to feel a little better.

"Should I really?"

He smiled again, in pure amusement.

"Certainly, you can. It may amuse you to know that you are following in a very famous mediaeval tradition. When there had been a great dynastic marriage, and no heir was produced, both the male and the female members of the union had to submit to an ordeal. The man had to sleep with a female virgin, chosen for the occasion, and the girl had to sleep with a male virgin similarly chosen.

"If a birth resulted from either coupling then they knew who was responsible for the infertility, and if it was the girl, the marriage was annulled, and the girl wife was sent off to a convent. Well, it certainly seems from this that you won't have to be sent to a convent!"

I didn't know whether to laugh or cry.

Maxim said very earnestly,

"Don't you see what this meant, Jeanne? You've proved that the fact we couldn't have children was not your fault, as you thought, but mine. When this war ends, I shall go to one of your expensive clinics, and let them do all the tests they want, and discover the reason for our infertility. If we sort it out, we can have several children, just the two of us. But we wouldn't have known that but for Junior here. Do you like the idea of half a dozen children?"

I was too happy to speak. Maxim had lifted the burden of my guilt.

*

I did my best to meet Maxim's military deadline of forty-eight hours, and only missed it slightly, giving birth on the evening of the third day. Maxim was still there, and was present at the birth. There were good military reasons for the delay, he said. They had blasted their way through all German opposition (not that there was much, the Germans seemed anxious to surrender to the British), all the way from Paris to the Auvergne, and could go on to effect a juncture with the French forces coming up from the south, as had been the plan. But the war between the Maquis and the Germans was continuing with unabated ferocity, and if Maxcol was diverted westwards they could mop up several German garrisons, and moving with all speed might take the SS Panzer division in the flank.

He had sent a signal back to GHQ, putting forward this alternative plan. In the meantime, while they waited, Maxcol could do necessary repairs, and get into a state of greater readiness. The answer came on the third day, just as I was going into labour, real labour, not the false pangs that I had thought I felt in the barn.

The orders were succinct: stick to the original plan, effect a juncture with the forces from the South, and then go hell for leather back to Paris, to take part in the big push into Belgium and Holland.

The Maquis will have to carry on their fight with the Germans unaided, unless the army from the South could be diverted to their assistance.

Maxim swore. The *Comte* was with the Maquis, and they needed all the help they could get, quickly. But orders were orders.

In the two days that we had together, Maxim entertained me, probably to stop me from brooding about the impending birth of Junior, by telling me how he had fared since leaving me in Paris.

Once the escape network had conveyed him over the Spanish border into Andorra, and hence into Spain, his problems were over. He had money, and his Swiss papers, sewn into his cost. He was able to shave off his beard, get some smart clothes, and take the train to Burgos and thence to Madrid.

In Madrid, from a good hotel, he was able to phone Coppelius and get more funds transferred to him, and Coppelius was able to give him a contact name for Carton's Organisation in Lisbon, Maxim going by train there, having secured a passport from the Swiss Consulate.

Carton's man in Lisbon had pulled strings, with a result that Maxim was able to get from Lisbon to Gibraltar, and was flown from there to Egypt, where the Duke of Cornwall's Mounted Infantry were now stationed.

General Auchinleck, a much underrated General in Maxim's view, better than many of his subordinates, was still in charge of Egypt, and had built an admirable defensive ring, which later commanders were able to take full advantage of. Shortly after Maxim arrived in Egypt, Auchinleck was replaced by General Alexander as supremo, and Montgomery as commander of the Eighth Army.

Alexander, knowing Maxim's worth, wanted him back on his staff, but Maxim only wanted combat experience. In the end they compromised. Maxim would join his regiment, but would be available to help Alex, whenever Alex sent for him.

"It was a daunting experience rejoining the regiment," Maxim said ruefully. "We were both dead scared of each other. I arrived with the temporary rank of Major, which soon reverted to Captain. I'd been on the regimental books as a "ghost officer", since 1938, but had been on special duties since then. I came with the reputation of being a good staff officer, and with having escaped from the Germans in France. They were rather in awe of me. At the same time, I knew that my knowledge of actual regimental and battle duties was rather less than the rawest recruit. So I expected we would be in for a sticky time."

Maxim was posted to be intelligence officer to the First Battalion, which had light tanks and were attached as a support unit to David Stirling's long range desert group. In that capacity they ranged over no man's land in the desert between the two armies. Maxim had the good fortune to be given command of one of the companies, whose commander had gone down with dysentery.

"I called my sergeant in, who was a battle-hardened veteran, and I said to him, 'Look, I've been a staff officer, but I know nothing about actual warfare. But you know it all, and I have common sense, and I can learn. Can we work together?' And he said, 'Blimey Captain, I've waited twenty years to hear a staff officer admit his ignorance. Stick with me, Cap, and we'll work it out all right.' And we did."

Just before El Alamein, a few months later, Maxim's nerve was put to the test. On a reconnoitring mission with the LRDG, the Dukes were caught by a larger force of marauding tanks, and in the ensuing combat, the Colonel was killed, and the second in command badly wounded.

As Maxim was the oldest by several years of the company commanders, despite his relative inexperience, he was chosen by the surviving officers to take temporary command of the battalion. Aided by his sergeant, he managed to gather together the scattered and demoralised forces, and brought them back to base. He acquired the nickname of 'Sniffer Dog', because he had a sort of sixth sense as to where the minefields were, and could bring the depleted battalion back through them.

"I found I could look at a map and at the terrain, and see, in my mind's eye, the Germans planting the mines, very logically and systematically, at predetermined intervals. I knew the German mind, you see. So I could envisage exactly where he would put the holes in the minefields, in order to escape out of them. It is a little like painting a floor; you don't want to paint yourself into a comer."

So Maxim returned to Cairo with his reputation enhanced, and for several weeks commanded the battalion, until a replacement was flown out from England.

"I listened to my Sergeant, and the other veteran NCOs, and did what they advised. They commanded the battalion as much as I did."

From this evolved the idea of a participatory command, in which the officers and NCOs were on an equal footing, in conferences and decision making, something that was very much a feature of Maxcol.

After Alamein, Maxim was very much working for Alexander, questioning the prisoners. Among the prisoners he had to interview was von Ahremburg who recognised Maxim from Switzerland, and laughingly related all the trouble he had gone into, on my behalf, to discover the missing Major John de Winter.

Like all the other officers, von Ahremburg, now a Colonel, was totally disillusioned at the way he felt his hero, Rommel, had been betrayed by the German High Command, who had starved him of oil and other supplies, at the vital juncture of the campaign.

Maxim said he had questioned von Ahremburg as to Rommel's methods and tactics, especially in the French campaigns. While von Ahremburg as a patriotic German would not fight against his comrades, he was happy to give all the details of Rommel's chain of command, exact concentration and mix of forces, and other details. Between them they evolved the idea of a flying column, tanks, artillery, lorries, supply network, replicating and improving on Rommel's methods.

When they had a blueprint, Maxim went to Alexander with the idea for a flying column. Maxim said he had no idea that he would command it. But Alex knew his man, and promoted Maxim to be temporary Brigadier, to command the force, christened Maxcol after its commander.

Maxcol had its baptism of fire in the desert, and in the Tunisian campaign. It was utilised in the Italian campaign, and throughout 1943 Maxim was working on the concept, a modern day version of the mounted infantry principle.

By 1944 Maxcol was back in England, and took part in the invasion, being part of the forces that broke out through the German ring of steel, and helping to encircle the German forces in the Falaise Gap.

As the forces approached Paris, Maxcol was chosen to make a detour round the capital, and open up the roads to the south, along which the forces which had landed in the South of France could come, securing the bridges and roads, and wiping out the opposition in a swift surprise move.

Did Maxim have a sixth sense that I was trying to get back to the château, and had diverted his forces accordingly? Maxim said no. It was a move directed solely at bringing help to the Maquis, if he had been permitted to do so. He thought he would find the *Comte* at the château and could get from him a proper appraisal of what the French Resistance forces needed, in the way of logistical support.

The *Comte*, who had to be an adviser to the Resistance, would be the best person to tell him. But the *Comte* was already away, helping co-ordinate the Maquis in their battle to prevent the Panzer divisions from getting from Toulouse to Normandy. But why had he directed his forces to pick up the refugees?

"To get first-hand information on the battles around Châteauroux, Maxim said. But I was not so sure. I felt Sniffer Dog Maxim had managed another coup.

I won't weary you with details of my birth labours, which were much like any other woman's, but let it suffice to say that I had Maxim holding one hand, and Mike the other, when Junior finally made his appearance.

Later on, they brought him to me, angry at the experience, and looking just like Winston Churchill. Maxim was at my side, though Maxcol already had its orders to march, and he was soon to leave me.

"The last of the de Winters!" he observed.

"The first of the half dozen you've promised me!" I said.

He laughed.

"What will you call him?"

I had forgotten my childhood agonies as 'Smelly Mellie'.

"Benedict..." I began.

"Good. Let's acknowledge his true father."

"Adrian..."

"After Carton de Wiart. I thoroughly approve."

"Xavier, after the *Comte*..."

"Very proper," he said. "Anything else?"

I pondered. And then the inevitable followed.

"Maximilian."

So Ben was known throughout his junior schooldays as Bax-Max, or 'Back-Smacks', for which, he tells me, he will never forgive me.

Coda

I always liked the tradition of eighteenth century and nineteenth century novels, where the writer ties up the loose ends. Maxim returned to me after the war was over, after Maxcol had distinguished themselves in the race through Holland to reach the Airborne Division at Arnhem, and later they broke through, as the German forces disintegrated, crossing the Rhine and careering through South Germany and Austria, as far as Klatovy in Bohemia. Had they been allowed to stay there, or move on to Prague, this part of Czechoslovakia might have remained this side of the Iron Curtain. But power politics dictated, in another Munich-like appeasement, (but of Stalin, this time), that they had to withdraw.

Maxim was a useful behind-the-scenes operator at the peace talks, and later at the Nuremburg Trials, where he received a curiously complimentary offer from Marshal Tito, to come and set up a Maxcol, a mobile force, to police the warring communities in Yugoslavia.

So for about five years, from 1948 to 1953, our home was a chalet on the banks of Lake Bled, close to Tito's summer residence, and Maxim and I added Slovenian and Serbo-Croat to our repertoire of languages Our eldest, Ben, spoke Slovenian before he spoke English, his nurse being from Ljubljana.

Yes, we were able to have a family, after Maxim and I visited a high-powered clinic in Geneva. Another three children were born to us, a boy, Gerald, and two girls, Anne-Marie and Irene (pronounced the French way). We still live in our chalet by the lake in Switzerland.

By some curious alchemy, Ben has grown up to resemble, in looks and personality, Maxim rather than his true father, Mike. From his earliest childhood he has had only one ambition, to rebuild Manderley, and he endeared himself to his Polish American grandfather, the builder of skyscrapers, by stating this ambition to him, on a visit to New York.

He further endeared himself to Grandfather Victor, who spoke Polish in the family circle, by addressing him in careful Slovenian, which is closely allied to Polish. The old man, delighted, swears that he will bring young Ben into his building business, Burr Construction, and will work with him to rebuild Manderley when he is grown up. [See the sequel to *Jeanne de Winter at the Wars*, *The Mistress of Manderley*.]

Gerald, who is my favourite, has paradoxically the droll humour and laid-back manner of Mike, and thinks he will be an actor, "or a barrister, which is much the same thing," when he grows up.

If there is a wild de Winter – a staid de Winter in one generation, a wild one in the next generation – it is our daughter, Anne-Marie. She is the bosom companion of Rose's daughter, Caroline, and Rose and I have a certain difficulty with the girls' habit of sunbathing, *au naturel*, on the terrace in summer time, a practice which we both try vainly to discourage. Irene is like me, a placid, biddable child, with a talent for the piano.

Over the years we have been visited by many of our old friends from the wartime adventures. Isaak, our musician from Paris, came earliest of all, and has often returned, giving Irene a great insight into music. He survived the war by being concealed in a Jesuit seminary in Paris, posing as a retired Jesuit, and becoming the organist for the seminary. He has developed a great regard for the Jesuits, for whom he feels a great affinity. "They are just like the Jews," he says, "always being persecuted for being too clever by half."

Carton, now retired to Ireland, has visited us. He had a good war, commanding the forces in the Norway campaign, taking part in the war in the Middle East, though he was captured early on by the Germans, and not released till 1943, after which he went to China as an adviser to General Chiang Kai Chek. When last we heard of him he was writing his autobiography, *Happy Odyssey*, but we made him promise not to bring us into it.

Mike visits us often, sometimes with Gabrielle-Pauline, more often not; she has a certain sensitivity and awkwardness when Ben is around. They have two boys, but the elder, Henri-Xavier, has become one of the staid and pompous de Langlades, conscious that he will become *Comte* de Winter when his grandfather dies. His ambition is to be a career soldier. There is some resentment that Ben is now Grandfather Victor's favourite grandson, and heir apparent to the Burr Corporation millions.

Many of my friends from the German Paris HQ survived the war, and the post-bomb plot *putsch* by the Nazis. They often visit us, especially Colonel von Ahremburg, who is now our near neighbour on the lake. We sing the old songs, especially '*Spiel, Zigeuner*', loudly if a bit unmelodiously, the music echoing across the lake.

Llew has visited us, with his new French wife. He still has his electrical business in Paris, the security side of which is especially prosperous, and Marie's husband – I still cannot remember his name is the managing director. He says darkly, "I have the taxman, instead of the Gestapo, to contend with nowadays."

But it is now evening over the lake and I must conclude my tale. Never leave over till tomorrow what you can do today, is Maxim's constant advice to the children, especially the wild one, Anne Marie. *Morgen ist viel zu spät!*